Benjamin Sorrow: One for Sorrow

By P. G. Challis

Text copyright © P. G. Challis 2016
Design copyright © Alexandra Paise 2016
All rights reserved.

P. G. Challis has asserted his right under the Copyright, Designs and Patents Act 1988 to be identified as the author of this work.

No part of this book may be reprinted or reproduced or utilised in any form or by electronic, mechanical or any other means, now known or hereafter invented, including photocopying or recording, or in any information storage or retrieval system, without the permission in writing from the Publisher and Author.

First published 2016
by Rowanvale Books Ltd
Imperial House
Trade Street Lane
Cardiff
CF10 5DT
www.rowanvalebooks.com

A CIP catalogue record for this book is available from the British Library.
ISBN: 978-1-910607-07-7

Chapter One

'Come on!'
'No.'
'Come on!'
'No!'
'You mis'rable bastard! I've got money; no good for you is it?' slurred Borell.

'Look, you've had more drink than you can clearly handle. Folk are leaving 'cause of you,' said the bartender, keeping a cool head.

'Kiss mine, there are other —'

Borell came to, lying face down on the icy cold autumn pavement outside the pub. The bartender clearly knew how to deal with problem customers. Slowly getting to his knees, rubbing a sore and bleeding head, he could feel the extent of his forceful ejection from the pub in his lower back.

'You have been keeping yourself busy, I see,' said a voice, towering over him. A tall, silhouetted gentleman wearing a bowler and distinguished clothes was taking a drag from a silver-piped cigarette holder that glinted in the warm light from the gas-powered street lights.

'I can offer you somewhere more comfortable to kneel if you can tear yourself away from the pavement, Borell,' he said.

Borell let out a painful breath. 'You have me at a dis'vantage, sir.'

'We have a mutual acquaintance, which is all I'll say for now.' The silhouetted man dropped the cigarette from the holder. 'We have a job that requires your particular skills. There is a warm bed, pay and all the beer you can drink waiting for you —' he chuckled '— *if* you complete this task for us.'

The silhouetted man faded in and out of view as Borell's eyes slowly succumbed to his severe intoxication. He managed two words before passing out completely.

'Why not?'

***

Borell awoke in a firm but comfortable bed, his head sore from the night before. Sitting up, he also sharply remembered the pain in his back.

'Can still see, then. Isn't as bad as I thought,' he said through an achy jaw. He rubbed his head, and found a sore spot that made him wince. He noticed his elbow had been carefully bandaged, so someone had clearly looked after him when he got — wherever he was now. Looking around, he didn't recognise the room or anything in it. He had a vague recollection of meeting someone, but that was as far as his memory would allow him to probe right now. He decided, rather unwisely as it turned out, to stand up and look out of the window. His knees gave under him and he staggered to the chair opposite, managing to recover from a graceless fall.

'Okay, maybe it *is* as bad as I thought,' he muttered.

Knock, knock, knock.

'Good morning! Are you awake?' called the unknown voice from beyond the door.

'Who's asking?' he replied with a hazy stammer. The unlocked door slowly opened and a very beautiful woman entered. Standing comfortably in her six-foot tall, slim, heavily bustiered frame, she smiled at him.

'Good morning, Borell,' she said. 'I've been sent to make sure you have recovered from your evening, and bring you up to speed on the task required of you.'

Borell sighed. 'That's great, but I'm gonna be needing some breakfast before getting down to anything too strenuous at this point,' he said, both in an attempt to delay reality creeping into his waking head, and because his hangover craved food.

'I am well aware of your usual morning requirements,' the unknown woman replied, and opened the door to the room again. Two men entered sporting a tray of pastries and pies, a flagon of beer and coffee and unfaltering smiles. They set the tray and drinks down on a side table and left as cheerfully as they entered.

Borell was starting to recall the reason for the kindness through the haze that was his morning grey matter. Usually the tasks that followed were not at all pleasant, so his employers had come to learn that starting him off on a sated stomach garnered his full attention.

'I will return in one hour. We will then discuss our needs,' the woman said, then left him alone with his breakfast. Borell hobbled over to the chair next to the food and started to eat. He was sure that this job would indeed be horrendous. Normally the food was acceptable and the accommodation tidy, but this was a level above his usual expectations.

***

Borell drank the dark, thick coffee from the large mug whilst gazing from his room's window. Breakfast satisfied his hangover, and he was just waiting for the woman to return. She was certainly a sight for sore eyes this morning. Well, any morning really. He could see from the city's clock tower through his window that she should be due any time.

Knock, knock, knock.

'Come in,' Borell called. The door opened and the same slim woman entered carrying a small folder of papers.

'I hope breakfast was to your liking?' she said.

'Very much so.'

'My name is Loren.' She gestured for Borell to sit. Still hobbling a little, he managed to move to one of the plush armchairs and sit down. Loren took one of the other chairs and sat in front of him.

'Let's get to the business at hand,' she said with little enthusiasm for further pleasantries. 'We need you to recover an item for us; there is no need to be discreet about it. We have been looking to acquire this item for some time now, and recently it fell into the hands of — well, people who aren't us.'

'Who *is* us?' Borell interrupted again.

Loren let out a small sigh. 'Don't trouble yourself with that. The point is, we want you to recover this item for us, and we don't care how you do it. The Society has been supporting the man who built the device, and is now readying their operatives to locate it. They are more than slightly concerned that it has disappeared.'

'So I've got competition? Does anyone know where to start looking?'

'According to our sources, the Society have no leads. We have heard, however, that a man who calls himself The Grey Hand has information of the whereabouts of the item, and will sell for a price. We don't intend to pay him, but we are happy to leave the details of this *transaction* in your capable hands. The Society may uncover this information before you get to him, or they may already have — in which case, you will need to source the information another way.'

Borell smirked. 'Understood. Get the information, kill him, avoid getting killed in the crossfire, kill someone else if necessary.'

'It goes without saying that anyone else looking for this item is fair game. We don't want to know, just get the job done.'

Loren stood and handed Borell a small brown pouch with a leather drawstring threaded through the neck, containing his payment, and placed a folder of papers on the table next to his breakfast.

'One half now, one half when you put the item into my hands. Understood?'

'Yeah, I get it. I ain't no rookie.'

'Very good. You will find a woman named Bethany at the Broken Arrow Inn. She will pass on your message when the job is done. If you are caught, you better hope they kill you.'

Borell's face changed from a smirk to one of contemplation at the statement, but it soon changed to back into a grin. As Loren opened the door, she turned and said, 'Don't enjoy the facilities, we don't expect you to be here for long,' and closed the door behind her.

Chapter Two

Benjamin Sorrow sat in his darkened study, staring at the ornate typewriter on the desk in front of him. It stared back at him, waiting for his inspiration to become lasting imprints in the sheet of paper cradled inside it. The lights in the study were low, illuminated by old gas lamps that gave the room a warm, comfortable feel, with the quiet hiss of the burning fuel.

Shadows moved slowly across the dimly lit walls as the early morning sun rose through the large window overlooking the front gardens. Benjamin liked it this way; it allowed him to centre his thoughts and encourage his ideas to flourish. His father had taught him the technique as a child as way to focus his mind on his studies. Unlike his father, Benjamin had never achieved the same level of focus and would often just fall asleep when he tried. He relearned and mastered the technique later in his early twenties, which helped him on long arduous assignments for the secretive government agency, the Society.

He had been spending time trying to write his memoirs since he took an indefinite leave of absence from his job with the Society. Since his parents' death two years ago, he'd decided he needed a change of pace. The day-to-day assignments had taken a toll on his body and mind. He felt worn and tired. His forty-year-old body was still recovering from the years of abuse it had taken.

Benjamin's fingers hovered over the keys, his eyes closed, willing the words to seep from his subconscious into his conscious mind.

He waited.

The world turned a little more.

Benjamin sighed and removed the sheet of paper from the typewriter, laying it back on the unused pile. He stood, stretched his arms and then made his way out of his study towards the living room.

'How about a nice cup of tea and some breakfast?' asked Mary, the housekeeper, who caught him in the hallway.

'Thanks, Mary, that would be great.'

'I'll see what I can do,' she said, and walked off to towards the kitchen.

Having a housekeeper like Mary freed Benjamin from the unnecessary complication of day-to-day tasks, but it was also the done thing. A wealthy person in Trellern wouldn't be caught dead dealing with everyday matters of cooking and cleaning. But Mary was much more than a housekeeper. Having worked for his family for as long as he could remember, she *was* family as far as he was concerned.

Benjamin walked to the front door just as his morning paper was being delivered, sliding through the letterbox and landing heavily on the mat. He picked it up and wandered in to the living room, glancing at the headlines as he went.

The light from the rising sun illuminated the city's hexagonal clock tower through the main window in the living room, giving an impressive skyline view. The majestic tower that rose high above the peaks of houses had been built more than a hundred years ago and could be seen by nearly every house and estate within the inner city limits — hardly surprising that it was also the centre for local government.

The private docking tower at the clock tower's peak, reserved for officials, was currently engaged in a tango of manoeuvres with a large airship. Judging by the light armaments, it was a government ship, probably escorting one of the higher ranked ministers to their hideaway in the mountains.

The capital city of Menillis was also a bustling port for trade, commerce and all the matters a city does not want to admit to. Everything from food to technology came through Trellern. Most goods arrived by the main River Whyle by ship or barge. Some of the more lucrative goods traders, who were wealthy enough to be able to afford air transport, arrived at the large trade hub upriver by airship.

Many trade routes existed to the other cities and towns of Menillis and its neighbours, but Trellern was universally agreed to be the hub of commerce across the kingdom.

Benjamin looked at the clock on the mantelpiece and adjusted the hands, correcting the time in accordance with the city clock.

'Here you go,' said Mary as she walked in to the living room, handing him a cup and saucer.

'Thanks, Mary. What would I do without you?'

'Live in squalor and go hungry,' she said, smirking.

He chuckled. 'Agreed!'

'Breakfast will be ready shortly.'

'Thanks, Mary.'

***

Benjamin looked up from his cup of tea, across the kitchen to the clock above the stove. It showed just after eight thirty. He had always been an early riser, usually up and out of bed by six o'clock. He had been trying to use this time recently to work on his memoirs, to little success.

The kitchen table was sparsely covered with breakfast; he didn't have a great appetite first thing in the morning. Tea, toast, jams and his newspaper were all he needed.

He had not taken breakfast, or any of his meals, in the main dining room since coming back to the house after his parents passed away. It seemed like an awful waste of a room, but there was nothing but a cold, unwelcome atmosphere in there without the family he remembered.

'Anything in particular you would like for dinner this evening?' asked Mary from the sink, where she was washing dishes.

Benjamin looked up from his newspaper and thought for a moment. 'Do we have any steak?'

'No, but I can pick some up from the market this morning.'

'Thanks, Mary.'

He returned to his newspaper, the *Trellern Chronicles*, and skipped the sensationalised headlines. He glanced at the business pages, more companies being closed down and bargains to be had if you were so inclined. A new aerodrome tower in the works, yet another blight on the skyline as he saw it, but such is the price of progress.

He read for a few minutes then closed and folded the paper.

'Mary, I'm going out to see Jackson,' he said, downing the last of the tea in his cup.

'Say "hello" from me. Tell him I'll bring him his favourite pie on Thursday.'

'I will,' Benjamin smiled.

'Dinner will be at seven sharp.'

Benjamin smiled a thank you as he walked out of the kitchen. He took his coat and hat from the hallway stand and put them both on to brace himself for the autumn chill outside.

Benjamin regularly went to see Jackson Burns, once a week on a Monday morning. Since taking leave from the Society, Jackson's particular skills were not required as often as they used to be. He wasn't just an inventor, in the absent-minded, 'let him potter about, it'll keep him busy' sense of the word, but a brilliant scientist and craftsman. He kept himself a low profile, as he only worked for those who he trusted.

The hallway bureau was antiquated and hid things the unknowing burglar wouldn't find. One of these was a secret panel in one end that contained Benjamin's pistol. He kept it cleaned and oiled and always took it with him out of habit; Trellern had its share of troubled citizens. He tucked the weapon into the integral holster in his coat, collected some rounds of ammunition and closed the panel again.

Descending the steps leading from the front door, he walked along the path, crossing thirty yards of front gardens to reach the gates leading to the main road outside. It was only a fifteen-minute walk to Jackson's shop in the trade district of the city. It was a bright autumn morning, cold and fresh but he didn't mind. The traffic was humming with people on their way to work.

As he walked along Elm Avenue, he noticed the same airship docked to the private docking port on the clock tower; it looked even more menacing during the light of day.

Enjoying the cool autumn sunshine, Benjamin continued his walk to see Jackson.

Chapter Three

Benjamin arrived outside the shop that Jackson called home a little after nine o'clock. The understated signage, attempting to dissuade the average passer-by from calling in, was starting to look very dated. Benjamin pulled the doorbell and waited. He tried to peer in through one of the windows, but they were so grimy it was impossible to see anything inside. Part of the charm of having a shop that no one wants to go into is that you can keep to yourself, but still have a certain trade with those that need it.

Strange, thought Benjamin as no one answered the door. He pulled the doorbell again. Still nothing. He tried the handle and to his surprise found that the door was unlocked. Benjamin instinctively put his hand onto the grip of his pistol inside his coat and cocked the hammer.

'Jackson?' he said as he slowly opened the door and peered inside. He pushed the door, feeling the resistance of the small table placed against the inside. 'You in here somewhere, old man?' The echo-less shop front was the only thing to greet him.

Benjamin slowly walked in and closed the door behind him. He could see why the door was unlocked now. Part of the doorframe on the inside was splintered, so there was nowhere for the lock to home. He drew his pistol and looked around the shop. It was unremarkable but warm; there was a tidy counter, sparsely laden shelves with various run of the mill items, all clean and surprisingly free from dust. There was many a time he came here looking for merchandise and impossible to obtain items for his assignments. No one else in Trellern could provide the items Jackson could.

Thin shafts of sunlight shone through the grubby windows and an eerie glow reflected from the highly polished copper counter top. Benjamin continued to look around.

'Ben?' came Jackson's voice from behind him, making him spin around, gun poised.

'Hell, old man, you scared the shit out of me!' Benjamin said with a smile, and holstered his weapon. 'What happened to your door? Are you alright?'

'Oh, could be worse. Just a bump to the head and a few scrapes. Come, let's have tea and I'll tell you about it,' said Jackson, wandering off towards a doorway in the rear of the shop. Benjamin pushed the table back against the door, looking at the damage more closely, then turned and followed Jackson.

The back part of the shop looked more like a house than a shop, with thick but worn carpets, warm wooden panelling and a sofa that looked like it had been slept on many times. Jackson had lived here for as many years as Benjamin had known him, and the room had not changed much in all that time. A stove fire at the opposite end of the room was burning low and comfortably. Jackson placed a kettle onto the stove and ushered Benjamin to sit down.

'So what happened?' asked Benjamin again.

'I'm a little hazy on some of the details. Biscuit?' Jackson said, offering Benjamin a small tin.

'No thanks. The door?' Benjamin prompted his distracted friend.

'Hmm? Yes, well I was in my workshop when I heard a crash, which I found out later to be the doorframe. I turned around and saw two — at least I think it was two — large men come charging towards me from the shop front. They clocked me on the head. After that, I don't really remember too much. I woke up with a bloody forehead and a cracking headache.'

'At least that's all they did to you. Why didn't you call me, I would have been here in a heartbeat.'

'I didn't want to trouble you, they didn't take much. I'm alright, really.'

'I take it you reported this to the authorities?'

'Yes, yes. Has all been dealt with,' Jackson said clearly avoiding answering.

'What did they take?'

'Oh, you know my work. Bits of this, bits of that,' Jackson said dismissively.

'Come on, Jackson. I've known you for too long to think they were just after "bits and pieces".'

Jackson wandered over to the fireplace, staring at it for a moment deciding what to tell Benjamin. He knew he could trust his friend, probably more than he could trust anyone, but he also knew there are secrets that have to be kept, even from friends.

'Jackson?' Benjamin said, looking at his friend staring into the fire. 'Was this Society work? Is that why you won't tell me?'

Jackson sighed and looked at his friend. 'Oh, it's nothing really.'

'Jackson,' Benjamin said in a parent-to-child tone of voice.

Jackson picked up a cast iron poker, prodded at the fire for a moment, then returned the poker to its stand. He desperately wanted to tell Benjamin, but knew the consequences of involving him in secret Society work, even if Benjamin used to be an operative. He stood at the fireplace and fought with his conscience. For Jackson this seemed like an eternity; for Benjamin it was a moment or two of desperate concern for his old friend.

Jackson finally decided that he would tell Benjamin — damn the consequences, he would just come out with it.

'Many years ago, when your father and I worked together, I theorised a device. A device that could produce vast amounts of energy, way beyond what we had at the time — or even now. I had kept this to myself, never sharing it with anyone, other than your father.' Jackson paused, stoking the fire again and thinking. 'I didn't believe in the theory enough to take it to my colleagues at the Society.'

'But you did start to believe in it?'

'After some time, yes. I reworked my ideas, the calculations; it ended up being somewhat of an obsession. I started building a prototype, on my own, in secret. If nothing came of it, nothing was lost.'

'Did you get it working?'

'Yes and no,' Jackson said. 'The prototype did produce masses of power, enough to power a small town like Farneville. But it was unstable. It would burn out the core after a few hours. This was an improvement on my original, which lasted mere seconds. I needed more resources, so contacted an old colleague from my Society days for help. That was my first mistake.'

'The Society found out and wanted to take control of the project,' Benjamin said confidently.

'Yes. Elliot is a good friend, but terrible at keeping secrets as it turned out. The Special Projects Division came calling and offered me all the resources I needed. We wanted the same goal and now that they knew about it, there was little point hiding it. I was reluctant to work under oversight again, but knowing how easily they could just take my work, well... they persuaded me.'

'So someone inside the Society leaked information about the device, probably for money,' said Benjamin.

'It would seem so, yes,' Jackson said as he spooned two sugars into his cup.

'But you called them. They came and saw you?'

'Yes. I sent a message to Special Projects and reported the theft of the prototype. They sent someone to see me within minutes. Strange fellow. What was his name...?' Jackson said, furrowing his brow and trying to remember.

'Bone, I think he said his name was. Not met him before, but he was Society. Knew all about the project.'

'And he didn't leave any agents here to look after you, or repair your door?' Benjamin was angry.

'He said more Agents were on their way, to tidy up and go over details. To be honest, I couldn't remember much anyway. It all happened so fast.'

'Clearly they didn't show up.'

'No. I'd started to tidy the shop anyway, then time just ran away from me.'

'Something isn't right. If the Society were invested in a project like this, they would have moved you some place safe or at least left some Agents here to watch over you.'

'I refused to work at Special Projects. Told them I was too long in the tooth for all that again. They eventually agreed to let me work here. They said that security had been taken care of. I guess not.' Jackson sighed again.

The realisation struck Benjamin. 'The device can be weaponised, can't it?'

'Yes, easily, which is mostly why I kept it a secret all these years. But the thieves didn't take all the parts they need to make the device work. I am sure they will realise this when they try to power it on.' He allowed himself a sly smile.

The kettle started to whistle. Jackson poured the water into a strange looking teapot, and Benjamin asked about the missing part to the device.

'Well, even I know that you don't keep all your eggs in one basket. I guess our leak inside the Society didn't know about the initiator. Without it, the device just won't work. I was somewhat selective with some of the details about my work — force of habit.'

Jackson walked to the mantel over the fireplace, pushed what appeared to be a knot in the wood and a small compartment dropped open underneath. He took out a small octagonal item, no larger than the palm of his hand and about as thick as his finger. It looked clear to the eye, but appeared to contain slowly swirling clouds inside when you looked closer; an interesting illusion.

'I've always kept this hidden, except when testing the device.'

'We need to get you and this —' Benjamin said, nodding at the initiator '— somewhere safe. Away from those people who will no doubt come looking for it.'

'I have never run from anything before. I don't intend to change that now,' said Jackson in a stern voice.

'You need to listen to me on this. Whoever they are, they will be back. And I guarantee that if this initiator isn't wrapped up in a bow, sitting on the counter in your shop waiting for them, they'll not hesitate to beat you into submission to find it.'

Jackson looked Benjamin in the eye and saw that he was serious. 'What did you have in mind?' he said reluctantly.

Benjamin thought for a moment, pacing from the mantel to the stove.

'My estate is secure, and I can find people I trust to watch over you whilst I look for your device.'

'But you are retired. Do you think the Society will let you look for the device on your own?'

'Let me worry about that,' Benjamin said confidently. 'Get together whatever you need. I'll contact the Society for help. I know one person I can trust.'

Jackson went through a door leading down to his workshop, which was neatly concealed behind a section of bookcase. He began collecting tools, papers and other items he needed to continue work elsewhere. He found a large leather bag, which had not seen the light of day in well over a decade, dusted it off and started loading it with items. Before long, the bag was full.

His muffled voice travelled up to the lounge where Benjamin was waiting. 'I could do with a hand down here. I seem to have packed rather too much for me to carry.'

'Be there in a minute,' Benjamin replied through the

open bookcase door. He took an empty capsule from the Perpetual Post-box on the lounge wall, and set the numerical dials to that of the Society's border offices.

Perpetual Post was a quite brilliant invention. Instead of taking hours for a message by courier to be delivered, you could send the same message in minutes to anyone in the network. Trellern was the pioneer city for this postal system and the technology had been used to connect the rest of Menillis for many years.

Unfortunately, technology had moved on and a telephone system was beginning to establish itself amongst the homes and businesses of Trellern. Perpetual Post was still more secure, as some unscrupulous individuals found ways to listen to conversations on the new telephone wires.

The border office would manually relay any messages from there to the Society; no direct message could be sent via Perpetual Post. There was always the threat of someone finding the Society's address and sending something dangerous to them. The border offices were equipped to handle such events, so nothing untoward should ever get through.

He wrote a note in code, rolled the paper up and inserted it into the capsule. The ornate post-box in Jackson's lounge was reminiscent of the early post-boxes connected to the system. In the very early days, you could easily set the destination address incorrectly, and the capsule containing your message would bounce around the system for days — hence the name that it was given. Not long after its creation, a fail-safe counter had been added to each capsule. Each time the capsule passed a relay point, the counter would count down, and when this reached zero, the next relay point would drop the capsule into a bin. Someone would then take the capsule and send it back to where it came from with a little note saying 'Sorry, that's an unknown address,' or, if the operator was having a really bad day, 'You are an idiot, don't try again.'

He placed the capsule inside the post-box, closed the cover and the capsule disappeared with the sound of rushing air. It would take about twenty minutes for his message to be delivered to its final destination. He quickly wrote another message to send to a carriage company, so they would have transport to his house. With another rush of air, that capsule disappeared too.

'Good grief, how much stuff have you packed?' exclaimed Benjamin as he lifted Jackson's bag. 'I hope we don't need to make a quick getaway carrying this!'

'It's been many years since I left here for any length of time, I didn't really know what to pack.'

'Don't worry, we'll manage,' Benjamin said with a kind smile.

Benjamin walked with Jackson to the front of the shop and kept an eye out for their carriage.

***

The warmth of the late morning sun was starting to creep into the alleys and passageways of the trade district as an unremarkable carriage pulled up outside of Jackson's shop. The two horses pulling the carriage didn't seem bothered with the chill in the air, and stood patiently as the driver signalled Benjamin that their ride had arrived, with a short sharp whistle.

Benjamin opened the door slightly and looked through the gap to check that their exit was clear. The limited view worried him, so he told Jackson to wait whilst he had a quick look outside. Hand poised on the butt of his pistol concealed under his jacket, he slowly opened the door fully and peered through. The road outside was empty, apart from a few pedestrians going about, what appeared to be, their normal daily activities. He didn't see any obvious danger, but knew not to always trust his eyes.

'Come on, let's get moving,' he said. Without looking behind him, and keeping his eyes sharp for any threats outside, Benjamin hoisted the large leather bag over his holster shoulder and stepped outside, holding the door for Jackson.

'Nice day for it,' Jackson said absent-mindedly as he followed Benjamin outside and locked the shop door, Benjamin's temporary fix to the doorframe holding firm.

The pair walked casually across the pavement towards the waiting carriage. The driver, Arthur Bourne, acknowledged Benjamin with a tip of his hat. Arthur had driven for many operatives of the Society in his nearly twenty years as an Agent; he had worked with Benjamin on many occasions.

The heavy leather bag was pushed into the open door of the carriage, closely followed by Jackson. Benjamin took an extensive look around, noticing different people walking about, new carriages stopping up and down the street.

'Where to?' called Arthur from his perch above the carriage.

'Home, please, Arthur. Take the scenic route.'

'No problem,' Arthur said as he geed the horses on.

Their extended route away from the trade district took them along Appletree Drive and then, shortly after, right into Docklands. They continued along Docklands for about two minutes, passing ships and boats overladen with goods moored along the riverbank. The smaller traders, who dealt with cheap, everyday goods that were offloaded to the poorer areas of the city, usually managed these vessels. The very exclusive goods were supplied by the wealthiest of traders, and many of those favoured airships over boats; they could afford them.

The main dock was reserved for all the large ships and paddle steamers that brought the bulky goods to Trellern, such as grain, oils, metals and timber.

They were now about a twenty-minute journey away from Benjamin's estate, and the relative safety therein. Hopefully his message to the Society had been delivered by now, and help was already on its way to meet them. With any luck, they would already be in place and no one would be the wiser.

'How's Lilly getting on at Browne?' Benjamin asked to pass the time and distract Jackson.

'Oh, she's doing very well. Top of her class in the sciences this semester — must take after me,' he beamed. 'She's coped well since her mother passed. I do try and keep in touch, but it's not as often as I'd like.'

'Still no word of her father?'

'No, the Society still have people looking. Still no sightings or information about what happened to him. Fortunately Lilly can't remember him too well, but we'll have answers one day.'

Lilly's father had disappeared without a trace when she was a small child, and since her mother's death she had been living at the University of Browne, continuing her studies in the city of Dolare. Her grandfather, Jackson, was the only real family she had left.

'Prob'ly best to get out up ahead,' Arthur called from above. 'I'll carry on as decoy, just in case. You can cut through the park from here.'

Benjamin looked out of the window as they slowed to a stop alongside one of the main entrances. It would only take them a few minutes to walk through the park, with Benjamin's estate being just on the other side. Carriages and horses were not allowed in the park, which gave them the advantage of being able to mingle with the other pedestrians.

'Thanks, Arthur. I owe you one,' Benjamin said as he stepped down, giving Jackson a helping hand. Benjamin and Jackson took a steady walk through the park, pulling their jackets tight against the chill air.

'So, is there anything else you can remember from the break in? You saw, maybe, two large men? Did you hear anything? Anything else that could be helpful?'

'No, not really. Like I said, it all happened so fast

before I passed out,' Jackson said thoughtfully. 'No, wait!' he blurted suddenly, grabbing Benjamin's arm. 'There was something that I've just remembered. Maybe it's all this fresh air.'

They stopped, and Benjamin looked at the old man concentrating on this new memory.

'There was a smell. I never thought about it until now, but there was a strong smell of lavender. Does that mean anything?' Jackson said hopefully.

'I don't think so, but if small details like that come back to you, then others might later.'

'Sorry Benjamin, I'm not much help am I?'

'Don't worry.' He smiled.

As they continued their walk through the park, it was a nice distraction to see families playing with their children, friends gathered around tables, talking, and those just generally taking the fresh air. Above them, airships bound for the aerodromes further out in the city could be seen pushing leisurely through the clear blue skies.

'I've never been in an airship,' commented Jackson as his skyward gaze caught Benjamin's attention. 'Never got round to it, I suppose. Amazing things, aren't they, just hanging there. Although, knowing what they are filled with, I'm also kind of happy with my feet on the ground.'

Benjamin smiled. 'Never?'

Jackson chuckled, looking more relaxed than earlier.

Benjamin could see his estate now through the main gate they were approaching. Four main pathways, each of which had a large wrought iron gate preventing everyday traffic from entering, quartered the park. The gate on Elm Avenue had ornate Elm trees entwined into the bars, something that he had seen every day on leaving his house. He pushed open the smaller pedestrian gate and held it open for Jackson. Across the road, he could see the safety of home.

They stood on the pavement waiting for a gap in the traffic, which didn't take long. Benjamin saw that his message to his friends at the Society had made it in time. He could see two ex-colleagues blending into the surroundings; one of them was sweeping leaves, the other was working on the gate to Benjamin's estate.

Benjamin held onto Jackson's elbow and ushered him across the now quiet road.

'Will have ya' gate running as slick as a whistle in about three hours, Mr Sorrow,' the man working on the hinges said as they approached.

'Three hours? That long?' Benjamin countered.

'Aye, unfortunately these hinges can be a tricky business,' he replied. 'I may need to get parts. Three hours minimum — two and a half at a push.'

'At a push would be appreciated,' said Benjamin as they headed up the path to the main house.

'Aye, sir, will do me best,' the man called out behind them.

As they approached the main entrance to the house, Jackson asked, 'He wasn't really fixing your gate, was he?'

'Yes and no. The squeak will keep him looking busy. The bad news is that we have a couple of hours before the rest of our support gets here. I'm guessing some are out on assignment.'

'All that for me?' Jackson asked feeling a little embarrassed but also relieved.

'I'll find out more when I see Kodey in a couple of hours, as soon as backup arrives.'

Chapter Four

The long corridor ahead of Kodey Twill was adorned with portraits and photographs of current and past prefects of the Society. He smiled as he passed the photograph of his father, a prefect before him. The Society had seven other prefects as well as him and, being autocratic, a principal overseeing everything. The government relied on the Society to deal with everything to do with maintaining the security of their kingdom.

As Kodey approached his office, he noticed the door was ajar. *I'm sure I closed that,* he thought to himself. Pushing the door open, he saw the back of a figure wearing full-length black robes standing behind his desk, looking through his window to the city outside.

'Kodey,' said the figure, without turning around.

'Damn it, Emmerson, does the sanctity of another man's office mean nothing to you?' he exclaimed, gesturing with his hands.

'Nope, not even if you lock the door.'

'I *did* lock the door,' he said, his voice breaking a little at the frustration.

'There you are then, you have your answer.'

'What the hell do you want, Emmerson?' Kodey and Emmerson's history wasn't pretty, but their relatively senior positions within the Society meant they tried to keep their differences private. They had come to blows, but this was always somewhere away from prying eyes.

Emmerson Lamont turned away from the window to face Kodey, his ceremonial robes perfectly pressed and immaculately maintained.

'Well?' asked Kodey again. 'What *do* you want?'

'I hear you had a meeting with the principal earlier.'

'You really are a nosy bastard, aren't you? Do you mind?' Kodey gestured to Emmerson to move away from his desk. Emmerson obliged, raising his eyebrows and clasping his hands behind his back as he did so.

'Indeed...' he said as he walked away.

'So is that all you wanted? To know what my meeting was about? You know I can't talk about assignments and I wouldn't tell you shit anyway,' Kodey said, sitting down and dropping the folder of papers he was carrying on his desk.

Emmerson smirked, clearly knowing more than he was letting on.

'I do so enjoy our little *get-togethers*,' Kodey said through gritted teeth. 'Now if that's all, bugger off.'

Emmerson tipped his head in acknowledgement and left, closing the door behind him.

'What an asshole,' Kodey muttered under his breath.

He placed a folder in front of him that was sealed with the Principal Insignia; it had been handed to him directly when he met with the principal earlier that morning. Kodey knew better than to leave things unattended like this. He opened his desk drawer, removed a silver letter opener, and used it to break the wax seal. Removing the dozen or so pages, he began working his way through the detail of his assignment outlined by the principal himself. It detailed Jackson Burns' device and contained information about its history. There were several pictures, which showed it sitting on a bench from various angles. It looked like a complex mess of wiring and tubing, sitting about twelve inches high, but for all the complexity there was also a form of beauty.

Kodey continued working through the pages until he had read all that was available to him. The last line of text on the last page of the documents simply said:

Destroy completely.

He scooped up the handful of pages and photographs and took them over to the fireplace in the far wall. The fire burned fiercely for a moment and then died as the pages were consumed.

Chapter Five

Inside Benjamin's house, Jackson looked around the hallway and noticed the immaculate furnishings and tidy abode. 'Mary, still keeping you well I see. Where is that sweetheart anyway?' he said.

'She's out at the market. Should be back before too long and I am sure she will be pleased to see you. Come on, Dad's old workshop in the basement will be the perfect place for you to work. No one has been down there since — well, for a few years anyway.'

'That would be ideal.'

They headed along the hallway with its large double doors on the left for the dining room, the single door on the right to Benjamin's study and another on the left to the kitchen. They passed various other doors to rooms that didn't get a lot of use either, until they came to one on the right with a plain handle and no visible lock.

'Do you remember how this works?' asked Benjamin.

'Of course. Let me see...' Jackson said as he stood in front of the door and studied its wooden panels. 'If I remember correctly —'

He pushed the top right panel in the door, which recessed about half an inch. He let go and the panel split across the middle and slid apart to reveal a row of four cylindrical dials forming a combination lock. The dials were a finely finished brass affair, with painted embossed numbers ranging from zero to nine.

'As long as you haven't changed the code,' Jackson said hopefully, 'the combination is; four, seven, one and two.' He rotated each dial to the correct position. The row of dials slowly moved away from him and the panel that had split apart closed again. They heard the sound of mechanical locks moving behind the door and they could both feel the vibrations in the floor as the locks made their final positions. Benjamin turned the handle and pushed the door open.

'I always did like this door,' Jackson commented on his own handiwork as a warm, glowing electric light came on inside to illuminate the wooden staircase leading down to the basement. Benjamin walked through the door first, carrying Jackson's leather bag, carefully negotiating the steep steps without overbalancing on the way down. Jackson followed close behind, firmly gripping the bannister.

Reaching the bottom of the stairs, they both looked around at the workshop that had once been such a hive of activity when Benjamin's father was alive. The benches, tools, cupboards and furnishings were all ghostly, covered by once white dustsheets.

'This should do you, then?' asked Benjamin, taking a moment to remember watching his father at work.

'Perfectly, thank you.'

'Well, let's get this cleared up and get you settled,' said Benjamin, indicating to the dustsheets, 'I'll have Mary sort a bedroom for you later.'

Benjamin put Jackson's heavy bag down and suddenly felt as light as a feather. He wandered over to the main bench along the far wall, grabbed hold of one of the large dustsheets and gave it a gentle pull. A cloud of dust leapt into the air, hanging there like moisture on a misty morning.

'Best not breathe too much of this in,' Benjamin said, pulling the sheet off completely and laying it on the floor to fold away. The bench was spotless. All the tools were all in their designated places. Little bins containing various materials and components hung on the wall above the bench.

One by one, Benjamin and Jackson removed the dustsheets and folded them away, and soon the entire room looked to Benjamin exactly as it had many years ago. A large oak worktable stood in the middle of the room, which had previously been the assembly table for many of Benjamin's father's projects. Benjamin could see the years of tool marks made in the surface, more than some of which he was responsible for as a boy.

To the right of the main bench stood a small smelting furnace, used by Benjamin's father when making his own parts and components for his work. Ladles of varying sizes were hanging from a board on the wall next to it, along with a heavy pair of leather gloves and various sized smelting pots on a bench. A much worn, but surprisingly comfortable, sofa sat in the corner of the room. Benjamin remembered he had fallen asleep on it more than once as a child when watching his father work.

'If those thieving bedlice manage to get my device working,' said Jackson with a pained look on his face, 'we ought to have some way of knowing about it. I could modify the apparatus I was going to use to measure the power it produced. It might allow us to track it down. Of course, they would have to switch it on first.'

'Let's hope we can find it *before* that happens,' Benjamin said. 'You said it would take some knowledge of your work to get the thing going? I can't imagine the ones who stole it would have the knowledge, or even the intelligence. We should be okay until it reaches the hands of those who paid for it.'

'I'll do what I can, Benjamin.' With that, Jackson started to unpack tools and equipment from his bag. All manner of tools in neat, leather and deer suede roll-up containers and pouches soon found new homes on the benches. The apparatus Jackson spoke of was carefully wrapped in a leather bag which, when removed, was also wrapped in a blue satin cloth. He left what little clothes he had packed for himself in the bag.

'I may have underestimated the clothing side of things,' he said, looking at the handful of mismatched items in the bag.

'We'll find you something; Dad's clothes are in boxes somewhere. Mary will look after you.'

Benjamin lit the stove in the corner of the room, taking the chill from the air.

'I was lucky to have worked with your father, and now it seems I'm also lucky to be looked after by his son.'

'Nothing is going to happen to you. You have my word.'

Chapter Six

Borell's motor carriage bumped along the main road towards a town called Farneville ten miles outside of the city limits. His hangover had caught up with him, and the ride of the carriage wasn't being kind to his mood or his stomach. He was trying to look through the notes given to him at the inn, but sore eyes and the motion of the carriage made it too difficult. Closing the folder, he pulled down the window and took a deep breath of the fresh country air as they left the city limits.

From what Borell had managed to read, The Grey Hand, as he called himself, was reported to be a small-time smuggler living in Farneville. His real name was James Stroud. He had been arrested on many occasions by the law, but had always covered his tracks too well to be prosecuted. His dwelling was small and modest which, based on his reported occupation, suggested he had somewhere more lavish to retire to in secret.

Borell was heading for the home address given in the folder. With a bit of luck he would be the first one there and could obtain the information before his competition did. He decided to rest his eyes for the remainder of the journey; putting his feet up on the opposite bench in the carriage, he closed his eyes.

Rest turned into sleep.

***

Borell's carriage stopped with a jolt. He scrambled about on the seat whilst he regained his composure.

'We're 'ere,' called the driver. Borell opened the door and stepped down. Looking around, he was standing outside a cottage on a sparsely populated road of houses. He put his hand in his pocket and removed a handful of coins. Picking out sixpence, he tossed it skilfully up to the driver, who deftly snatched it out of the air.

Borell closed the carriage door. 'Wait!' he shouted to the driver as he was about to put the carriage into motion. Opening the door and reaching inside, he grabbed the folder of papers from the seat and closed the door again. 'Right, off ya go,' he said to the driver who looked at him with a blank expression clearly *thinking* of something he wanted say aloud. The carriage shuddered into motion and disappeared in a cloud of dust as Borell folded the papers and put them inside his jacket.

Looking at the house behind him, he couldn't tell if anyone was home or if anyone had beaten him there. There was only one way to find out. Pushing open the white gate guarding the short stone path to the front door, he slowly looked around for anything out of the ordinary. The path was uncomfortable to walk on, the stones large and uneven — not at all inviting. Which was probably the whole idea.

Knock, knock.

'Anyone home?' Borell called through the closed front door. He wasn't worried about an invitation, but it is less conspicuous if the door is opened for you.

No answer.

''Allo?'

Still no answer.

'Right'cha are then,' he said to himself as he tried the door handle, looking towards the road as he did. A quick jiggle of the handle revealed that it was firmly locked. Not wanting to draw too much attention, he decided against kicking the door in and stepped back to look at the front of the house again. One of the main windows to his right caught his attention. On closer inspection, with his nose pressed up against the glass, he realised why.

'Ah shit,' he said as he saw a broken body lying on the floor of the living room. Presuming there was a rear way into the house, he made his way around the side, following the uneven path. He slowly pulled out a knife from inside his jacket when he saw the back door was ajar.

He crept along with his back to the wall, listening intently for any noises coming from inside. Not hearing anything, he reached out his left hand and pushed the hinged side of the door gently. It slowly swung open. Peering inside without showing too much of himself, he didn't see anyone in the kitchen, so went in as quietly as possible.

The kitchen table was clean, save for an empty bowl for fruit or vegetables. The kitchen looked unused — either that or the owner was an obsessively tidy person. The door to the lounge was open and the sun shining through the front window illuminated the body on the floor. Putting his head through the doorway into the hall, Borell checked to make sure he was alone. A quick check of the bedroom, bathroom and dining room confirmed he was by himself.

Well, nearly. Borell took a photograph from the folder he was carrying and checked it against the face laying in front of him.

'What are ya' gonna tell me now *Mr Grey Hand*?' said Borell standing over Stroud's body. He knelt down carefully and noticed a lack of blood on the floor. Whoever had been here first presumably had the information they wanted through some kind of torture, he thought. Stroud was lying with his neck turned more than a neck should, and his eyes were shut tight with a contracted post-mortem expression. He noticed that there were two puncture marks on Stroud's neck. Only a tiny amount of dried blood had escaped from the wounds and had left tear drop stains on his pale, almost white skin. The lack of blood on the floor suggested that his blood had been drained.

'Creepy,' Borell muttered to the corpse, 'what the hell did they do to you?' He checked Stroud's pockets. There would probably be nothing of worth left, but there may be some clue to help. After a few minutes of searching, he decided there was nothing that would help and cursed.

Not wanting to miss an opportunity to add to his own collection, he took the pocket watch he found in Stroud's jacket pocket, sating his compulsion with timepieces. He stood and looked around the living room. It looked as immaculate as the kitchen; Borell assumed Stroud didn't spend much time here.

'So where else do ya' go then?' he said as he looked through the items on the mantelpiece. A few neatly organised trinkets, a photograph of a pretty woman and a newspaper. He spent the next twenty minutes carefully searching the rest of the house, but all that he found were more tidy rooms and few personal possessions.

Taking a last look around, he tipped his hat to Stroud and headed for the kitchen and his exit, closing the kitchen door behind him as he left. He casually made his way around the front of the house towards the road; he looked around to make sure he wasn't being watched, and closed the little gate behind him as he stepped out onto the pavement.

Walking along the street, he took the folder Loren had given him from his jacket pocket and looked for Stroud's work address.

'Carter's Mill,' he said. 'Won't take long.'

Chapter Seven

Benjamin's bedroom was bright with the midday sun. His window overlooked the rear garden of the estate, and offered a pleasant view that he had enjoyed since childhood. The furnishings were comfortable and not at all lavish. His large closet wardrobe contained lots of hanging bags with clothes and outfits he had used in his many years working for the Society; the item in particular he was looking for wasn't something that would be easily discovered.

Opening the doors and sliding other hanging items out of the way, Benjamin pulled on two hooks either side of the rear wall. A door latch released, opening a secret panel that contained, amongst other things, a substantial black canvas bag hanging from a solid looking hook on the back wall of the compartment. A zipper running its length kept it neatly closed.

The bag was heavy as Benjamin unhooked it and laid it on his bed. Unzipping it, he took a second to look at the equipment that had saved his life many times. The body armour that Jackson had created for him many years ago still bore the scars of more than one attempt to impale, shoot or slice him. Unfortunately, the clothes he had been wearing over it hadn't fared so well, but he was still alive to appreciate the craftsmanship.

He slipped off his shirt and lifted the armour over his head, letting it rest on his shoulders. The straps around his waist mostly buttoned up as they used to, but Benjamin had to use the next button along to give himself a little more breathing room.

'Guess I'm not as slender as I used to be,' he said to himself as he pulled the straps as tight as he dare. Jackson had made the armour as lightweight as possible, creating some new techniques for layering the materials and metals that protected him, but he still knew he was wearing it. Fortunately, it still fit snugly enough to offer no restriction in his movement.

A concealed ankle holster complete with pistol was next to be strapped on. Finally, a long leather coat was all that was left in the bag. He didn't put it on, preferring to drape it over his shoulder instead. Benjamin closed the compartment, leaving behind the larger weapons hanging securely inside. He was sure he wouldn't need them just yet.

Fully dressed again, he headed back downstairs. With all his gear on he felt like his retirement had started to get the better of him and he was in for one hell of a workout if he had to run anywhere.

As he walked down the stairs, he could see a new message waiting for him. He had not heard the bell from the Perpetual Post-box, but could see the little indicator light blinking diligently in its single solitary task. He threw his coat over the arm of a chair and opened the message. He unrolled the paper and read the message, which was in code. It simply said:

2pm K.T.

Benjamin appreciated the brevity of the message, saving him a headache deciphering a complicated code. He looked at the clock on the wall, *a quarter past one*. Just at that moment, the front door handle started to turn and Benjamin span round with a start, drawing his gun from his holster as he did.

'Arrgghhh!' screamed Mary as she pushed the door open, dropping her bag of groceries on the welcome mat.

'You scared the life out of me, Benjamin. What the heck is going on?'

'I'm so sorry, Mary.' Benjamin holstered his gun and helped Mary pick up the bags, putting some of the spilled vegetables back as he did so. 'I'm a little on edge at the moment.'

'I did wonder what was going on. You didn't tell me someone was coming to fix the gate. And I did think it was a bit strange that he knew my name!'

'Ah, yes. Mostly to do with our guest. I trust you'll look after him.'

'Him? Who is *him*?' Mary inquired.

'Well he*'s* down in the workshop at the moment, and I'm sure he'll be looking forward to a good home cooked meal. He did say he missed your stew.'

'Jackson is here? What's wrong? Is he all right?' Mary looked like a deer caught in headlights.

'He's fine. Just needs a bit of protection for now. Couldn't think of a safer or more familiar place for him to stay. I'll let him know you are home.'

'Well then, I'll get this stuff into the kitchen and put on a nice pot of tea. Will your friends outside be wanting any?'

'Unlikely. Might blow their cover if they get too comfortable. You know, with tea and cakes,' Benjamin smiled.

'Right'cha are then,' she said, popping off to the kitchen fully laden again with bags.

Benjamin took a deep, calming breath. Clearly although his reactions were still as sharp as ever, maybe his nerves were a little frayed. He headed down the hallway to the workshop. Jackson had certainly been busy in the time Benjamin had been away. The room suddenly seemed to have come to life. Lots of equipment that belonged to Benjamin's father was now being useful somewhere on one of the benches or tables.

'Been busy, I see,' Benjamin said as he reached the bottom of the stairs.

'Oh yes, indeed.'

'There is someone upstairs who's keen to say "hello".'

'Hmm? Oh, Mary's home? That's wonderful. I have been looking forward to seeing her. I suddenly feel in the need of some liquid refreshment,' he said, putting down a screwdriver and wiping his hands on his apron.

They headed upstairs, where Jackson took his apron off and hung it on the coat rack in the hall and Benjamin headed for his study.

'Would you like me to ask Mary to fix you some tea as well?' Jackson asked, just before Benjamin made it to his study door.

'No thank you —' but Jackson had already turned and headed through the kitchen door before Benjamin could complete his reply. He smiled at seeing Jackson so happy. He knew Mary would love the company too; anyone to fuss over would do it.

***

Benjamin looked out of the window at the front of his study, stretching and getting used to the weight of his heavy undergarments. The clock on his study wall showed a little after two o'clock.

'Almost right on time,' he said as he saw a carriage pull up on the road outside the front gates.

He turned and headed into the hallway. Opening the front door, he saw three men carrying large brown canvas duffle bags walking down the path towards him.

'Benjamin,' said the man at the front of the trio, nodding his head in greeting and extending a hand to shake.

'Rallon. It's been a few years. How's the knee?' he said, smiling at the man who greeted him and shaking his hand. The last time they had seen each other, Rallon had twisted his knee badly on a mission. Benjamin had saved his life; Rallon was indebted.

'Healed nicely,' Rallon replied.

Benjamin looked at the two other men. 'Carter, Donald,' he said. Both men nodded back.

'I've got to go and see Prefect Twill shortly. I assume you have been briefed?' Benjamin asked.

'Yeah. We'll take good care of the place. Just the subject and your housekeeper inside?' Rallon asked.

'In the kitchen. Come in and I'll introduce you.'

The three men followed Benjamin through the front door. Carter and Donald quietly went their separate ways and began the task of setting themselves up for the duration; Rallon followed Benjamin into the kitchen.

'Mary, Jackson,' Benjamin said, patting his friend on the shoulder, 'This is Rallon. He's here to keep an eye on you and the house for a while.'

'Afternoon,' Rallon said, smiling and nodding his head.

'I have to go out for a while. I trust Rallon with my life. He'll make sure you are safe,' Benjamin said with a smile.

'Our driver is waiting for you,' Rallon informed Benjamin. 'He'll take you where you need to go.'

'Thanks, Ral.'

Benjamin left them in the kitchen and headed back to the front door, putting on his coat and his hat that he had left on the chair earlier. Walking towards the waiting carriage, he could see the man still working on his gate. He nodded towards Benjamin.

A traditional horse and carriage stood waiting by the curb, the driver looking cold in his thick coat and uniform.

'Hornwell Street entrance, please,' Benjamin said to him as he climbed into the carriage, closing the door behind him.

Chapter Eight

Nearly two hundred miles away in the university town of Dolare, Lilly Jansen stared hard at a man sitting at the bar.

'Twenty one. Torken. Single. Studies —' Lilly paused.

'Come on, Lil,' whispered Renae, 'there's a shilling riding on this one.'

'Okay, okay. Studies Mathematics and Horticulture,' Lilly said finally.

'Horticulture! Really? Where did that come from?' said Mia sitting next to Lilly, a little louder than she had planned.

'Look at the boots. Dull and worn soles, scuffs around the toes, brightly polished leather.'

'He could just walk a lot,' retorted Renae.

'Yes, but they've been polished in a hurry. You can still see where he's not cleaned the dirt off first,' Lilly explained. 'He's trying to impress or hide the fact he's a gardener or both.'

'Nope, not buying it. Torken — I'll give you that one. That's pretty obvious,' said Mia. 'But if that's what you're sticking to, I'm quite happy to take your money.'

Torken men were slim and mousey, normally suited to less physical work — another reason Lilly's statement about horticulture made no sense to Mia and Renae.

'Well, one of you two will have to go and find out. And I will have another ale half when you come back with my shilling.' Lilly grinned confidently.

Renae and Mia looked at each other for a quick second, then Mia shouted, 'Not it!'

'Damn it, Mia, I hate asking,' Renae exclaimed.

'Should be quicker then, my dear.' A smile beamed from Mia's face.

'Fine. But you're wrong, Lilly,' grunted Renae as she pushed her chair back and stood to make for the man at the bar.

The Crab and Basket was a pub in the main square of the University of Browne, where most students drifted towards after their studies like moths to a flame. A spacious lounge area, set up perfectly for the hundreds of students to descend upon, made it the ideal place to unwind. Tables ranging from one chair, for the more solitary students, to large round tables with a dozen or more chairs catered for the larger groups and parties.

Lunchtimes were usually busy, but not as packed as just after the first evening bell. Fresh food was always available at the Crab and Basket, and considering it was affordable for students, it wasn't actually that bad when it came to taste. On nice warm days, the front of the pub was open to the elements, allowing for plenty of fresh air and sunshine to lift even the lowest of educational spirits. Today was too cold for that kind of exposure, and several open fireplaces kept everyone warm and cosy inside.

'Mia, who's that guy at the bar? Near the stairs at the back,' asked Lilly, deliberately looking at Mia with an expression that said *don't look too hard*. 'He's been looking over here on and off since we came in.'

With a casual lean back in her chair, Mia craned her neck, pretending to stretch, and caught a fleeting glance of their mystery admirer.

'No idea, but he's not someone I'd want to introduce myself to. Did you see the bulge in the side of his jacket?'

'Yeah, not the friendly looking sort is he. As long as he stays over there, he'll be safe,' Lilly looked at Mia and chuckled moderately loudly; Mia sniggered a response.

'Have you heard from your brother recently?' Lilly asked.

'Yeah, I got a letter from him this morning actually,' she said, rummaging in her jacket for the envelope. 'He's found himself a small loft in Rannor and has been able to get work in a bakery just down the street. Says he's going to come and visit when he has saved enough money.'

'When was the last time we saw him? A year ago?'

'Thereabouts. I really miss him,' Mia said with a look of sadness on her face.

'At least he's out in the world doing what he loves. Making people fat,' Lilly said, which made them both laugh.

A half shilling coin landed on the table and span to a stop, followed by three glasses of ale clinking together and making a puddle of foamy drink on the table.

'Fine, you win, Lil,' said Renae as she distributed the glasses around to where Lilly and Mia were sitting, 'One of these days, I'll stop wagering you.'

'And one of these days I'll stop taking your money,' Lilly smiled. 'Pony up, Mia.'

'He studies Mathematics *and* Horticulture?' Mia asked Renae as she took her original seat next to Lilly.

'Yeah, his father is an accountant and wants to add *'and son'* to the family business. Our Torken friend over there has other ambitions. He would rather be outside in the fresh air, so is taking studies that his father doesn't know about. It'll all end badly, for him,' Renae chuckled.

'Where is he going to do that? Torke isn't exactly a fertile place,' wondered Mia.

'Don't care; he is ugly as sin up close. Certainly won't be going back over there to ask him anything else.'

'Renae, we really need to work on your people skills,' Lilly said with a furrowed brow and a smirk. Mia fished around in her purse and handed Lilly her half-shilling coin.

'How did you know he was studying mathematics, Lil? Lucky guess?' said Mia.

'Maybe, maybe not. If I told you how, there would be fewer shillings in my pocket.'

***

The lunchtime gathering was beginning to thin as the three of them reached the bottom of their drinks. Most students had afternoon classes, but today Lilly was free. Mia and Renae were not so lucky.

'Meet you here after six tonight? I hear that dream singer from the arts department is performing again. Want to get a good seat for that, if you know what I mean,' Renae smirked.

'We always know what you mean, Ren. Are you sure he'll sing again after you put him off last time with your outrageous flirting?' asked Lilly.

'It *was* outrageous, wasn't it!' Beaming a huge smile at Lilly and Mia, she stood up and drained the last of her drink. 'Right, off to have a sleep in Humanistic Disciplines. See you at six.' Sweeping her long auburn hair in an overly flirtatious way, she turned and left.

'She'll never learn.'

'But she'll have fun trying!' said Lilly, smiling.

'Walk with me to class?' asked Mia, as she put down her now empty glass. 'That guy is still giving me the creeps.'

'Sure. I've only got an afternoon of relaxation and reading to look forward to,' Lilly said smugly.

'Hate you,' Mia said lovingly.

'You too,' Lilly replied in kind.

The man standing at the bar wasn't looking at them as they stood and turned towards the doors, but Lilly caught a glimpse of him in the reflection of a glass cabinet as they made their way outside. He seemed to be watching them. She didn't say anything to Mia; she was on edge enough about him as it was.

'Who have you got this afternoon?' Lilly asked.

'Hibbit for Chemistry. One of the few classes I actually enjoy at the moment.'

'It helps that you like the subject,' said Lilly, keeping Mia distracted from the man at the bar.

The front of the Crab opened on to a large square with an ornate water feature in the middle, small vendor carts dotted around, selling everything from delicate foods to stationary supplies, and the main dormitory at the far end. Some of the other students and visitors to Dolare sat outside in the chilly sunshine, drinking steaming mugs of something or other and chatting their cares away next to flaming braziers.

The pair made their way across the square. Some of the poorer merchants simply had their wares on the wagon hitched to their donkey; others, with clearly more wealth, had modest mobile cabins with a roof and a multitude of goods hanging out for a more prominent display. One of these vendors, selling fine silks and materials, called to the girls as they walked past.

'Lovely day, ladies! Can I interest you with fine silks that pale in comparison to your beauty?' A cheesy opening line.

'Come on,' said Lilly, pulling on Mia's arm, knocking her slightly off her stride.

'Lil, I'll be late!'

'Won't be but a moment, I want to see what this fine gentleman has to offer us today,' she said in an overly showy stage voice.

'But you don't —' Mia received a quick dig in the ribs before she could finish her sentence.

'Now then, ladies, what will it be today? Fine silks from the monks of Fallon? Velvets as soft as a new born baby...?' Lilly had stopped listening at this point and was using the cover of the cabin to look back towards the Crab to see if they were being followed; she was only vaguely aware of the man continuing his sales pitch.

'Well, Lilly? You buying something, or am I going to be late for no particular reason?' said Mia with a not too subtle annoyance clearly audible in her voice.

Lilly turned to the man, who was now sporting a frown at being paid such little attention.

'Alas, my good man, we are but simple students, and have not the means to afford your luxurious wares. But I will tell all of my friends of your merchandise and a good word in this town goes a long way, as I'm sure you are aware,' Lilly responded in a playful voice.

'Indeed it does, but you ain't getting nuffin' for free, you know,' replied the man. 'Now bugger off if you're not buying anyfin''

'It's amazing how quickly they revert to their true nature isn't it, Mia,' Lilly said as she again pulled Mia's arm walking her away from the vendor.

'What was that all about, Lil?'

'Just checking.'

'Checking what?' exclaimed Mia. 'How late you can make me for class?'

'I was making sure our admirer from the Crab wasn't following us. He was paying us an awful lot of attention when we left. Looks like he's not following us, so he was probably just drunk and horny.'

'Eeewww, Lil, that's horrible!'

'It's not the first time we've had some unwanted attention in there. You know some people think university girls are easy,' Lilly said. 'And then there are those who don't do anything to curb that stereotype.'

'Yeah, Renae can be a bit much, but that's just who she is.' Mia laughed, making Lilly smile and shake her head with amusement.

Lilly and Mia continued walking past other stalls and street performers and caught some of the cold spray from the fountain as it drifted across the square in the afternoon breeze. Instinctively turning down Portland Lane, to head for the side entrance of the university, Lilly had an uneasy feeling well up in the pit of her stomach.

The narrow lane was quiet. Looking behind them, Lilly saw two shadows stepping out from a doorway. Mia turned to see what Lilly was looking at. She slowly turned back to Lilly and squeezed her arm, hard.

'Lil,' Mia whispered loudly, as if the men wouldn't hear her.

The two men didn't speak, but Lilly and Mia could see that they were armed with small coshes not too covertly hidden up their sleeves.

'What do you want?' demanded Lilly, turning to face the men. 'We have little money. Or, if you're after something else, we're pretty dirty and full of disease.'

'Lil!'

'They might as well know what they're getting, Mia,' Lilly said loudly, in a hope to put the men off their attack, if only for a moment.

The two men stepped forward in unison, slowly at first, and then suddenly rushing the pair. Lilly pushed Mia to one side; her friend tripped and fell into a doorway, but she was at least out of the line of attack. The first man fell a moment later, cradling the cosh in his stomach as he bent over double, groaning with pain.

The second man swung his cosh at Lilly, who dodged, putting the man off balance and, turning around to grab his weapon, brought her foot down hard on the back of his legs.

He crumbled to the floor crying out in pain.

'Run!' Lilly shouted as she helped Mia to her feet.

Mia was now ten steps down the narrow street before she turned to see Lilly wasn't following.

'Lilly! What are you doing?' she shouted.

'Just run!' Lilly said as she turned and started to follow. The two men on the floor had started to regain some composure and got to their feet.

'Go left!' Lilly shouted as she caught up to Mia at the end of Portland Lane. Mia ran down Barber Street as fast as she could and Lilly headed in the opposite direction. She looked behind as she ran to see the two men giving chase.

'Shit,' she shouted as she turned to look where she was going, moments before running into a horse and carriage, getting some angry shouts from the driver as he hurriedly calmed his horse.

Making her way as fast as she could through the mill of people and vehicles, she could now only see one of the men following her, visibly tiring from the chase. Lilly was faring better; her training in the Torlen defensive arts kept her fit. She took a turning down another side alley she knew branched in to several others in an attempt to lose the man.

Lilly turned a corner too fast and slid across the slippery stone paving, crashing into a wall and screaming in pain as her shoulder connected with a protruding brick. Picking herself up, she ran as fast as she could down an alley that was an obstacle course of washing and clothes hanging to dry. If nothing else, it would slow her pursuer down as well. Pushing sheets and rugs out of her way, she started to feel damp and cold from the water clinging to the material. Rubbing her face with her wet hands was refreshing and gave her a spur of energy.

As Lilly pushed past a large bed sheet blocking most of the alleyway, she was grabbed by a pair of hands she couldn't see off to her right. Her momentum and temporary blindness from the sheet caught her off guard and she tumbled sideways into the open doorway.

***

'Lilly, be quiet,' came a familiar voice, as the door they had tumbled through was kicked closed. Lying on the floor with an arm around her waist and a hand over her mouth gave Lilly a new sense of fear. She was tired from the pursuit, and it took a moment for her to regain her composure and to recognise to whom the voice belonged.

'Andris?' she said, the word muffled by the hand over her mouth.

Lilly stopped wriggling for a moment, just in time to see a pair of feet run past from a gap under the door.

Andris removed his hands and Lilly got to her feet, leaving Andris laying on the floor.

'I thought you were one of them,' she said, bending over with her hands on her knees, panting. Lilly had known Andris for a few years at the university. He studied mechanical engineering or some such thing she didn't understand and had met through mutual friends.

'Why was he chasing you? He looked the particularly unpleasant sort.' Andris sat up and dusted off his hands.

'That's a very good question that I don't have an answer for. He was watching us in the Crab.' Lilly suddenly realised that Mia was also on the run from the other man. 'Oh shit, Mia! I've got to go.'

'I'll come with you,' Andris offered as he stood up. 'You might need an extra pair of hands if she is in trouble.'

'Thanks all the same, but I'll deal with this on my own.'

'Like you dealt with it just now?'

'Hey, I've already taken them down once. Well for a few moments anyway,' Lilly said, feeling a rage build up inside her. 'I can take care of myself.'

'Fine, but at least let me get you back to the university, in case the men are still outside somewhere. You may need a distraction.'

'And you'd take them on, would you?'

Andris smiled. 'Let's just say I'm a sucker for a good cause.'

'Fine, just don't get in my way.'

Andris nodded in agreement.

Lilly moved closer to the door to look out into the alleyway, trying to see if the man was still out there somewhere.

'I've got a better way, come on,' Andris said. 'These houses have more than one way in and out, and we can get to the university quicker if we go — up.'

Lilly looked at him for a moment and thought about being able to see more from up higher. That and the fact the men wouldn't be looking up there for her.

'Okay, let's go.'

Andris turned and headed up the stairs in the corner of the dark and cramped room. The sunlight coming through the window boards afforded some visibility. The room was virtually too full to move in; bags of coal, some broken crates, a roaring furnace, pieces of furniture, stacks of logs and lots of dust.

'Up here. We can get on to the roof this way,' Andris said.

The stairs creaked as they both climbed together; Lilly had a death grip on the banister. The adrenaline was subsiding, now that she was calming down; worry for her friend starting to fill the void that remained.

The first floor hallway was much tidier and brighter. They walked into Andris' room to their right, containing his bed, large enough for one, a writing desk on the back wall and very few personal possessions. A door to the left of the stairs was ajar, and Lilly could hear voices discussing perhaps poetry or literature inside.

'Who's that?' Lilly asked.

'Friends of mine from the university. They are writing a play, or something. I'm sure they spend more time here than at the campus...' He smiled. 'Come on, this way,' he said as he opened the double windows and climbed out onto the narrow balcony. More washing hung between the two rows of houses over the alley on the first floor, gently blowing in the breeze. Lilly stepped out and looked up to where Andris was pointing. 'We can get up there and then cross over to the other side,' he said. 'It's a bit of a height. I hope you're okay with that?'

'I'm sure I will be.'

'Good.'

Andris used the brickwork to the right of the balcony to climb to the roof. The bricks had been laid in a decorative fashion, which also made it quite easy to climb.

'You do this a lot, do you?' called Lilly behind him.

'Yeah, don't you?' Andris joked.

Lilly climbed the last brick and stepped onto the flat roof. 'Wow, it's amazing up here.'

'Yeah. Not many people come up here, except to get some sun in the summer; it's too much effort most of the time. Handy though if you know where you're going. I've got to and from the engineering quarter without ever stepping foot on the ground.'

Lilly was only partly paying attention; the rest of her attention was wandering around the rooftops, taking in the view of the town. Towards the university, she could see the campus quite clearly. The cathedral-like building that housed the physical sciences; the huge, almost entirely glass building of the library; a dark grey building, billowing smoke from its three chimneys, which was unmistakably the engineering quarter.

'So which way to the fall that will kill me then?' Lilly asked, suddenly coming out of her daze.

'Come on,' Andris said, smiling at her and offering her his hand. 'This way.'

Lilly let her hand reach out towards Andris without thinking, then realised what she was doing.

'Just get going, I'll follow,' she said waving her outstretched hand in a dismissive gesture.

'Yes, boss,' Andris said, tipping an imaginary hat to her and turned towards the direction Lilly had run down the alley earlier.

***

After only a couple of minutes of walking along the rooftop, they came to a beam that was attached to a small dormer roof. It reached out across the alley to a similarly protruding roof on a house the other side. Hanging underneath were various remnants of festival bunting and decorations, long lost to the weather. The beam was nearly five inches wide, just enough room to walk across — provided you had a head for heights.

'And how many times have you crossed this? Seems a bit — narrow.' Stress showed in Lilly's voice.

'Lots. The trick is to look ahead at the chimneystacks in the distance. I'll go first and then you can focus on me if you're scared.'

Lilly gave him a serious look. 'I'm not scared of heights,' she said, looking over the edge into the alley below. 'It's the hitting the ground bit that I'm not fond of.'

'Don't worry. It really is easy.' Andris put his right foot onto the beam and balanced there precariously for a few seconds, just for dramatic effect.

'Not funny,' Lilly said, trying to stop the corners of her mouth from making a smile.

Andris casually walked across the beam, making it seem as easy as he said. After only a few seconds, he was at the other side looking back at Lilly. 'Come on then, I thought you were in a hurry?'

Lilly looked at him and screwed her face up in mock amusement. Looking down again, she stepped closer to the edge of the roof, and put one foot up on the beam. She had a great sense of balance, her Torlen training saw to that, but she had never used it forty feet from the ground before.

'Remember to look at me. Don't look down,' Andris called from the other rooftop.

Lilly lifted her other foot onto the beam, arms out for stability. Once she was on the beam, balance was easy, but she did listen to his advice and didn't look down. Slowly, she made her way across to Andris, who offered his hands again for support; this time she accepted.

'Thanks. Do we have to do that again anytime soon?' she asked with a sigh of relief.

'No, it's all rooftops from here — maybe a small jump here and there.'

'Well that's *mostly* good news then.'

Still holding her hand, Andris headed off along the rooftop with Lilly in tow. They followed the path of the street below, which for now was the quickest route towards the university. They passed Portland Lane where Lilly had first encountered the two men, and headed in the direction of Barber Street.

They soon came to an alleyway ahead of them, 'Gonna have to jump this one!' Andris said as he started picking up the pace into a run. He held on to Lilly's hand as they both leapt over the narrow gap. Suddenly, Andris found himself being pulled backwards as Lilly abruptly stopped just the other side of the gap.

'Hell, I thought you'd fallen!' he said, catching his breath. Lilly was too busy looking down into the darkened alley to notice Andris. She let go of his hand and knelt at the edge of the roof.

'Mia,' she whispered, a muffled cry sounding more than her words. Tears welled up in Lilly's eyes as she looked down at the growing crowd of people standing around her friend's motionless body. One man was on his knees pressing his hand onto a wound on Mia's abdomen.

'You! Put your hand here and keep the pressure on,' the man shouted at a woman standing nearby, looking on. 'I need someone to run to the university's medical quarter and fetch help now,' he shouted again, the stunned onlookers staring blankly at him. 'Go NOW! Someone, anyone!' he said in a calmer but equally loud voice.

'I'll go,' said a boy in his early teens standing at Mia's feet. 'I know where it is.'

'Good lad. Tell them to bring a trauma team. Or just say someone's been stabbed. Bring them back as quick as ya' legs can carry you. She's not dead yet.'

The boy disappeared in a flash.

'Where are you going?' Andris said as Lilly headed towards what looked like a ladder on the far side of the roof leading down to the adjacent alleyway. She ignored him as she stepped onto the first rung of the ladder.

'What if that man is down there waiting?' he said.

'Why would he be? Even if he was, there's a dozen

people down there. What's he going to do?' she said, exasperated at needing to justify her actions. Lilly quickly climbed down the first ladder, which stopped at the first floor, then headed down the second ladder that finished several feet above the alley below. Clinging to the last rung, she braced herself and dropped to the floor, staggering sideways against the wall with the impact. Had she looked up, she would have seen Andris following close behind, but she was already across the alley to Mia's side.

'Mia? Come on, wake up, Mia,' she said as people looked on.

'You know her?' said the man, holding Mia's wound.

'She's my best friend.'

'What's your name?' he asked her in that polite but firm voice.

'Lilly,' she replied.

'Okay, my name is Doctor Hann,' he said. 'Help is on the way. Just keep talking to her and hold her hand. Let her know you are here.'

Lilly did as the doctor asked as they waited for help to arrive.

Chapter Nine

Borell stood across the road from Carters Mill, casually leaning against a lamppost, smoking a rolled up cigarette. His eyes followed the men and women coming and going. There were two main entrances at the front of the building facing the road. One for vehicles arriving and leaving with goods, and one smaller entrance for workers on foot.

Several trucks had arrived with grain and left with sacks since he had been watching. Although there were a number of people going in and out of the Mill, it would be too risky using the front entrances. Once inside, he could pass for an official or clerk, but didn't want to have to explain himself to anyone on the front gates if they stopped him.

A quiet looking alleyway ran alongside the building; he hoped this would be a quieter way inside. He took a hefty drag on the cigarette and flicked it into the road. As casually as he could, he crossed the road, avoiding traffic, and meandered his way towards the alleyway.

Looking down the alley from the main road, there didn't seem to be anyone with which to concern himself. The wall that bordered the Mill was a good twelve feet tall on his right, but the opposite wall was more manageable. Making his way down the alley, he picked his moment, scrambled up the lower wall, then lunged across to the Mill wall. Hanging precariously for a moment, he pulled himself up and peered over into the yard.

A roof sat a few feet below the wall on the other side. From his vantage point, it looked like a coal shed, or some kind of outside store. He pulled himself up and over, landing as quietly as possible on the corrugated roof. Borell quickly made his way to the side of the roof and dropped down behind some large sacks.

He had not been spotted and from here, he could see the whole yard.

The yard was large and it easily accommodated ten trucks with room to turn and manoeuvre. They were lined up with their flatbeds reversed into bays, ready for the large burly men to load with sacks of flour, or lined up in front of chutes to tip their grain for milling. As one truck started to tip its load, the noise from its engine and the pouring grain was deafening.

Not somewhere I'd want to work all day, Borell thought.

He let out a breathy sigh. Looking around, he could see a doorway where the suits were coming and going. It looked like a good place to start. Brushing his jacket down with his hands and straightening his tie, Borell stood up when no one was looking made his way to the doorway. He didn't look out of place, even going as far as nodding greetings as he passed people. He wouldn't be memorable to anyone.

Getting close to the door he spotted earlier, it opened and a large, heavyset man wearing a bowler hat and a thick coat walked through.

'Af'ernoon,' the man said in a raised voice, barely audible above the din of the yard.

Borell smiled and nodded in response. It didn't seem like people were concerned by him being there. The man held the door for Borell as he walked inside, and then closed it behind him.

Silence — almost. The door did a great job of blocking the sound from outside. His ears rang a little as they adjusted to the quiet. The door had opened into the middle of a corridor running from left to right with a set of stairs leading to the next floor opposite him. A large brass sign on the wall in front of him simply said 'Mill' pointing to the right, and 'Office' pointing upstairs.

He climbed the stairs to the first floor where the corridor was full of doors; some of them were open, and he could hear voices engaged in conversation coming from within. Slowly walking along the line of doors, he listened to the various conversations as best he could.

'I don't care if they refuse to pay because their shipment was a little late. It arrived, so they pay,' one voice was saying to another in the first room.

'You should have seen him the next morning,' said a voice in the next room. 'There was no way that bet was going in his favour. I have never seen anyone so hung over —'

Borell kept walking, looking at the name plaques on the doors and listening to patchy conversations. After about a half dozen doors he came to the one labelled with James Stroud's name. He turned the handle casually; the door was unlocked.

Peering inside, this office looked much like the others. But unlike many of the other offices, this one was pristine. Stroud was obviously as meticulous in his work life as he appeared to be at home. The folders of paperwork on his desk sat in neat piles, with labels protruding so that you could see what they contained. The surfaces were clean, not a hint of dust anywhere. The walls were pale green with numerous maps and pictures, evenly spaced around the room.

Borell crept inside and closed the door behind him. He locked it, not wanting to have someone walk in on him. Looking at the maps on the walls, they appeared to be trade routes for the various shipping companies. A map of the mainland was the largest of them all, Stroud had used pins and different coloured string to map out the routes. Borell guessed that the routes changed from time to time, based on the pin holes scattered around the map. Nothing made much sense from the maps, Borell assumed the various colours indicated different companies, but he wasn't interested in that.

He turned his attention to Stroud's desk. Looking at the pile of plain coloured folders, he opened them one at a time, quickly scanning them to see if there was anything of use inside.

After several minutes of looking at shipping manifests and Bills of Lading for everything from perishable goods to heavy machinery, nothing looked out of the ordinary. Although if Stroud was as expert a smuggler as he was reported to be, then this was probably his normal every day work.

'Where would you hide your personal stuff,' he pondered aloud. Stroud was obviously running his real job shipping legitimate goods, but if he was also using the company to move his own illegal goods, he must have been keeping his records elsewhere. Borell spent the next fifteen minutes looking through well-organised filing cabinets of documents containing more of the same.

Frustrated at the apparent dead end, he sat in Stroud's chair and sighed. Looking around the room, nothing stood out to say that the occupier was involved in anything illicit. Glancing down at the waste bin next to the desk, even Stroud's rubbish was neatly folded or torn into small evenly sized pieces.

Then he noticed it, but almost didn't. A tiny patch of the table leg was worn — not overly noticeable but definitely worn. Borell looked at the rest of the finish on the desk. It was nicely polished and clean.

'Hello,' Borell said, getting up from the chair and kneeling next to the table leg. It was clear from looking closer that the varnish had been worn from something rubbing against it repeatedly. As none of the other legs showed this sort of wear, it prompted closer investigation.

The area affected wasn't very large. Borell rubbed his finger along the worn surface. There was no sign of a hidden panel or lever. He pushed and prodded anyway; tried to move the table leg which was fixed to the floor firmly; then sat back in the chair staring.

'I'm wasting my time,' Borell said. And then it hit him. 'Time,' he said, quickly looking around the room again. Just as he thought, there were no clocks or timepieces anywhere. Rummaging in his jacket pocket for Stroud's pocket watch, he realised the simplicity of it all. He held the watch out and sure enough, it was about the same size as the mark on the table leg. Placing the watch against the worn wood, he anticipated a secret draw opening or a hidden panel in the desk appearing.

Nothing.

Noticing how the watchcase was flatter on one side than the other, he flipped it around and tried again. This time there was nothing as dramatic as a magically appearing draw or panel, but the sound of a dull thud from the filing cabinets behind him caught his attention.

'Clever boy, Stroud,' he said with a wry smile on his face. 'I knew you were hiding something.'

At that moment, Borell was turned around by a knocking at the door; the handle rattled.

'James. You in there?' came a man's voice from the other side. A few more knocks, then Borell heard footsteps heading down the corridor. He removed his hand from the knife under his jacket and got up. He heard the same dull thud again and assumed the lock had automatically closed. He placed the watch against the table leg again and listened for the sound.

This time he could pinpoint where the sound came from and quickly started pushing and pulling the filing cabinets. The first two didn't move and then, 'You beauty!' he exclaimed as the third cabinet moved backwards into the wall, revealing a hidden room. He kept pushing the filing cabinet until it stopped dead, leaving a small opening for him to enter.

The hidden room was well lit and about as large as the main office. He assumed that Stroud had split the room in two and everyone just thought the office was small. There were four filing cabinets along one wall, a bench along the other wall and what appeared to be a boarded up window on the back wall. This interested Borell, as next to the window was a length of knotted rope hanging by a hook. On closer examination, the boards covering the window were hinged on one side. A quick peek behind the boards revealed the original window.

'You *were* a clever boy, Stroud,' he said closing the boards again. Through the opening into the main office, Borell could hear voices and knocking again. Deciding that he could use Stroud's escape route, he slowly pushed the filing cabinet back until he heard the thud as the bolt locked the cabinet in place again.

Now that the room was sealed, it was deathly quiet. It wouldn't matter what Stroud's colleagues did in the other room now; he would be safe for a while. Borell started looking through the neat stacks of papers on the bench. These looked like documents and orders for the illegal goods he had been supplying. There were sheets of paper with customer requests — mostly, it seemed, for things like tobacco and alcohol. They detailed the people requesting the items, the location that the items would be delivered to or left discreetly and notes about where to source them.

It didn't take Borell long to read the papers laid out on the bench. They appeared to be orders in progress or new orders that would never be fulfilled. As he was nearing the end of his reading, he came across a folder containing more paperwork. He opened it and realised he had found what he was looking for.

'This looks more like it,' he whispered to himself.

The folder contained details about Jackson Burns; his shop, the basic outline of the item to be acquired and details of security arrangements in place.

'So that's what I'm after,' he said, looking at a blueprint of the device that had been acquired. It was evident that Stroud was getting his information directly from someone with access to Society files, possibly an Agent.

Stroud's notes detailed the thugs he hired to break in and steal the device and Borell presumed, by the red line drawn through their details, that they were either dead or no longer a viable line of enquiry. It also contained the location of the handover of the device to the buyer.

This was due to happen very early this morning. Borell had to assume that Stroud made it to the handover, but didn't make it into work afterwards. So now, he needed to find out who the buyer was and track them down.

Borell closed the file and tucked it inside his jacket. He took a final look around the room for anything else that might be of use. When that came to naught he opened the hinged panel covering the window and looked outside. It was quite a drop to the ground, but it appeared that Stroud had chosen a nicely secluded escape route. Nothing overlooked this side of the building, just the river and an unused dock area below.

He dropped the rope through the window and took a deep breath.

Chapter Ten

Lilly stared out of a window on the fifth floor of the medical quarter across the expanse of the university as she waited to hear news from the doctors. They had rushed Mia here minutes before and, in all the choreographed commotion, Lilly had been told to wait for news outside of the operating room.

'She'll be okay,' Andris said as reassuringly as he possibly could.

Lilly just continued to stare out of the window. She was still trying to work out why the man had tried to kill Mia and why the other had continued to chase her down. It made no sense to her.

'If they were after me, why did they keep chasing Mia? If they wanted Mia dead, then they would want the same for me. Right? We had both seen the men...were they just covering their tracks? What did they want?'

Andris looked at her, trying to make sense of it too.

'I don't know. Anyway, there's a constable coming,' he said pointing down the corridor. 'Let them work out what the men were after.'

Lilly looked to her right, down the corridor and saw a uniformed constable approaching, baton in hand. A second later, the man who was chasing her earlier turned the corner and appeared behind him.

'Shit!' Lilly said as she turned on her heals and ran past Andris. 'It's him!'

Andris instinctively jumped up and ran after Lilly, fearing for his own life in that split second decision.

'You two, stop right there!' shouted the constable as he began running down the corridor after them, Lilly's attacker in close pursuit. They rounded a corner further down the corridor and ran into medical staff, pushing them out of the way. Their only way out was the stairs at the far end of the corridor, but as they drew closer, they could see another constable waiting with the other man, who'd stabbed Mia.

'Now what?' Lilly shouted.

'In here,' said Andris, as he kicked open a door just ahead of them on their left. Once inside, Andris bolted it shut, knowing it wouldn't keep the men out for long.

'Great, why did I listen to you? Now we're stuck in here!' Lilly said, panicking.

Andris ran to the back of the room, which was full of laundry, and pulled open a chute in the wall. 'It'll be a wild ride,' he said, pushing lots of the loose linen down the chute first, hoping for a soft landing.

'You're kidding!'

'You'd rather stay in here?' Andris said, looking less than confident in his escape plan. He held open the chute door, which was easily wide enough to accommodate someone much larger than either of them. 'Okay, I'll go first —'

'And leave me up here? Like hell,' Lilly said as she stepped up on a crate and used Andris as support, sitting herself on the lip of the chute. They both turned and looked at the door as men outside started banging and shoving it.

'Go!' shouted Andris as he gave Lilly a not so gentle shove, waiting for a few seconds then diving into the chute headfirst, following Lilly's screams; the chute door closing solidly behind him. The metal chute was shiny and smooth from repeated use and they quickly slid down the five floors to the basement laundry room, ending up in a heap of bed sheets and clothes at the bottom.

Andris scrambled to his unsteady feet and grabbed

Lilly's hands as she floundered in the linen.

'Come on, there's a back way out of the basement,' he said, pulling her up.

'How do you know?'

'I've been here before, trust me.'

Lilly followed him across the basement room, to the astonished looks of women washing linen in large vats.

They found a set of stairs that took them up into the yard behind the laundry and wasted no time in getting as far away from the hospital as they could. They ran along the main roads leading away from the hospital, not really thinking about who else might be pursuing them, down some smaller side roads and through more main streets.

'Wait, wait,' called Andris as they ran through some of the surrounding gardens. His legs had given up on him and he had to stop to catch his breath. Lilly saw him stop and breathe heavily, so stopped and ran back to him.

'What are you doing? We've got to get out of here,' she said.

'I just need to catch my breath.' He took a moment and stood up straight, letting his breathing calm before speaking again. 'So now the law wants you too? What's going on, Lilly?'

'I wish I knew,' she said. 'Those constables were working with the men that attacked us, that's clear. So I doubt they were acting lawfully. Who knows how many others are out to get us.'

'Us?' Andris said, looking ashen.

'You ran away too, and they shouted for us both to stop. I guess they figured you know about the attack on Mia and me. Another loose end.'

'That's great. So what do we do?'

'We can't stay here. We've got to get out of town. We need to find somewhere safe.'

'Where do you suggest?'

Lilly thought for a moment. 'Trellern,' she said.

'Why there?'

'My family is there. Unless you can think of anywhere else?'

Andris was quiet for a moment. 'As good a place as anywhere, I guess.'

'Right, then it's settled. We'll find my grandfather and get help there,' Lilly said, making the decision final. 'How much money have you got on you?'

'Not much, probably enough to get to the train station,' he said.

Lilly put her hands in her pockets and fished out what money she had left after lunch at the Crab and Basket. She found the shilling she had won from Mia and Renae.

'I've probably got enough for one ticket and taxi fare. That's not going to work,' she said.

'We might be alright. A friend of mine works the station. He owes me a favour.'

Lilly grabbed Andris by the hand and got him moving again, heading towards the main road they could see in the distance.

After a couple more minutes of laboured running, they flagged down a taxi carriage and climbed aboard.

'Train station please,' Lilly shouted to the driver.

Andris sat back on the bench seat, holding a stitch in his side and panting.

***

The large clock above the station office showed a little before three. Lilly and Andris sat on one of the platform benches as far away from the other passengers as possible. So far, they had not seen any constables, but they were still on edge.

A large-chested man in a conductor's uniform shouted in their direction, 'Three o'clock Trellern direct arriving in one minute.' He then shouted it again in the opposite direction for others to hear.

Lilly slunk down onto the bench as much as she could;

it made her feel less exposed. In the near distance, Lilly and Andris could hear a rumbling of wheels on the steel tracks as the train approached the station.

'Boarders make ready,' called the conductor as the train pulled up alongside the platform, steam venting from ports under the carriages. Several doors opened on the carriages as people got off, the people waiting to board standing clear to give them room.

'All aboard,' the conductor called as he looked at his pocket watch, checking the time of departure. Once the doors were clear, the two dozen or so people wanting to get on made their way aboard to find a seat. The carriages were not particularly busy today.

Andris quickly walked over to the conductor with Lilly following him closely. 'Frank.' He held out his hand to shake.

'Andris, you scurvy dog. Good to see you,' replied the conductor, shaking his hand.

'Listen — I need a ticket gratis and quick.'

'Can't you buy one like everyone else?'

'I could, but you owe me. Remember Susan?'

'Oh. Yes. I suppose I do owe you for her,' Frank said with a grin. 'Here,' he said, pulling out a pad from his jacket and tearing off a ticket. 'It's a return ticket, too. I owe you at least that much.'

'Thanks, Frank. Say hi to Susan for me.'

'I will. Best get aboard, she's leaving in one minute,' Frank said, ushering them towards the carriages, looking at his watch again.

Andris and Lilly sprinted to the train and climbed in to the nearest carriage. Finding seats wasn't hard; they quickly found two seats with a table. Andris sat opposite her and looked out of the window.

'So, who is Susan?' Lilly asked.

'Frank's lady friend. I set them up a few months back. He's never been so happy. He said he owed me; I thought it was about time to collect.'

'Ah I see. A matchmaker too,' Lilly said with a smile.
'I have my moments.'

One by one the doors on the carriages were closed by the conductor as he quickly walked the length of the train. He blew his whistle and the train started to move. Wheels span on the tracks as the locomotive tried to gain traction, followed by a jolt as they bit into the steel and pulled the carriages along.

Through the windows, countryside started to drift past, slowly moving faster and faster as the driver let the locomotive loose for a good run to Trellern.

Andris massaged his sore elbow.

They began to relax a little.

Chapter Eleven

As the driver was 'whoaing' the horses to a stop on Hornwell Street, Benjamin grabbed his hat, opened the door and climbed down onto the pavement.

'Much obliged,' he said to the driver as he closed the door. As the driver worked for the Society, he didn't need to be paid for the fare, but Benjamin knew a happy driver was a friend, so tossed a coin up to him.

'Thank you, sir,' the driver said, catching the coin before geeing the horses into a trot and heading off down the street.

The visitor's entrance on Hornwell Street was a subtle affair. A worn looking door in the side of the building that didn't stand out at all; in fact it looked just like the many other doors along the street. Benjamin knocked twice and waited. He had not needed to use this entrance for many years.

A few moments later, the door opened and a large, well-dressed doorman stood in front of him, showing no discernible expression. He stood to one side and Benjamin walked in. The antechamber was clean and sparse in decoration. To one side, behind the door, was a desk where the doorman sat when not dealing with visitors.

In front of him were two doors and a small blacked out window. The right-hand door led into a corridor that made its way to this office of the Society. The other would produce half a dozen men at a moment's notice if needed for any reason. Although Benjamin couldn't see through the window, he knew the men on the other side could see him.

'Weapons please, sir,' asked the doorman in a voice which made it clear he wasn't really asking. Benjamin took out his pistol, unloaded it and handed it to him handle first. Remembering he was also wearing a pistol on his ankle, he quickly handed that over too.

The doorman walked back behind his desk, placed both guns into the draw, and closed it. He handed Benjamin a slip of paper. He then proceeded to check for any other weapons. A quick search revealed nothing else of interest to the man.

'Who are you here to see?' he asked.

'Prefect Twill. He's expecting me.'

The man walked back behind his desk and took out a ledger from another drawer. 'And your name?'

'Sorrow, Benjamin Sorrow.'

He opened to today's bookmarked page and scanned the lines of appointments. 'Ah yes, so you are. Through the right hand door,' he said politely. The entry in his appointments list indicated that Benjamin didn't need an escort, so he didn't get one.

'Thank you,' replied Benjamin as he headed to the door, nodding to the blacked out window as he went.

Once through the door, the corridor beyond was well lit but long, the walls plain and featureless. The floor sloped down taking him underground for a short while and then gave his legs a workout as the incline took him back up to the surface.

After about a minute he reached the end of the corridor and heaved opened the large steel door to the Society offices. On the other side, a bright clean room with a desk and clerk on either side awaited. Lots of natural light flooded the room from the overhead light tubes that extended from this room to the roof, several floors above. The two clerks were busy filling out forms and paperwork, but acknowledged him with a polite 'good afternoon.'

Two large elevator doors faced Benjamin at the other end of the room, with an elevator operator standing between them at attention. The operator summoned an elevator by pressing the button located between the doors. Benjamin always thought this was a bit showy, and unnecessary, but he wasn't about to argue about a job with someone who clearly enjoyed his work.

The elevator arrived promptly with a distinctive *ping* and the doors slid open. Benjamin stepped inside and pressed the button for the sixth floor. The doors closed in front of him and the quiet hum of the elevator consumed him as he felt it pick up speed as it ascended.

Ping.

The elevator stopped and the doors opened at the sixth floor that was reserved for prefects. Above them would be the senior prefects and at the top of the building would be the principal. A strict hierarchy existed in the Society and stature was all-important.

Walking along the corridor, Benjamin took a passing interest in the pictures on the wall. He spotted a familiar face and smiled. 'Still leaving your door unlocked then, I see,' he said unceremoniously as he walked in to Kodey's office.

'Ben!' Kodey exclaimed, getting up and walking over to Benjamin. The pair shook hands and gave a brief old-friend embrace. 'It's good to see you.'

'You too, Kodey.'

Kodey closed the door behind Benjamin, turning the large key in the lock and ushered him towards a chair in front of the desk.

'Can I get you a drink?' Kodey said with a childish grin on his face. 'I have some of that Portabello Scotch that we used to drink at The Long Lance Club.'

Benjamin smiled. 'I'll pass. You know what that stuff does to your brain.'

'Yeah, I remember all too well,' said Kodey smiling. 'How is Jackson? I only learned about the theft this morning.'

'He's okay. Still shaken up, but he's a tough old coot.'

'Good. I take it the help arrived quickly enough? I mustered the best men I could at short notice.'

'Thank you for that. Rallon was a good choice. Jackson and Mary are in good hands.'

'I had a meeting with the principal earlier. He chose me to liaise with you on this issue. My instructions are to keep this as quiet as possible, for as long as possible.'

'Any ideas why he wanted me? I am retired, you know.'

'And how is that working out for you?' Kodey said in a jovial voice, sitting down at his desk. 'The principal knew that you would get yourself involved somehow, and decided to make use of your skills.'

'He's family. I just wish he'd contacted me sooner.'

'Did you learn anything from Jackson about his device? I was only given an outline of the project. I guess I'm still on a need to know basis.'

'Jackson gave me the headlines, nothing too specific. That was dad's area of expertise,' Benjamin said, smiling. 'I would have thought the Society would have been all over this the moment Jackson was robbed. Why would they sit around doing nothing whilst the device was being moved to who knows where?'

'A very good point. Jackson would have reported it — or, at the very least, whoever was in charge of the project would have. Did he say anything about our involvement after the robbery?'

'He said that the project was very low key and that he assumed that it was being dealt with. He mentioned an Agent Bone that came to his shop to investigate.'

'Come on, we need to speak to Agent Bone.'

'He was my next stop. I want to know why he left no agents to look after Jackson and didn't even get his door fixed!'

Kodey opened his desk drawer with a tiny key hanging on a pocket watch chain from his waistcoat, took out a small bunch of keys and stood up. He unlocked his office door and extended his hand for Benjamin to go first, playfully slapping him on the stomach as he walked past. 'Just checking to see if it's armour or retirement,' he said, grinning broadly at Benjamin.

'There's a bit of both in there,' Benjamin said and smiled back, casually punching his friend in the arm for his quick wit. 'How is your father?' he added as they passed by the picture of him on the wall.

'He's as stubborn and cantankerous as he always was. But *he's* actually enjoying his retirement. He and mum just found a little house in the country away from everything. It's a nice place to take the kids — you know, get away from the city.'

'Margret and the kids are good?' Benjamin continued their catch up chat as they walked down the corridor.

'They are. Lucy and Miles are growing up so quick. The family life still doesn't appeal to you then?'

'I have been thinking about it more recently, but you know how hard it is to find the right girl. I'm not sure if she's even out there for me,' Benjamin said with a mock glum expression on his face.

'Here,' Kodey said, pulling out a thick envelope from his waistcoat pocket. 'Your directive and reinstatement papers from the principal. You'll need that to get access to any resources you need. You'll also need this,' he said, taking out Benjamin's badge from his jacket pocket. 'Welcome back.'

Benjamin took the leather wallet with the Society crest on the badge, looked at it and smiled.

'Didn't expect to see this again.'

They stepped into the elevator at the end of the corridor and pressed the button for the fourth floor.

***

The door to the elevator opened at the fifth floor and a smartly dressed man wearing his day robes stepped inside with his hands behind his back looking pensive. 'Ah — Mr Sorrow,' he said. 'I heard a rumour that you were back amongst us today.'

'Prefect Hoyt. It's been a while,' Benjamin replied. Cornelius Hoyt was a senior prefect, but he let the slip of his title pass this once. The doors closed and the elevator descended again.

'Prefect Twill,' Hoyt said.

'Sir,' Kodey replied.

Ping.

The doors opened to the fourth floor and a wash of sound hit them. There were people amassed in the corridor as well as security officers, other prefects and medical staff.

'What's going on?' Kodey asked Hoyt.

'Foul play, I'm afraid. One of our agents has been found dead.'

'With permission, sir, we'd like to join you,' Benjamin said.

'Fine, fine, just don't get in the way,' Hoyt said with his air of seniority and a dismissive wave of his hand.

The fourth floor was where most of the senior agents worked. There were small single offices and several generous offices that contained various specialised teams of agents. The mass of people were congregating around an office near the end of the corridor. Benjamin had no idea who it belonged to, but he had a hunch that it was Agent Bone's.

They made their way through the throng of staff, nodded a hello to a few agents and stood outside the office under scrutiny. The body of the agent lay slumped over his desk with what appeared to be an ornate letter opener protruding from his left ear, a pool of dried blood on the desk. The medical team had checked him over and confirmed he was dead. He appeared to have been this way for about a day, one technician said. The smell seeping from the locked room had finally attracted some attention from his neighbours.

Benjamin looked at the nameplate on the door:

Hadleigh Bone — Senior Field Agent

'I want everyone out of here, now!' shouted Hoyt as he emerged from the room. The security team started to usher those that were merely looking on back towards their offices.

'That includes you, Mr Sorrow,' Hoyt glared at Benjamin.

'With all due respect, sir, I believe this may be relevant to a matter that I have been assigned to investigate,' Benjamin said maintaining the proper levels of decorum.

'Like hell it is,' Hoyt blasted. 'Get out of here now or I'll have you removed forcefully.'

Benjamin put his hand into his jacket pocket and removed the Principal's Directive. 'In that case, you give me no choice,' he said, handing it to Hoyt. Kodey stood back, watching the annoyance on Hoyt's face grow. He tried to hide the small pleasure he took from it, mostly succeeding.

Hoyt snatched at the letter and opened it. His face fell and his eyes narrowed immediately, his expression now one of pure annoyance and darkening like an approaching storm. He moved close to Benjamin. 'Friends in high places today, *Agent* Sorrow,' he said in a hushed voice. 'Get in the way and, Directive or no Directive, I'll have you *removed*. Understand?' The last part was completely rhetorical. Benjamin took the Directive from Hoyt's hand and smiled.

'I want the autopsy complete this afternoon,' Hoyt shouted at the medical team. 'See that I'm not kept waiting'. He turned his attention to the scene technicians who were examining the office. 'Your report had better be on my desk in one hour. If *he* —' he pointed at Benjamin '— touches or moves anything, it'd better be in your report in black and white.' With that, Hoyt turned on his heels and strode towards the elevator, glaring at Kodey as he went.

'That man has got a huge bug up his arse,' said one of the technicians examining the office for evidence, once Hoyt was out of earshot. 'He seems to have it in for you, my friend.'

'We have a history, I'm afraid. He still doesn't like me very much,' said Benjamin.

'Pissed him off, did ya?'

'Actually it was the other way around. Then he didn't take to kindly to me holding his career back a year or two. Not that he seems to be struggling now.' Benjamin offered his hand to the technician.

'M' name's Bastion. Any enemy of Hoyt is a friend of mine,' he said with a chuckle.

'Benjamin Sorrow,' he said, shaking Bastion's hand.

'It is an honour, sir. You're a bit of a legend around here. I thought you'd retired?'

'So did I.' He smiled. 'Have you found anything?'

'Not really. Doesn't seem to be any physical evidence apart from the weapon. Maybe the corpse guys can tell ya more when they get their hands on him.'

'Mind if I take a look through his diary?'

'You go right ahead. Anything you want to do is fine by me. My report will be pretty thin by the looks of it anyway. No need to pad it out with everything you do in here,' Bastion said, continuing to work his way around the room. Kodey stepped into the office doorway after speaking to some of the other agents who were milling about outside.

Benjamin turned the cover of the diary on Agent Bone's desk. He had no appointments scheduled for today. He looked back through the days. Nothing of interest.

'If you find anything else that might help me with my enquiries, would you send it here?' Benjamin asked, offering Bastion a small card with his name and post-box number on it.

'It would be a pleasure to help, sir.'

Benjamin said goodbye and made his way out of the office.

'What the hell is going on?' Kodey whispered to Benjamin as they walked back towards the elevator.

'Two guys break into Jackson's shop, steal the device, then someone kills the agent who investigates?'

'Must be an inside job?'

The offices along the way to the elevator were a buzzing with conversation about Agent Bone's death. It appeared that no one had been to his office over the weekend, but Benjamin and Kodey saw a woman being consoled after discovering his body today.

'We need to find the message that Jackson sent. See if anyone else was showing an interest. Might be our only lead,' Kodey suggested. 'I know someone in administration who can help.'

'After you.'

***

Benjamin and Kodey walked across the administration floor looking for Jessica. She was a petite woman with shoulder-length strawberry blond hair and a girlish face. Kodey had known her for several years and she often brought her two children to Kodey's house to play with his own children.

'Jessica,' Kodey said, catching her attention.

'Hi, Kodey,' she said with a huge smile showing off her pearly white teeth.

'This is Benjamin. He's helping me with an investigation.'

'Nice to meet you, Jessica,' Benjamin said.

Jessica smiled back and shook his hand.

'Jess, we need to know about a message that would have arrived yesterday morning from Jackson Burns. It was intended for Agent Bone.'

'I just heard. I can't believe it, someone killed inside our building?' Jessica said. 'Come on, I need to check the message logs.' She took them over to her desk and she grabbed a file from the shelves behind. She flipped through the pages until she found the message Kodey was interested in. 'Here it is. A coded message from Jackson Burns for Agent Bone.'

Kodey and Benjamin both looked at the entry.

'Do you remember who the runner was that took the message to Agent Bone? It's important we speak to them,' Kodey said.

'Sure. Sunday would have been Tom. He's over there by the bookcase. Is he in trouble?'

'No, we just need to ask him some questions,' Benjamin said in a reassuring way.

Jessica smiled again, seemingly lost for words.

'Margret is looking forward to you and the kids coming over at the weekend,' Kodey said to her. 'I'll speak to you later.'

Jessica said goodbye in an overly bubbly way, waving her hand towards Benjamin like that of a young schoolgirl. Benjamin looked at Kodey with a suspicious expression on his face.

Kodey smiled deviously. 'Later...'

'Tom,' Kodey called as they walked towards the boy sitting engrossed in a book.

'Yes sir?'

'I'm Prefect Twill and this is Agent Sorrow. We just need to ask you a couple of questions.'

'Me, sir? Have I done something wrong, sir?' Tom stood up, expecting a telling off.

'No, not at all. Do you remember taking a despatch to Agent Bone on Sunday?' Benjamin asked.

'Yes, sir.'

'How did Agent Bone seem to you when you gave him the despatch?'

'Oh, I didn't see him, sir.'

Kodey and Benjamin looked at each other.

'Why not?' Kodey asked.

'Well you see, sir, I was waiting for the elevator to go

up to the fourth floor. A prefect appeared next to me — out of nowhere he came, honest. He saw the despatch in my hand and said he was heading to see Agent Bone and would take it for me.'

'So you gave him the despatch?'

'Yes, sir. Saved me a trip up there and back.'

'Do you know who the prefect was?' Benjamin asked.

'Prefect Abner, sir.'

'Are you sure it was him? We need you to be absolutely sure.'

'I am, sir. I've met him lots of times. S'why I didn't think it would be a problem giving him the despatch to take for me. Although to be honest —' Tom leant closer, lowering his voice '— it makes me feel a bit sick being around him for too long. That smell... it's enough to make a bee puke.'

'Remember you are talking about a Prefect, Tom,' Kodey replied, a little more sternly than he had intended.

'Yes, sir. Sorry, sir.' Tom hung his face and looked at his shoes.

'What was the smell, Tom?' Benjamin asked in a friendlier tone. 'Come on,' he said to Kodey with a smile. 'Cut the kid some slack.'

Tom's face lit up a little at the humour in Benjamin's voice and said, 'Stinks like flowers dunt'e.'

'What do you mean? What flower?'

'Lavenders and stuff.'

'Thanks, Tom,' Benjamin said. Just as Kodey was about to say something, he pulled him away and they began walking back out of the room.

'Now do you want to tell me what that was about?' asked Kodey.

'Jackson was a bit muddled, but he said he remembered smelling lavender in his shop. What if Abner went in place of Agent Bone, to make sure there were no loose ends? We're already pretty sure the people that robbed Jackson were large, thuggish men, so I doubt Abner did any heavy lifting. Maybe something went wrong and Bone was just a diversion?'

'That's pretty thin, Ben, but you have a point,' conceded Kodey. 'Killing Bone and taking his place would mean that any follow up would lead to a dead end — literally. I'll have someone look after Tom for a while, just to make sure he's out of harm's way.'

'Good. I'll go and find Abner. Although I suspect he's long gone.'

'His office is just along from mine. I'll come with you.'

***

'So how we gonna do this?' Kodey asked Benjamin as they stood a few doors down from Abner's office.

'I was hoping you had a plan. Wouldn't mind a weapon, just in case he's armed.'

Kodey gestured towards one of the security officers he had ordered to assist them, signalling him to give Benjamin a weapon. The look on his face said he wasn't sure, but he didn't want to argue with a prefect who was going in first.

'Thanks,' Benjamin whispered to the officer as he checked the gun, and cocked it ready.

'He shouldn't be too much trouble. I've got your back,' Kodey said.

'Thanks. So I'm going first, then,' Benjamin said, curling the corner of his mouth into a smirk. 'Just like that time in Baszan?'

'Hell, I hope not. At least this time there should be only one person inside. Maybe a secretary as well, but I'll take care of her for you.' The smile on Kodey's face almost reached each ear.

'That's a great help — thanks.'

The pair slowly made their way along the plush hallway until they stood either side of Prefect Abner's office door; the two security officers stood back, a little further down the corridor, as instructed.

Benjamin put his ear as close to the door as he could to listen for any sounds inside. He looked at Kodey and shook his head. He put his hand on the doorknob and turned it slowly; the door was unlocked.

He mouthed to Kodey, 'One — two — three,' then shouldered the door open and burst inside. Kodey followed closely behind and covered Benjamin as they both surveyed the room through their gun sights. The reception room was empty. Abner kept a secretary, but it didn't look as if her desk had been occupied today.

They moved quickly towards the door leading to Abner's main office.

'It's locked,' Kodey whispered, trying the handle gently.

Benjamin stepped back from the door and slammed his boot hard against the lock. As the door edge exploded into splinters, they burst in to Abner's office and surveyed it for any occupants before looking dejected and holstering their weapons.

'Good to know I can still do that,' he said to Kodey, rubbing his knee. 'How come he gets a reception room?' he added as a joke.

'I got the better view,' Kodey replied, perfectly seriously.

Abner's office was smaller than Kodey's, due to the addition of the reception room, and view wasn't nearly as pleasing — they both agreed upon that. The room was cold and still with no signs of life. Benjamin walked over to the fireplace. 'Stone cold,' he said.

'I'll have security search the lower floors and arrest him if they find him, although I doubt he's been in today,' Kodey said.

Chapter Twelve

Lilly gazed out of the window at the countryside whipping by. Things were slowly becoming more industrial as time passed and they approached the city. The motion of the train was enough to put Andris to sleep, but Lilly didn't mind; it made her smile. They had passed the time chatting and talking about their families and hometowns. The shock of the whole situation with the men back at the university and the constables was at the back of her mind for now.

The conductor walked along the aisle, calling, 'Fifteen minutes to Trellern. Fifteen minutes.'

'Hmm, what?' Andris woke from slumber wiping his eyes. 'Sorry, that was bad form, falling asleep,' he said.

'That's okay. It's nice to just watch the world go by.'

'I'm looking forward to seeing Trellern first-hand with the hustle and bustle of the streets. Is it really that different to Dolare?'

'In many ways it is. The same in others. It is much larger and everything seems to be happening at a faster pace. You'll love it,' Lilly said, rolling her eyes in a playful way.

'Shouldn't we have told your grandfather that we're coming?' Andris said.

'If we did, who knows who might have intercepted the message before we got there. Besides, he'll love a visit. He'll be easy to find too — he's always at his shop.'

Fifteen minutes flew by quickly for Lilly with the anticipation of seeing her grandfather again. She was sure that the men who were after her in Dolare wouldn't be following her to Trellern. Why would they?

'Look at all the airships!' Andris blurted out as the train swung gently around a bend in the track, revealing the city of Trellern. 'It's even better than I thought!'

'You are easily pleased, aren't you?' Lilly giggled.

'Hey, knock it off. I've wanted to come here for a long time now,' he said with an awestruck expression on his face. 'Just never had the time, what with studying and apprenticing.'

Lilly spent the next five minutes listening to Andris getting excited about all the industry and technology he saw as they approached the city centre. The large industrial buildings on the outskirts of the city bellowing smoke and steam into the afternoon sky. The construction sites of new hangars being erected, to house the biggest airships that were being built here. The smaller aerodromes and the larger airports were a choreographed dance of landing and launching airships and planes.

As they drew closer to the terminal, the surrounding buildings grew denser. The country skyline was now replaced with the sprawling residential structures of houses, stately homes and mansions.

'How long will it take to get to your grandfather's shop?'

'I think it's about ten minutes by carriage. I'd feel safer moving quickly instead of walking.'

The train began to slow as it approached the terminal. The conductor hurried past them to get to the head of the train for disembarking. The windows of their carriage were suddenly dark as they clattered through a short tunnel and appeared the other side in a long glass-domed station terminal.

Glancing out the windows, they could see that everything had slowed to a standstill as people waited patiently on the platforms for everyone to disembark.

'Come on then — unless you want to stay here all day,'

Lilly said, lightly slapping Andris on the shoulder.

They joined the other passengers and made their way slowly to the doors.

'Thank you,' Lilly said politely as she passed one of the conductors standing by the door.

'Miss,' he replied, tipping his hat.

Once on the platform, Andris followed Lilly's lead. She had at least been here before and knew where she was going. They pulled their coats tight against the chill air. The huge terminal was a wonder, the likes of which Andris had not seen first-hand before. Majestic columns rose from the platforms supporting the expanse of glass that made up the domed roof. The terminal at Dolare was tiny by comparison and the station in his hometown was smaller still. His knowledge of these engineering marvels was mostly from books at the university, he had explained to Lilly. Getting out into the real world was always something he'd planned to do — later.

'We can get a carriage over there,' she said. 'The sooner we get moving again, the happier I'll feel.'

'No arguments there.'

They made their way through the waiting passengers and pushed past the slower ones who had got off the train ahead them. Some seemed to be standing idle, waiting for others or looking lost. Tourists, Lilly thought.

'Come on, there's a carriage,' she said, pointing towards three of them waiting beside the entrance to the terminal. The driver of the lead carriage saw them approach and opened the door for them.

'Where to, miss?' he asked, blowing into his cold hands.

'Merchant Drive, in the trade district please.'

'Yes, ma'am,' he said as they climbed aboard. The horses raised their heads at the shift in weight behind them, instinctively ready for work. The driver motioned the horses forwards, keeping them at a steady trot until they'd left the cover of the terminal.

Andris hung his head out of the window on his side of the carriage for a minute, taking in as much of the city as he could, until his face burned with the cold wind. Lilly relaxed a little more as the driver picked up speed and drove out onto the main road, knowing she was on familiar ground and minutes away from someone she trusted. She was sure her grandfather would be able to find them somewhere safe to stay for a while.

The driver took all the familiar roads that Lilly knew. Now on Appletree Drive, Lilly could see the clock tower on the other side of the river. She pointed it out to Andris, who watched as an airship was undocking from the top of the tower and beginning a manoeuvre away to the north.

A few minutes later, the carriage began to slow as the driver negotiated a left turn onto Parsons Lane and then again onto Merchant Drive.

'Whereabouts do you wanna be, miss?' called the driver through a hatch in the front of the carriage.

'The place is about halfway down on this side. I'll tell you when I see it.'

'Right'cha.'

Lilly looked out of the window ahead of them, looking for the familiar frontage of her grandfather's shop. Things had changed little in the few years since she was last here.

'Just up ahead, on the left,' she shouted up to the driver.

They heard the horses being 'whoaed' and the carriage slowly came to a stop outside the shop.

'Come on,' she said to Andris as she opened the door and climbed out. She took out her purse and handed the driver some coin.

'Thanks, miss. Good day to ya', he said as he made a clicking sound with his mouth to move the horses on.

'The shop looks a bit run down,' Andris commented as they both stood on the pavement outside.

'It always looks like this. Inside is a different picture.'

Lilly walked up to the door, pulled on the doorbell and waited. No answer. She tried again. Still no answer. Lilly tried the door handle, but the door wouldn't budge.

'Strange,' she said. 'Grandpa wouldn't be out for lunch this late in the day.' She had just assumed he would be here as he rarely left his shop.

As Benjamin had done the day before, she peered through one of the grimy windows, looking for any signs of activity inside.

'Maybe he's asleep?' Andris offered unhelpfully.

'He may be old, but he's got as much energy as you or I,' she said. 'Well, he used to have anyway.'

She knocked again, harder this time, and tried the handle a few more times.

'Maybe he's just out then. Is there somewhere else he might go? A friend, your family?'

'There is my uncle, Ben,' she said. 'Well — he's not really my uncle, but he's a very good friend of Grandpa's. I've not seen him in a while, but he may know where Grandpa is.'

'Then that sounds like as good a place to look as anywhere,' Andris said, offering his arm to Lilly. 'How far is it to his house? Do we need a carriage?'

'We can walk, it's not far.'

***

A quarter of an hour's walk later, Lilly apologised for the third time.

'I really thought it was closer than this,' she said.

Andris didn't mind the walk; the sun was shining and the air was clear, even if his nose was feeling a little numb.

'It is beautiful once you get to some of the green spaces, isn't it,' he said. 'Your uncle must have quite a bit of money if he lives in an area like this.'

'It's family money really. His parents died a few years back — I remember Grandpa writing about it in his letters. Some kind of airship accident I think he said. Uncle Ben travelled a lot for business, but I'm not really sure what he does now.'

The pair walked along Elm Avenue, marvelling at the gardens of the houses and mansions as they went. They stopped at a couple of houses and peered through the gates to get a better look. Some of the topiary were beautiful, and some were just plain fantastic. They took a moment to stop and look at a family of elephants that stood proud, endlessly watching the path to the main house on one property. Andris had never seen anything like it.

Finally, they reached Benjamin's house, where a man was working on the front gate. He eyed them cautiously as they walked past.

'He sure has got a nice house, Lilly. I wouldn't mind staying here for a bit,' he said to a dig in the ribs from Lilly.

As they walked down the path to the front door, Lilly couldn't help but feel as though they were being watched. She casually turned her head back towards the man they had just passed. He was still scrutinising them; she met his stare.

'I've got a bad feeling,' she said.

'You've just got a bunch of nerves in you after what happened at the university.'

'Thanks for the reminder.'

They climbed the steps to the front door and Lilly pulled the doorbell twice. After about twenty seconds, she heard the dragging of a bolt and the door slowly opened. The face of an older woman wearing a white apron appeared through the gap.

'Miss Lilly?' exclaimed Mary. 'What in the devil's name are you doing here?' She didn't give her time to respond as Lilly opened her mouth and tried to form an answer. 'Never mind. Come in, come in.'

Lilly looked at Andris, who looked happy to be welcomed in, and then back to Mary.

'Mary? You still work here? Well of course you do. It's good to see you again,' Lilly suddenly found herself babbling. She had always got on well with Mary when she was a child. It may have been because of the treats Mary would hide for her when she came to visit; feelings of home and belonging came back to her. She gave Mary a firm hug.

'Now now, child, there's someone else here who would enjoy a hug like that. Come in.'

As Mary opened the door wider Lilly jumped back to see two men standing in the shadow of the entrance with pistols drawn.

'Put those things away immediately,' Mary barked at the men. 'Lilly is family and will be treated as such.'

'Yes, ma'am,' Rallon replied, holstering his weapon, as Carter did the same. 'Miss — sir,' Rallon said as the men returned to their post.

'Mary, what's going on? We've just been to Grandpa's shop and he's not there. Is something wrong? Has something happened?'

'My my, you *are* full of questions today,' Mary said as she ushered Lilly inside. 'And you would be?' she said, looking squarely at Andris and avoiding Lilly's question.

'Andris Tar, ma'am,' he replied. 'A — a friend of Lilly's from the university.'

'Well, any friend of our Lilly is welcome here.'

'Lilly?' came a quiet voice from along the hallway.

'Grandpa!' Lilly shouted as she turned to the familiar figure walking towards her. She rushed over and threw her arms around him.

'I thought I heard your voice. What are you doing here?' he asked, holding her tightly.

'We had some trouble at the university. We needed somewhere safe to go,' she said.

'Well you've come to a safe place; I'm just not sure about the timing.'

Lilly let her hug loosen a little. 'Grandpa, what happened to your face?'

'Come, let's sit and I'll try and explain.'

Jackson headed back towards the kitchen with his arm still around Lilly.

'Master Andris, you look like you could use a nice hot bath after your journey,' Mary said indicating towards the stairs, skilfully diverting him away from Lilly and Jackson.

'That would be wonderful, ma'am'

'And less of the "ma'am" if you please. Call me Mary like everyone else,' she said with a dismissive wave of her hand.

'Mary — that would be wonderful.'

***

'So what is really going on, Grandpa?' Lilly asked as they sat in the comfortable chairs in the corner of the kitchen. Benjamin had moved some of them from the lounge to be comfortable when sitting with Mary in the mornings.

'Where to begin really...' Jackson sighed. 'I seem to have got myself into a spot of bother,' he admitted.

'A spot!' Mary exclaimed as she walked back into the room. She had left Andris to soak his bruises in a hot, steaming bath upstairs.

Jackson smiled, 'Okay, a lot of bother. I've been working on something for a while now. Has great importance for the Kingdom — the world, really. Unfortunately, my work turned out not to be as secretive as I had hoped. Some people broke into my shop yesterday whilst I was there and stole something from me.'

'Okay, that explains the bruises, but why are you at Uncle Ben's house? And what about those men?'

'How much do you know about what Benjamin does for a living?'

'Not much really. I know he travelled a lot. His parents were kind to me when I was growing up. I think he was something to do with cartography?'

'Nowhere close, my dear,' he said with a smile. 'He did travel a lot, I'll grant you that, but I guarantee you he wasn't involved in map making.'

'What was he doing then?'

'That is a good question. He did everything — and nothing. To most people, he was merely a wealthy traveller. To the Society, he was one of their best agents.'

'What? An agent — Uncle Ben?' Lilly said incredulously.

'Indeed he was. He took a leave of absence after the nasty business of his parent's death,' he said. 'But recent events have brought him back to the Society. Hence my presence here and the heavily armed men outside. They're here to protect us, Lilly.'

Lilly sat open mouthed for a moment, then screwed up her face in disbelief. 'So you work for the Society as well?'

'Not really. Some of my work is funded by them, but I have always maintained my independence otherwise. Unfortunately, one of my projects has now caused more trouble than I had planned for. I knew there would be some disruption when it was finished, but I hadn't anticipated this.'

'So what were you working on?' she asked, not sure she would understand the answer.

'The less you know, the safer you will be,' said Jackson, trying to avoid explaining the project. 'But I *will* say that all the work I have done was for what I believed would be a better future for us all. Fortunately, the men that stole my work didn't get everything they needed. That's why Benjamin brought me here — to keep me and my work safe.'

'I'm sure you had the best intentions at heart, Grandpa,' Lilly said, taking hold of his hands. 'No one could blame you for that.'

'She's right, you old fool. If I know my Benjamin, he'll have this sorted in a tick,' Mary said, trying to lift everyone's spirits. 'Now who's for tea and cake?' she added, looking at Jackson and Lilly.

Lilly's face lifted, but she wasn't entirely sure if she should be relieved, hungry or scared now. As Mary poured tea for the three of them and served up a slice of cake,

Jackson suddenly remembered he had not asked Lilly why she was in Trellern.

'I don't really have an explanation for what happened,' she said. 'I just know *what* happened.'

She began to explain the attack on Mia and herself and Mia ending up almost dying. She told them of how she had found a rescuer in Andris, and how they had escaped from the constables.

'I didn't know who to trust,' Lilly said. 'It seemed like anyone could have been involved if the law was. I needed to get away from my friends, somewhere safe so they wouldn't get hurt because of me.'

'Well, you came to the right place,' Mary stated matter-of-factly.

'After hearing your story, I can't help thinking they were trying to kidnap me — to get to you Grandpa. It makes perfect sense.'

The colour drained from Jackson's face. He had never thought that his work would affect his family and the idea made him feel ill.

'Jackson? Are you okay, dear?' Mary asked as Jackson sat back in his chair.

'I — I —' he started to say, but couldn't find the words.

'It's okay, Grandpa, I'm safe here with you now.' She looked at Mary for reassurance. 'Right?'

'Right'cha love. We've got some of the best men your uncle knows watching over us right now. Nothing is going to happen to anyone, not whilst I'm still standing.' The horizontal line of Mary's mouth in a firm expression somehow made Lilly feel more at ease, but it clearly didn't have the same effect on Jackson. 'And your uncle will be home later. He won't let anything happen, either,' Mary added.

'Thanks, Mary,' Lilly said with an earnest smile.

'I'll sort you and Andris out some rooms for tonight. You're staying here until this all blows over. Separate rooms, mind,' Mary said, a devious expression on her face.

'Hell yes!' Lilly said, making Mary giggle.
'Come on, dear, I'll draw you a nice hot bath too.'

Chapter Thirteen

Borell had taken a carriage to a part of town he knew all too well. The sort of place frequented by thieves, rogue traders, guns for hire, assassins and, frankly, people like him. He knew he stood little chance of finding the current owner of the item he needed, but there were enough rogues in this part of town to know what was happening on the shadier and downright dark side of the law. Many a time he had been sat at a bar whilst drunken men regaled their friends with stories around him, of deals made and lives taken. Someone would talk about the sale of an item as big as Jackson's device.

He stood outside of the Crooked Barrow, a pub notorious for its nasty clientele, the perfect place to make some friends. The smell of fresh vomit rose up to meet his olfactory senses as he looked around at the bodies lying on the pavement outside; some crawling on hands and knees, calling to whatever god they believed in; some unconscious, with empty bottles of liquor in their hands or smashed into pieces nearby. There were always plenty of drunks in Trellern, you just needed to know where to look; it wasn't very hard.

'Excuse me,' Borell said as he stepped over the legs of one man who was trying to steady himself in preparation for an attempt to stand up. The motion was denied as his legs gave way under him, adding another body to the pile.

The front door to the Crooked Barrow was open and loud jeering and voices poured out into the street. Borell staggered in and headed straight to the bar. It would help to have a drink in hand, and exaggerating his state of inebriation would make conversations flow easier.

'A pint of stout, my good man,' he shouted, holding up a coin for the barkeep to see. He propped himself up against the bar as the man behind it pulled a thick draught from the taps and put it down in front of Borell.

The barman wasn't in a favourable mood. It looked like things had become ugly in here earlier, as a pile of broken furniture stacked in a heap in one corner was being used as firewood. Borell couldn't help but smile; he had been involved in many taproom brawls and had enjoyed every one of them.

He recognised a man sat in a group by a window, chatting loudly and excitedly. Taking a large mouthful of his drink, Borell wandered over to the table and sat himself down without waiting for an invitation.

'Fellas,' he said, putting his glass firmly on the table in front of them. 'Don't let me interrupt; it was just starting to sound good.'

'And who the hell are you?' demanded a large man who had been listening to the story before Borell cut in, pulling his considerable weight upright in response.

'He's a low life thief. Someone who *would* piss on you if you were on fire — but only after he put out the match. Would rob ya' blind whilst you sleep.'

'Good to see you too, Sly,' Borell said.

'You know him?' asked the large man.

'Aye, we go back some. He's a'right.'

The others nodded a greeting or raised their mugs of beer to him — those that were still able to focus on their surroundings, at least.

'Well anyone with a character reference like that is welcome at our table,' slurred the large man. He raised his mug to Borell and took a large swig.

'I was jus' tellin' me friends here all 'bout the time I broke into the Parliament offices and took the ceremonial robes for a spin af'er robbing them of the week's wages,'

Sly said. 'Took 'em for a spin, then took a dump in 'em!' The table fell about laughing as he stood up and re-enacted the foul movements by rubbing his backside on the man next to him.

'One of your finer days, Sly, eh!' Borell said, joining in the laughter. 'That's nothing compared to what has been going on recently though, right?' He thought he would try the direct approach, as most of the men were fairly well intoxicated, and might not have been able to stay conscious for much longer. 'I mean, for someone to get hold of that thing and sell it on without being caught — I'd buy him a drink. Hell, I'd buy him a dozen!'

The men continued laughing, but his words soon started to work through the fog of booze.

'What 'ya on about, lad?' asked a stocky man hanging off the far side of the table.

'He means that business over at the s'iety, dunt he,' chipped in another man, a skinny red head, two drinks away from being unconscious.

'Oh that! Be lucky if that don't go to shit. I've heard that there are agents all over looking for it. Turning places inside out, I hear. S'posed to be something all godly, ain't it? Religious artefact or summin',' a blond man wearing scruffy clothes and eyes as wide as plates offered.

'Shame, I may have been generous with a drink if someone actually knew something. Guess there are other pubs and other thirsty drinkers...' Borell stood up to leave.

'Hang on, didn't say I know nuffin',' said the red haired man. 'I heard from a friend.' His eyes stretched out to some distant place in his mind. Borell slapped the man on the side of the face to regain his focus. 'Yeah, like I was sayin',' he continued. 'A friend overheard the innkeeper at the Lazy Boar talking about some men who rented out his entire inn, just so they could have privacy. S'posed to be going on until tonight.'

'That's it?' Borell said.

'Nah, they came in on a private boat. All la-dee-da and

shit. Flashy with their money too,' he said. 'That's gotta be worth a drink?'

Borell looked at him for a moment, and then downed the remains of his pint.

'So, where's me drink?' the red haired man protested.

'I said I *may* be generous. Be grateful you're still breathing.'

'See, told you he was a low life,' said Sly as Borell slapped him on the back.

The table erupted with laughter, all except the red haired man, who fixed Borell with a deathly stare.

'Bastard,' said the red head quietly under the laughter.

Borell heard and smiled at him. 'Yeah, that I am,' he said.

More laughter from the drunkards sitting around him filled the room.

'Barkeep!' Borell looked over his shoulder and shouted. 'Flagons of ale all round and be quick about it!'

A pretty young barmaid pushed in, leaned over and put her hands on the table between Borell and Sly.

'You want drinks, you better show me the shine of your coin first,' she said. The men opposite were trying hard to focus on the bosom staring them in the face.

'Today, I'm also feeling generous,' Borell said, handing her a newly acquired silver crown. 'None of that dishwater shit, if you don't mind.'

The table erupted with cheers and laughter as the barmaid stood, taking the coin from Borell.

***

The hazards of the streets surrounding the Crooked Barrow faded into a nicer class of thieves and robbers as Borell walked the ten minutes to the Lazy Boar. Only twice had would-be robbers approached him. Both of them hobbled away with less than good health.

Outside of the Lazy Boar, he could see a large man

loitering by the brazier that had just been lit on the front wall of the inn. Borell knew enough to recognise a bodyguard or mercenary when he saw one. This fellow looked like he fell into the latter category.

Borell straightened his hat and jacket and walked up to the door at the front of the inn. The mercenary moved to block him.

'Not tonight, fella,' he said. 'Private party.'

'Oh really? I was hoping to find a young lady here — if you know what I mean,' Borell said, leaning closer to the man conspiratorially for the last part.

'Well, you —' the man stopped mid-sentence, unable to make a sound. His eyes wide, he looked down to see a nine-inch slender blade withdrawing from his chest. Borell was almost surgical with his precision. A single thrust up under the rib cage, through the diaphragm and lung and into the heart, reducing the noise the victim could make before their heart stopped.

The mercenary's arms dropped to his side as the blade slid back into the mechanism strapped to Borell's arm, carefully hidden under his jacket sleeve. Borell caught him and sat him down with the help of gravity, placing the man's hat over his face and arranging him as if asleep. He tore the inside pocket and lining from the man's coat, and stuffed the cloth into the slit in the man's stomach to stem the blood flow. It would be a problem eventually, but it was getting darker so it would cover his tracks for now.

The windows to the lounge at the front of the inn were curtained so Borell headed around to the back to see if there was a better way inside. As he expected, there was another man standing by the back door, a fat dog asleep at his feet. Putting on a stagger, Borell bumped his way into the yard and slurred something incomprehensible at the man. The slim man just looked on without saying a word.

Borell had hoped he would come over and tell him to move on. Time to try a different tack. He leant into a corner and started to urinate against the wall.

Still the man looked on.

When he had finished, he turned and threw his arms open to the man.

'Hey, I know you!' he shouted. 'You're that guy — from that place.' He staggered closer to him with a face of recognition that the man didn't share. 'You 'member me! We did that guy in fer his shoes. 'member?!'

Finally, the man had seen enough, pulled out a pistol, and pointed it at Borell.

'Get the hell out of here before you lose more than your dignity. Not that you seem to have that much left to lose,' he said.

'C'mon... Dick, ain't it? Yeah, you're that Dick who —' Borell bent over, leaning against a wall, and vomited on demand. It was a dirty trick, but good enough to convince someone you are just a pathetic drunk.

'Shit, you're making a mess,' said the man. 'I've got to stand here and smell this all night!' He put his gun back in its holster and stepped towards Borell. He grabbed him by his arm and the scruff of the neck and attempted to drag him out onto the street. Clearly, the man was more cautious than his friend at the front door, as the moment he put his hands on Borell's arm he felt the bladed weapon underneath.

'What the hell?' he said, pushing Borell away. Borell lunged at him and knocked him to the ground, lying on him whilst the man struggled to reach his gun. Borell managed to get hold of the man's fingers and broke them in one clean motion as the man was fumbling with the holster.

The distraction of the pain was enough for Borell to gain the upper hand again. He head-butted the man hard enough to stun him, breaking his nose. The same blade he used before slid silently from his sleeve and the man went limp.

'Damn,' Borell said, sitting on the step next to the lifeless body of the man. The dog clearly had no allegiances to the dead man and rolled over, expecting his belly to be rubbed. Borell obliged whilst taking the handkerchief out of the jacket pocket of the corpse and wiping his mouth, then discarding it. 'I hate doing that,' he said to the dog.

He grabbed the dead man's wrists and dragged him unceremoniously down the two steps he was lying on and hid him in a corner of the yard, behind some empty crates. Looking up at the back of the building, he could see an easy route to the first floor. Climbing onto one of the crates and pulling himself up onto an outbuilding, it was then a simple job to scramble across the tiles to the large window on the back of the inn. He peered in through the window of the first floor landing. There was no one to be seen. *Perfect,* he thought as he slid a blade under the bottom edge of the sash to see if it would lift.

A grin wiped away the look of concentration on his face as the sash lifted, if a little stickily. Someone had forgotten to lock the window; he would have to remember to thank them later. Lifting the sash, he could hear voices inside, quiet enough to be too far away to hear him climb in.

It sounded like the meeting was in full swing, the voices becoming clearer as he climbed inside and closed the window behind him. Borell carefully placed his feet, feeling for the tell-tale movement of creaky floorboards. Side stepping a few, he moved closer to the source of the voices. They were coming from further down the hallway, around a corner. He took out a tiny blade from his boot and gave it a quick wipe on his trousers to buff the shine.

He crouched down just before the corner and slowly pushed the blade into the corridor he couldn't see. He could make out from the reflection a man standing guard outside a room, arms folded. Withdrawing the blade, he leaned his back against the wall. He needed a distraction, a way to get the man to come to him. A plan came quickly to mind. He lay down along the wall with his head about a foot away from the corner. He found the nearest creaky floorboard that he'd sidestepped before and placed his heel onto it.

Creak.

Borell waited and heard what sounded like a gun being removed from its holster and the hammer being cocked, followed by cautious footsteps towards him. Looking straight towards the ceiling, Borell waited for the man to approach. After a few moments, he saw the cautious guard spin round the corner, weapon aimed towards the man who should be standing there. Only he realised a second too late that he was looking in the wrong direction.

Borell thrust his arm up, extending the hidden blade, and stabbed the man through the groin as far as he could reach. The guard screamed in pain, letting off a shot that embedded itself in the wall; Borell needed to move fast. As quick as a flash, he got up and slit the guard's throat as he helplessly grabbed at his groin. Running for the door, Borell raised his arm with the spear-like blade taut and waiting for a release. He took a chance that someone would be looking to see what the noise was and let the power of the catapult mechanism on his hidden blade extend through the peephole in the door.

With a dull wet *thud,* the blade pierced the glass of the peephole and the head of the person peeping. The blade withdrew with a *ching* and Borell kicked the door open, prepared to deal with whatever remained of the party. By now the three men inside were scrambling for weapons as they realised their security was no longer effective. This gave Borell the upper hand, allowing him to stab and slice his way through the men in the confusion.

He stood in the middle of the room, panting and looking far too much like he enjoyed his work. He heard a groan from one of the men, slowly pushing himself up to sit. The man tried to put his hand to his gun, but found a heavy boot bearing down on his fingers, crushing his chest.

'Please, please I beg of you, don't kill me,' the man pleaded, spitting blood and struggling to breath under the weight of Borell's boot, the deep slash across his chest seeping blood.

'You've seen my face. It'll be quick.'

'Wait, my name is Jacob Abner,' the man spluttered, grabbing hold of Borell's foot with his other hand.

'So?'

'I'm Society. I can get you anything you want. Money, power, anything, just don't kill me.' Jacob began to sob. He watched as Borell lifted his boot, breathing deeply with the weight removed.

It was the last sound Jacob Abner ever made.

'Weasel,' Borell muttered, wiping the blood from his blades and retracting them before checking the room for the item he needed. The room was luxurious as far as inns went in Trellern. The lounge he was standing in was large and comfortably furnished. The innkeeper wasn't going to be happy when he had to clean this room, if the law let him before the blood stained.

Two of the slain men wore posh clothing and expensive jewellery; the third wore a smart but well used suit. His attention soon turned to the two boxes sat side by side on a table.

'Hello, my lovelies,' he said as he felt the warmth of the fire from behind the table. The left hand box was square, about sixteen inches along each side. It looked like it had a lid that lifted off, fastened on each side at the bottom by catches. The other box was a more traditional chest, longer than it was tall, but still only about two feet in length.

Borell undid the catches on the first box and lifted the lid.

'Wow. You're a pretty little thing, aren't ya?' he said, staring at Jacksons' device. It was inert, like a fancy table decoration. All brass, chrome and glass.

Borell slid the lid back onto the box. The other box was locked, but only took a handful of seconds to pick open. Inside were bags of heavy coin; payment for the seller, no doubt. Borell knew he wouldn't be able to take all the money and the device.

He picked up a bag of coin and weighed it in his hand. He decided that he could take two or three without unnecessarily weighing himself down. There is no point being sluggish and being caught — the money would be worth nothing then. Besides, he was expecting to be paid handsomely for the item anyway, so this was a bonus.

He tied three bags of coins to his belt under his coat, then added a fourth to balance the weight. He left the lid of the box open and emptied the coins from one bag onto the table. The innkeeper would need compensating for the mess. He had nothing against a hardworking man.

Greed is one thing; being greedy and dead is something else. Borell had a hunger for the former, but no desire for the latter. A woman's scream came from the street below. He looked out of the window and saw that a passing couple had stepped in the blood from the man lying outside; time to leave.

Borell's compulsion with watches gave him pause to check the fallen men for any timepieces he could add to his collection. A delicate gold inlaid pocket watch caught his eye, and then he took his leave. He picked up the box with the device and headed back the way he came, this time sporting extra coin and another new pocket watch.

***

Having hidden Jackson's device in a safe place, Borell walked into the reception of the Broken Arrow Inn. The interior of the Inn was decidedly plush, far nicer than any place Borell would stay in, if nothing else just for the cost of a room. The woman behind the reception desk looked over and smiled at him.

'Good evening, sir. My name is Bethany. How may I help you today?' she said in a friendly voice. Bethany was beautiful. Her brown silky hair was flowing over her shoulders, sitting freely on her bosom. She stared at Borell with her large brown eyes, making him feel unusually lost for words. 'I don't bite — that's extra!' She laughed playfully.

Borell took a moment and smiled back at her as he walked to her desk.

'Good evening,' he said, finally finding his words. 'My name is — Borell. I believe you are expecting me?'

'Ah, yes indeed we are. We have a room for you — room four,' she said, placing a key on the reception counter. 'It's on the first floor.'

'A room?'

'Yes, a room. It is *one* of the things we do here at the Broken Arrow Inn. Rather well, if I may say,' she said, giggling.

'I wasn't expecting a room. I was told to speak to you regarding a delivery.'

'My instructions are that you should go to room four and wait,' Bethany said with a courteous smile.

Borell took the key and Bethany pointed him in the direction of the stairs.

'She won't be long,' said Bethany, winking at Borell. He thought that maybe the Broken Arrow was used by high-class call girls; maybe that was just how the set up was supposed to look.

'Thank you,' he said, returning the wink. Heading for the doorway leading to the stairs, he turned a quick glance back to Bethany who was now looking down at her desk, reading a book. She paid no more interest to him.

Borell's first thought was that this was a set up. He was glad that he had left the device somewhere safe, having a suspicion that he wouldn't have left this inn alive had he brought it with him.

He climbed the stairs to the first floor and found room four. He turned the key in the lock. The door opened to a vacated room decorated for royalty — or, at least, the decoration was of a standard he assumed royalty would accept. The canopy bed took up a large portion of the bedroom, buried deep in the thick pile of the dark red carpet surrounding it. Closing the door behind him, he checked the bathroom to make sure there were no surprises waiting for him.

Whilst he waited for his visitor, he looked out of the window to see if there was a suitable exit route, should he need it. There was. A short drop on to a bay window roof below would see him clear of the room if the meeting went sour.

Knock, knock, knock.

That was quick, he thought as he walked over to the door. Looking through the peephole, he could see the familiar women whom he'd met at breakfast that morning.

'Loren,' he said, opening the door, 'come in.'

'Thank you,' she said, walking into the room alone and with the air of total control. 'I trust you have retrieved the item we requested of you?'

'Straight to the point. I like that.'

'Time is precious. No point keeping you hanging around, is there?'

'I appreciate that,' he said. 'The item you require is safe but, alas, not here.'

'Oh, I see,' Loren said with a disappointed tone in her voice. 'And there is a reason for this I assume? A bargaining chip for more money? You feel we won't keep our end of the deal?'

'Much simpler, I assure you. I was expecting to leave word for you here and to be contacted for a meeting somewhere else. Had I known we were meeting here, I would have brought the item, of course,' he lied.

'Very well, as it turns out our plans have changed somewhat since we met last. It would be suitable to have an alternative meeting place. Somewhere you would feel safer, more in the open, perhaps?'

'Where did you have in mind?'

Loren looked at her delicate pocket watch, 'Meet me at the aerodrome in two hours,' she said. 'Be mindful; if there are any tricks or foolishness on your part, you will receive none of your money and I cannot be responsible for the actions of my employer,' she said, slowly walking to the window.

'Fine,' he said, 'but as you mentioned money — I feel that the compensation for keeping an item like this safe is worth say...triple your original fee?'

'Ah, I somehow knew money would come in to this sooner or later. And you feel that you are worth triple what we agreed because...?' she said with a smirk of annoyance.

'Having seen the wealth of the men willing to buy this device, I think a tripling of my fee is a small price to pay.'

'Do you now?'

'In fact,' he said, playing the greedy thief card in an attempt to gain an upper hand, 'I believe there would be plenty of other buyers for such a device, at probably a better rate too.'

'You are pushing your luck, Borell. I had been led to believe you were a more professional thief than this.' Loren looked thoughtfully out of the window for a moment. 'And why shouldn't I just call for my associates and have them beat the location of the device from you?' she said calmly.

'You'd be surprised at the beating I can take. You'll never see your device if you try to take it by force.'

Loren turned to face him and laughed heartily. 'You are everything I have heard and more. You will have *double* your fee and no more, *if* you get to the aerodrome on time. Cross us and, reputation aside, your life *will* be over,' Loren said, still smiling.

Borell agreed to the negotiated rate. Loren bid him farewell and left the room.

Borell still smelled a trap, but open ground would be a little easier to deal with than being trapped in a room with a slim chance of escape. He had already made a sizable bonus; he had no idea what he would do with double the fee, if he managed to get it.

There was no fun without a challenge, he thought.

Chapter Fourteen

'I've just had a message from Benjamin. He'll be home shortly,' Mary said to Rallon as he watched the front of the property from the lounge. 'I expect you'll all be wanting something for dinner too?'

'We're not supposed to leave our posts, but the smell of a home cooked meal sure gives a man a distracting appetite.'

'Well, I'm sure I can find you something you and your men can eat whilst on duty,' she smiled.

'Very kind of you, Mary, thank you.'

Mary walked back through the hallway towards the kitchen. She enjoyed hearing the sounds and voices of people in the house; it reminded her of times gone by when Drummond and Claire, Benjamin's parents, were still alive. The house had always been busy back then, especially when Benjamin was younger. Recently it had felt too empty for just her and Benjamin, but Mary still loved her place here regardless.

'The room is amazing,' Lilly said as she came down the stairs and ran into Mary. 'Much better than I'm used to at the university.'

'You enjoy it, love. This house needs a few people in it to remind it of its roots.'

'How long *have* you worked here?' Lilly asked.

'Most of my life, dear. I started when I was about your age for Mr Sorrow — Senior. I have pretty much grown up here. It's as much my home as my job.'

'You must really like working for Uncle Ben to have

stayed here all that time?'

'He is like the son I never had, dear,' Mary said, putting an arm around Lilly. 'Come on, let's sort out what we're all having for dinner. That steak won't slice thin enough for everyone.'

'Where's Andris?' Lilly asked, looking about.

'Oh he went off to have a look around. You like him, don't you?' said Mary, squeezing her arm around her.

'What? No!' she exclaimed. 'He's a friend. He saved my life. I mean, I like him, but I don't *like* him — not like that.'

'Of course, dear. What was I thinking?' Lilly blushed and Mary smiled a warm, motherly smile.

'Come on, it's been a good while since I had someone to help me peel the veg. Your uncle is terrible at it.'

Jackson was working down in the basement with Andris. The door was open as Mary and Lilly walked past. They could hear industrious sounds and chatter drifting up the stairs. Back in the kitchen again, Mary pointed Lilly at a pantry with orders to find potatoes, carrots, swede and broccoli.

'You get started on the spuds then, there's a knife in the draw over there,' Mary said when Lilly returned with her arms full. She put the rest of the vegetables on the table and went looking for the knife.

Lilly found a suitable peeling knife after searching through a few drawers of cutlery and other kitchen implements. Sitting at the table, she barely focused on the peeling and was preoccupied with the events of earlier today again. Mary busied herself with preparing dinner, chopping the other vegetables and getting the oven to temperature. Lilly didn't notice Mary chatting away to her, lost in her own little world of thoughts.

'Lilly,' Mary's louder voice cut through the fog of her thoughts. 'Are you peeling those spuds or making pig feed?'

Lilly looked at what her hands had been doing. 'I'm so sorry.'

'It's okay, dear. Why don't you go and find the library? You used to like sitting in the large armchair and reading a book. Maybe the distraction would be good for your... distraction.'

'I am sorry. I've made you more work. I can finish them, I promise.'

'I do like the company, but you need time to work things out in your head. Run along, and don't come back until dinner,' Mary said.

Lilly smiled and got up from the table. 'What happened to the lights?' she cried as the room fell suddenly dark, save for the glow of light coming from the oven.

'The power has gone out,' came Mary's voice, tinged with fear and anticipation. 'Rallon!' she called. There was no answer. 'RALLON!' she shouted, much louder. 'Come here, Lilly,' she ordered. Lilly backed towards Mary, grasping the knife she had been peeling with firmly.

'What's going on?'

'I don't know, dear, but I think we should go somewhere else.' Mary pushed Lilly firmly towards the pantry. Lilly's legs needed some encouragement as they'd frozen in fear. 'Keep that knife handy, dear,' she whispered as she picked up a cleaver from the counter and held it firmly in her hand.

They crept across the kitchen, Mary guiding Lilly in the dim light. Another loud noise from outside, this time followed by screams that could have been Jackson or Andris.

'Hurry, dear,' she said.

'Who are they?'

'Not now, Lilly,' Mary said as they reached the pantry door. As they did, the main kitchen door creaked open and something was thrown into the room. It landed on the floor with the sound of a tin can then exploded into a wall of sound and blinding light.

Both Lilly and Mary were knocked backwards from the shock of the stun grenade. They struggled to maintain consciousness as two darkly dressed men rushed into the room. Lilly passed out, but not before concealing the knife in her sleeve.

One of the men picked her up and threw her over his shoulder. Mary tried to lift the cleaver to ward them off, but the butt of a pistol to her head put an end to her heroic action.

'Come on, leave her. She can burn with the house,' said a man with a husky voice, carrying Lilly. 'Set the charge on the table.'

The other man pulled an apple-sized device from his belt and wound the timer. As it started ticking, he placed it on the table in the middle of the kitchen.

'Let's get the hell out of here,' he said as they made for the door, Lilly hanging limp on his friend's shoulder. There were three other shadowy dressed men standing in the hallway, waiting for them with weapons drawn.

'All set?' one of them asked.

'Two minutes,' another replied.

'Set the other charges as we leave and don't hang around. We've got —' he looked at his wristwatch '— thirty minutes before the ship flies.'

The man carrying the incendiary devices took two more from his belt as he followed his companions down the hallway. He wound them both and dropped one into the open door leading down into the basement. The other he threw to the top of the stairs in the hallway, stepping over the body of Rallon as he went.

Outside, two more men were waiting. 'Come on, Sorrow is on his way,' said the larger of the two men. If Lilly had been awake she would have recognised him as Agent Carter, the guy she'd met at the front door with Rallon earlier. Carter was carrying his own cargo in the shape of a bound and gagged Jackson Burns over his shoulder.

Three mechanical carriages were waiting for them on the road outside the gates.

Chapter Fifteen

Borell's carriage pulled up just short of the aerodrome entrance and he jumped down carrying the wooden box he'd appropriated earlier. He paid the driver, who took off without saying a word. Borell scanned the open ground between him and the nearest departure lounge, looking for any surprises. Keeping the waist-high wall between himself and the concourse, he stepped forwards to better his view of the apron.

'Damn,' he said as he heard the click of a pistol being cocked at his temple. 'Where did you come from?'

'Put the box down and put your hands on the wall, my friend,' said the deep voice belonging to the pistol. Borell slowly put the box on the floor beside him, bending slowly to see if the pistol stayed pointing at his head — it did.

'Now get those hands on the wall.'

Borell straightened his back, his hands just above waist level. He still couldn't see the man behind him, but guessed from the position of the pistol that the man was taller than he was. Borell decided that he could catch the man by surprise and use his size to his advantage. Even if he was one of Loren's men, could she blame him for defending her prize? Borell thrust both arms behind him, bending double and releasing the blade mechanisms in each wrist simultaneously.

Chink.

'What the hell?' Borell said aloud, moments before the man's boot came down on his back, forcing him onto the floor with his arms in an awkward position, causing him to scrape his chin on the pavement.

'Was warned about you,' said the man as he let out a low chuckle. Borell rolled over and looked up at the man, who stood at least six feet eight inches tall at his best guess, and was about as wide. He opened his greatcoat with one hand whilst pointing the pistol at Borell with the other, and smiling. Borell could see that he was wearing solid armour plating from his collarbone to his waist. The metal was painted black, apart from the two flecks of steel he could see where his blades had glanced off it. The man was well armoured and more than a match for Borell.

'That's impressive,' Borell said, admiring the way the metal abdominal plates flowed with the man's movements. 'Bet that weighs a bit?'

'Shut up and take those off. Loren is waiting,' he said, pointing at Borell's spring loaded blades. Borell sighed and retracted his blades before carefully removing his coat and unstrapping the devices.

'Might just keep hold of these,' said the man.

'Be my guest,' Borell said, passing them up to the hulk standing over him, being in no real position to object.

'Get him up,' said the man to someone standing behind Borell.

Borell looked up and behind him. 'Shit. Where do they grow you guys?' he said, staring at another large man similar in stature to the one in front of him. The second hulk grabbed Borell by his shoulders and lifted him bodily to his feet.

'Get his gun,' ordered the first man, to which the second man obliged. He span Borell on his heels and put his massive hand around his throat whilst patting him down with the other. He tucked Borell's pistol into his belt, threw away his other knives and then let him go, satisfied he was no longer armed.

Borell choked an expletive or two and rubbed his neck, feeling where the sausage like fingers had left their imprints.

'Get moving,' said the man holding Borell's blades, pushing Borell towards the main gate.

With a gun in his back and a bleeding chin, Borell was escorted towards the one of the departure lounges nearest the gates. Various scenarios ran through his mind as to how he was getting out of this alive, but none of them looked favourable. However, he was alive for now so there was hope, or Loren may have other plans. Or it could be that the two men just didn't want to make a mess in public.

Borell opened the door to the lounge and saw Loren waiting inside, sitting casually on one of the large sofas intended for departing travellers. Half a dozen armed men, standing alert and watching him intently, surrounded her.

'All this for me?' Borell said as appreciatively as he could.

'Just a precaution,' Loren replied as the two men nudged Borell closer to her. 'I just wanted to make sure you were prepared to deliver our item this time.'

'And where did you get these two?' Borell said with a nod of his head towards his escort. 'They're a little conspicuous, don't you think?'

'What they are matters little. What they *do* is all that matters. Please, sit,' she said, pointing to a chair opposite her. 'I think we both agree that you are not going anywhere.'

Borell agreed and sat down. The hulk that was carrying the box brought it over to Loren and set it on the low table in front of her, then walked away and took station by the main door. The other hulk wandered over to a side-table and looked at his new toys.

'I do so hate playing games with suppliers, so thank you for not disappointing me this time.'

'My pleasure,' said Borell.

'I'm sure,' smiled Loren. 'As promised, your payment for services rendered.' Loren snapped her fingers and one of the men standing behind her sofa brought forward a box and placed it on the table in front of her, taking the box with the energy device in it away.

'Aren't you even going to have a look at the thing, now that you have it?' Borell asked.

'No. There is no need.' Loren stood and straightened her dress. 'We will honour our agreement for the *original* price. But —'

'Of course. There's always a *but*.'

'As you have caused us more than a little inconvenience and tarnished your reputation in the process, my colleagues here will help remind you of how we expect our suppliers to behave. Good day.'

Loren walked out through the doors to the concourse, followed by an escort of three men. The rest remained behind with Borell.

'So, I guess you guys are gonna' beat on me for a while right?' Borell said to no one in particular. The men just smiled back at him.

'Hey, how do you get these things to work?' shouted the hulk who was now wearing Borell's blades.

'Oh, you just need to squeeze your fists. That releases the —'

'Arrghh!' shouted the hulk as he made two fists. A row of steel spikes embedded themselves into the full length of his forearms. The spikes were angled from the elbow to the wrist so that you couldn't simply pull the devices off once they were deployed. Borell grinned. That was something he had always wanted to see put to use and he wasn't disappointed.

He jumped up whilst some of the other men rushed to the hulk's aid and made for the nearest soldier. He heard two gunshots, felt a blow to the chest and collapsed, sinking quickly into darkness.

'Get Cane on-board,' said the soldier who'd pulled the trigger. 'Get Mr Frederick to take a look at his arms. Leave this piece of shit here.'

Two large men helped Cane as best they could,

supporting him around the waist whilst he screamed in pain and hobbled towards the doors. The soldier who'd shot Borell kicked him in the chest as he walked past, grabbing the box of money before following the others outside.

Chapter Sixteen

Benjamin sat in the back of his horse-drawn carriage and watched the sun setting lower in the evening sky through a window. Even on a cold day such as today, it was still a beautiful sight. The carriage took a sharp corner, rocking him back on his seat with the change of direction. He had asked Arthur to make haste, so couldn't complain about the ride.

The carriage turned onto Elm Avenue moments away from Benjamin's home. Coming in the opposite direction in a muddle of dust and smoke, Benjamin could see three mechanical carriages tearing down the road. He couldn't see the occupants, as the curtains were draped.

A shockwave rocked their carriage as the windows on the ground floor of his family home exploded into a fireball, engulfing the floor above before dying back into a steady inferno. He threw open the door and stood out on the running plate.

'My god,' he shouted above the sound of the noise, as moments later Arthur pulled the horses up and stopped short of the front gates. Benjamin started running for the house, with Arthur following close behind.

There was another explosion that forced them both to cover their faces from the heat for a moment. It died down to a roaring fire as they started to make their way towards the front of the house again.

'You can't go in there!' Arthur shouted at Benjamin, holding him back.

He knew he wouldn't be able to get inside with the

fire burning as it was. His neighbours and passers-by had already started appearing at the front gates, watching the spectacle unfold. The fire had taken hold too vigorously to do anything about it now; the incendiary devices worked all too efficiently.

'Over there!' shouted a neighbour from behind them. Benjamin and Arthur looked in the direction he was pointing and saw a dark shape lying in the grass. They ran over, shielding their faces from the heat of the fire.

'Fetch some blankets!' Benjamin shouted to any of the onlookers that could hear him.

It quickly became clear that the shape on the lawn was the body of Mary and an unknown man. Benjamin ran to their side and pulled the man off Mary, rolling him onto his back. The man lay on the grass, groaning and holding his head in pain. Arthur pulled out his pistol and pointed it at the man.

'Who the hell are you?' demanded Benjamin whilst kneeling beside the unconscious Mary, checking to make sure she was still breathing.

'You must be Benjamin,' said the man.

'That's not an answer, kid. Who are you?' Benjamin said with more anger in his voice.

'Andris. Andris Tar. I'm a friend of Lilly's.'

'Friend of Lilly's? What the hell are you doing here?'

'Go easy on the boy,' Mary said, opening her eyes and suddenly reeling from the heat. 'He saved my life. He's been making a habit of that recently.'

Benjamin nodded at Arthur, who put his gun away and dragged Andris to his feet. 'Do you think you can get up, Mary?' he asked.

'One way to find out,' she said, sitting up and taking hold of Benjamin's hands. She was unsteady on her feet, but able to walk. Benjamin put her arm around his shoulder and helped her away from the house.

'What happened, Mary?' he asked as they approached the crowd gathered at the front gates.

'I'm not sure, dear. I was in the kitchen with Lilly —'

'Lilly? What was she doing here?' Benjamin looked confused.

'She ran into a spot of bother at the university. Our friend Andris here saved her life. Told you he had made a habit of it.'

'Then I am grateful to you, Andris,' he said putting out his hand to shake, 'for saving two of the most important people in my life.' Andris shook his hand.

'Mary, was anyone else inside? Where's Rallon and his men?'

'I don't know. I saw one of the men take Lilly before knocking me out. I can only assume they were after her and Jackson.' Mary rubbed the back of her head and found she was bleeding a little. Ever the resourceful person, she tore a piece of material off her petticoat, wadded it in her hand and applied it to the cut.

'Any idea where they were heading?' Benjamin asked.

'No, dear.'

'I heard one of them talk about a ship,' Andris offered. 'Said they had a half hour before it left.'

Benjamin turned towards Andris. 'Did they say what ship it was or where it was sailing from?'

'Not that I could hear. I was hiding at the time. Not very heroic,' he said, looking down at his feet.

'If you had been heroic, we probably wouldn't be talking right now.'

'Arthur, take Mary and Andris back to the safe house. I need to get to the docks.' Suddenly he remembered the mechanical carriages that had passed him at speed just before the house exploded, heading away from the docks.

Benjamin stopped Andris.

'Do you remember them saying anything else about the ship?'

'That's all I heard. All they said was, "We have thirty minutes before the ship sails."'

Benjamin nodded with disappointment, hoping the

carriages were somehow involved. Arthur started walking Andris and Mary to his carriage when Andris stopped and looked at Benjamin.

'He said "the ship flies" not "sails",' said Andris, searching his memory. 'Yeah, I'm positive that's what he said. An airship?'

Benjamin's face looked hopeful once more. 'Arthur, I'm heading to the aerodrome.'

'I'm coming with you,' said Andris, straightening his jacket and puffing out his chest a little, then deflating it when his chest screamed back in pain.

'Not a chance,' Benjamin said, shaking his head.

'I said I'd look after her. I can't let her down, sir.'

'You could do worse than let him help, Benjamin. He seems to have done alright by her so far,' said Mary.

Benjamin looked at Mary, who had always been a source of grounding for him, and sighed.

'Fine. Just stay behind me and don't get yourself killed. Lilly would never forgive me.'

'Yes, sir.'

Benjamin gave Mary a warm hug and shook Arthur's hand. 'I feel happier knowing she's with you, my friend.'

'She'll be safe until you return, you have my word,' said Arthur.

Benjamin and Andris took a shortcut across the front lawns to the garages that were at one side of the main house, fortunately unaffected by the fire for now. They both grabbed a handle on each of the two large wooden doors and pulled them open. Benjamin grabbed one corner of a large sheet and pulled, lifting several years' worth of dust into the air.

'Is that a Fortworth Oiler?' Andris asked excitedly, looking through the haze.

'It is. If it still works, we'll get to the aerodrome in no time.' Benjamin ran over to the Fortworth and climbed in, slipping a pair of goggles over his eyes. 'Crank the handle and we'll see what she does.'

Andris was beside himself with excitement, completely forgetting the situation they were in and the house burning behind him. A Fortworth Oiler was the prototype of an advanced internal combustion engine carriage; only ten or so were ever made before the Fortworth brothers moved onto airships instead. The cost was too great to be of any real use, they said, when horses were much cheaper and easier to maintain; they never made money in airships, either.

'Come on then, don't stand there gawking.'

'Sorry,' Andris said, firmly grasping the crank handle and turning it as hard and as fast as he could. A splutter of life, then nothing.

'Try again.'

Again, Andris cranked as hard as he could, this time with both hands, putting his whole aching body into the motion. Another splutter, then a cough, splutter — roar. Andris jumped back as the engine made the loudest sound he had heard from a machine that didn't take up a whole floor of a building. Benjamin fed the engine fuel and it ran like a child with raspy breath.

'It just needs to clear itself,' Benjamin shouted over the din of the engine. Sure enough, within a few seconds the engine was growling like a lion.

'Get in,' Benjamin shouted. Andris ran around to the other side and climbed into the cockpit. A cockpit was an accurate description, as Benjamin's father and Jackson had made quite a few modifications to the car, beyond the original design of the Fortworth brothers.

'This is fantastic!' Andris yelled.

'Buckle that strap and hang on.'

Benjamin pulled on the gear lever and put his foot down hard on the accelerator. The back wheels span but the Fortworth didn't move. He looked a little embarrassed. 'The brake,' he said, which he released and the vehicle charged forwards.

'You have driven this before, haven't you?' shouted

Andris whilst holding on to the console in front of him for dear life.

'Once or twice,' Benjamin confessed.

'Very reassuring!'

Benjamin pointed the vehicle in the direction of the gates at the end of the driveway and pushed a button on the centre of the cockpit's console. The gates sprang open just in time as the Fortworth darted through onto the road outside.

'Wireless gates?' Andris said, looking surprised.

'There have been a few... upgrades,' Benjamin shouted. 'There are some goggles in the front there — you might want to put them on,' he shouted again, pointing at the compartment by Andris' knees. Benjamin changed gear and accelerated down Elm.

'I'm sorry about your house,' Andris shouted as he found the goggles and pulled the strap over his head.

'Houses can be rebuilt,' Benjamin said matter-of-factly, focusing on the road. Andris was glad he put the goggles on, as dust and insects were soon bouncing from them as the Fortworth Oiler ploughed through the cold evening air. He pulled his coat tight around his face to stop it freezing.

Benjamin pulled hard on the steering wheel forcing the car left onto Appletree Drive. 'Hang on!' he shouted. Changing gear again, the Fortworth picked up an incredible rate of speed.

'My god, this thing is fast!' screamed Andris, and let out a *yeehaw*, as he had read that this is what plainsmen did when riding their horses at full tilt; it seemed fitting.

The Fortworth shot past the warehouse district, heading along Appletree, which followed closely to the river Whyle. Carriages and men on horseback were darting out of the way at the approaching wall of sound. The Fortworth handled exceptionally well for the large mechanical beast that it was.

'We should be there in a few minutes,' Benjamin shouted. Just up ahead in the distance, he could see the enormous outlines of the airship hangars against the skyline. He began to slow down as they approached the aerodrome. He was looking for the three carriages he saw earlier, sure that they were involved.

'If you see three black carriages anywhere, let me know,' he said, no longer needing to shout to be heard.

Benjamin pulled the Fortworth over alongside one of the buildings and switched off the engine. They suddenly noticed how quiet it was, even with the noise of airship engines. One airship was moored to a docking tower not far from them. Another was being towed into a hangar; it looked like it was being taken in for repair or maintenance. Two other ships were in the air overhead, slowly making their way to other moorings further down the airfield.

'They must be on that ship there,' Andris said, pointing at the one sitting quietly ahead of them.

'Come on,' Benjamin said, 'but stay behind me. If things go sour, find somewhere to hide and stay out of the line of fire.'

'By sour you mean, if they start shooting at us?'

'Most probably, yes,' Benjamin said, taking out his pistol and cocking it ready. 'You did want to come along, remember?'

Andris gave an audible swallow. Benjamin followed the line of the building they had parked behind until there was no more cover.

'We'll have to make a run for those crates over there. Ready?' He didn't give Andris time to say 'no'.

As they ran for cover, it struck Benjamin that things were all too quiet. Peering around the crates, he could only see three ground workers milling about and no passengers. From inside his coat he pulled out a miniature telescope and directed it at the main passenger gondola underneath the balloon.

'Not good,' he said. 'It doesn't look like there's anyone aboard. We have either beaten them here — or they have already left.'

'He looks official,' Andris said, pointing to a uniformed man walking across the apron. 'Maybe he can tell us when they left?'

'Come on.'

Maintaining as much cover as they could, Benjamin put his pistol away and they walked over to where the officer was now talking to a ground worker.

'Excuse me,' he said, addressing the officer. 'When does she leave?' He pointed at the ship above them. The officer turned to face them, tall and lean in his pressed uniform. He wore his authority comfortably.

'If you are travelling on the *Nightstar*,' he said, pointing at the moored ship, 'then I'm afraid you are three hours too early. She is due to leave at ten o'clock this evening. If you are not travelling on the *Nightstar* then your inquiry is for another purpose?'

'We are looking for a group of travellers,' Benjamin said. 'Have any ships departed recently, in the last thirty minutes?'

The officer fixed Benjamin with a hard stare, and then looked down at the clipboard he was carrying. He traced his finger down a list of items, looked up and said, 'No.'

'And you could have told me that without looking it up.'

'Perhaps,' the officer said, shedding his straight face for a large, toothy smile. 'Are you sure your friends are departing from this aerodrome? I assume you are looking for *friends*?' he said, reverting to his previous expression.

'Some of them. The others — not so much.'

'Then I fear you have come to the wrong place, and I have work to do.'

Benjamin turned to look at the moored ship and then at the other ships coming in to dock.

'Ah,' said the officer, spying Benjamin's pistol under his jacket as he turned back towards him. 'I see you are a man of means, and I didn't mean to offend you with my manner, sir,' his face melting to a softer, more pleasing expression. 'I don't want any trouble.'

'I am here on official business,' Benjamin said, showing the man his Society badge. Andris looked at the badge in disbelief, but quickly tried to hide it from the official, mostly failing.

'Ah I see, then I should point out that this is not the only place you can board an airship in the city,' the officer said.

'I know, but there is only one ship docked at the clock tower and from what I saw she is a government ship. The one we are looking for would be leaving any time now, with recent boarders.'

'If you and your friend would like to follow me to the observation tower, we have a log of all ships coming in and leaving Trellern. Maybe we can find the one you are looking for.' The officer gestured for them to follow him.

They walked across the apron of the aerodrome towards several buildings, which made up the observation tower, offices and workshops for the various crews. The buildings around the base of the mooring towers housed the luxurious waiting areas and bathroom facilities for passengers. The buildings Benjamin and Andris were heading for seemed to be devoid of such luxuries. They were utilitarian in form, clean and tidy, but not particularly pleasing on the eye.

As they reached the observation tower, the officer opened the door and stepped inside. He removed his hat and felt a gun barrel on the back of his head.

'You are as quick as they say you are. What gave me away?' the officer said.

'The tattoo on your neck. You almost had it hidden. If there were a next time, I'd say wear a scarf.' The officer fell in a heap on the floor as Benjamin struck him hard across the back of the head.

'What the hell was that for?' Andris said.

'Shhh, keep your voice down. He's nothing to do with the airport; that tattoo is a mercenary tattoo. He would as likely killed us before we reached the top of the tower,'

Benjamin said as he pulled the officer out of the corridor into a side room. 'Grab that rope and tie him up.'

'Why would he want to kill us?' said Andris. Benjamin looked at him for a moment and realisation dawned on him. 'Oh, right.'

'That ship must be the one we want.' Benjamin grabbed the clipboard from the unconscious man and looked along the list of departing ships. 'I thought so; it leaves in a few minutes. The destination is Nartill.'

'Why would they go there?'

Benjamin didn't have time to answer as they heard the sounds of engines starting outside. He finished tying up the man with Andris' help and dashed over to a window.

'Those damn carriages. I knew it. Come on!' Benjamin said.

In the blink of an eye, Benjamin was already back to the door of the observation tower and running across the apron. Andris was trying to keep up. The three mechanical carriages pulled up outside the departure lounge and their passengers unloaded in a hurry. Above, the engines revved as the pilot began departure checks. Benjamin could see two bodies, slung over shoulders, being rushed inside the departure lounge.

Bullets sparked off the ground near Benjamin's feet as he dived for cover behind the same crates as earlier; Andris was only a second behind.

'So things have gone sour then!' Andris shouted.

Benjamin pulled out his pistol and returned fire towards the source of the shots.

'You know those big balloon things above us are full of hydrogen don't you?' Andris said, panicked. 'Hydrogen explodes!'

'It's unlikely that a bullet will make it up there and do any damage.'

'Unlikely, but possible!'

Benjamin ignored him as he struck one of the men shooting at them in the chest. Another man with him pulled his body behind the carriage and continued firing. Benjamin pulled back behind the crates and reloaded his pistol. Bits of wood exploded from the top of the crate above them as they slid down closer to the ground.

'Wishing you'd stayed with Arthur now, aren't you?' Benjamin said with a wry smile, putting his hand around the side of the crate and returning a few shots. More shots exploded through the tops of the crates. 'Right, change of tactics,' Benjamin said to Andris, who was lying flat on the floor, keeping as low as he could. He unloaded the empty rounds from his pistol and took out three rounds from a pouch on his belt. Once reloaded, he cocked the hammer and snuck a quick peek around the crate, whipping his head back before he made an easy target. Taking a deep breath and letting it out again, Benjamin rolled onto his side, exposing himself to the onslaught of bullets, and fired two shots.

'What the hell was that?' cried Andris, putting his hands over his ears as the two rounds exploded.

Benjamin rolled back behind the crate. 'Two Jackson Specials.'

The gunfire had stopped and the only sounds, besides the ringing in Andris' ears, was the sound of the airship's engines above. They both stood up and looked around the side of their now dishevelled cover. The windows on the carriages were mostly smashed and the bodies of three men could be seen sprawled out behind them.

'Stun grenades in a bullet,' Benjamin said, reloading his gun with regular bullets again.

'Very effective,' said Andris as he followed him over to the fallen men. Benjamin checked to make sure they were unconscious. They were — apart from the man that he had hit square in the chest earlier.

Thump, thump, thump, thunk.

'No, no, no!' Benjamin said as the sound of the mooring tower gears released the airship from its grasp.

'We're too late,' said Andris.

They stared at the airship as it slowly drifted upwards, engines increasing in power and pushing it up, over the mooring tower, and away into the distance.

Chapter Seventeen

Borell woke up laying prone against a sofa in the departure lounge. Excruciating pain shot through him as he tried to lift his head to look at the injury to his chest. He didn't know if they had planned to kill him all along, or just teach him a lesson. It didn't matter now.

'Bitch,' he groaned as he fingered the holes in his waistcoat, checking for the damage. He felt two small holes in the material and pulled out a bullet from one of them. Being a cautious man, he had been prepared. He had stolen the ballistic proof vest he was now wearing on a previous job. It seemed like a good steal at the time and he was glad of it now. Slowly rolling onto his side to avoid the same pain as before, he got to his feet, holding the sofa for support. Poking around his ribs, he decided that more than one was bruised but none were broken — nothing he had not dealt with before.

He could hear the muffled sounds of engines outside. Looking up through the glass roof of the departure lounge, he could see the dark outline of the airship leaving. Borell sat on the sofa and took several slow, shallow breaths — deep breaths just hurt.

He got up and walked past the large picture window that looked out on to the apron of the airfield. He saw two figures checking the bodies of men laying scattered around the devastated mechanical carriages.

'Sorrow?' he muttered, hiding behind a wall as quickly as his achy frame would allow. Borell had avoided entanglements with him, barely by the skin of his teeth on more than one occasion. Benjamin and his companion had finished tying up the wounded men and Borell watched as they ran across the apron towards an airship that started to emerge from one of the hangers. This was a much smaller ship than the *Nightstar*, consisting of two separate gondolas hanging from the middle and rear of the balloon and one smaller pilot's gondola at the front.

It appeared Sorrow was setting out to retrieve the device. Borell wondered if he could tag along unseen in the hold and deal out some revenge at the other end. He had not received recompense for his efforts either, seeing that his money had been taken. His bruises would heal somewhat and he would be able to rest a little on the journey — if he could get on to that airship.

Chapter Eighteen

'Hey!' Benjamin shouted and waved at the ground crew as they walked out holding guy ropes. The smaller airship was being readied for service and was attached to a large vehicle with its docking tower holding the ship steady.

'What do you want?' replied one of the ground crew.

'Your boat,' said Benjamin. 'And I insist,' he added, pulling out his gun and pointing it at the man.

'Easy, fella,' said the man, putting up his hands as a reflex. In the process he let go of the guy rope and hesitantly grabbed hold of it again, trying to keep his hands in the 'don't shoot me' position. 'Who's gonna fly her? You?' asked the man incredulously.

Andris looked at Benjamin and asked the same question with a worried expression on his face.

'You're gonna have to start trusting me, kid. Climb aboard,' Benjamin said, pointing Andris towards the boarding ladder hanging from the front cabin. 'Here,' he said, handing Andris a pistol from one of the men they tied up earlier. 'Ask the pilot to leave — politely.'

Andris looked at the gun, then at Benjamin. Thinking about Lilly, he took the pistol and gripped it tightly in his shaking hand. He started to make his way towards the ladder, looking back at Benjamin a couple of times as he went. He couldn't quite believe he was about to steal an airship.

The ladder was about ten steps from the bottom to the cockpit — and a nice solid ladder too, none of this rope ladder business that Andris had never had much luck climbing. He poked his head inside and could see the pilot sitting in his chair, presumably running checks, but what did he know.

'Erm,' Andris stuttered, pointing the pistol at the pilot nervously. 'I would appreciate you, erm — leaving the ship, if you wouldn't mind.' He doubted the authority in his own voice.

The pilot turned his head to see who was offering such meagre orders. His face changed when he saw the pistol pointing at him, his hands assuming the same '*don't shoot*' position as his colleagues.

'Easy, easy son. You don't want to be shooting that thing off in here.'

'Yeah, tell me about it. Don't have much choice though, I'm afraid,' he said feeling a smidgen of confidence well up inside him.

'Okay, alright,' said the pilot as he stood up and waited for Andris to climb inside. This was easier said than done, but Andris managed it with a modicum of composure and managed to keep the pistol trained on his target throughout. He waggled the barrel at the pilot, who raised his hands again and sidestepped towards the opening.

'Off you go,' Andris said, clearly starting to feel the confidence of holding a gun. The pilot hesitated, but only for a second. He backed out of the doorway and stepped down the ladder, watching the barrel of the pistol until he was out of sight.

As soon as the pilot was gone, Andris took a deep breath and let it out slowly. A moment later Benjamin appeared at the top of the ladder and was inside the cockpit, hurriedly winding the handle that collapsed the ladder underneath its belly.

'Good lad. I wasn't sure you had it in you,' Benjamin said as Andris looked out of one of the windows to see ground crew releasing guy ropes.

'They're letting us go, just like that?'

'Not exactly. I gave them the keys to the Fortworth. I

also told them someone would be along to collect it and pay for the airship.'

'We're buying this thing?'

'*We're* not. My employers are. I can send them a communique once we are in the air. Pointing a gun at them helped persuade them quicker. I see you found the same persuasion worked with the pilot?'

'Ha. Yeah. Never fired a gun before, or even held one. I think I must have been somewhat convincing. I did worry I might accidentally shoot him or blow us all up, though.'

Benjamin took the gun from Andris and, pointing it at the ceiling of the cockpit, pulled the trigger. Andris dropped to the floor screaming and covered his head with his arms.

The only sound was the hammer hitting the empty chamber in the pistol.

'What? It wasn't loaded?' Andris said, uncovering his head and looking at the gun and then at Benjamin.

'I took the bullets out earlier. Didn't want you hurting yourself, or the pilot,' Benjamin said with an apologetic smile. 'Would have made it a lot harder to buy this thing with a dead pilot on our hands.'

Andris wasn't sure whether to be relieved or angry. He settled for a feeling weighted towards relieved.

'Here,' said Benjamin, handing the unloaded pistol back to Andris. 'Next time you may need bullets.' Benjamin headed towards the pilot's seat and ordered Andris to sit in the co-pilot seat next to him. 'We need to take a heading of ninety five degrees. That should get us to Nartill. We'll have to keep an eye out for their airship, as I don't know their exact heading or altitude. If we follow the normal flight path, we may get lucky. You'll be on look out once we get going, whilst I let my employers know they just bought themselves an airship and tell them where we're heading.'

'Is an airship something they want?'

'I doubt it, but they have little choice now,' Benjamin said with a smile.

A bulb illuminated on the console in front of Andris. 'What does that mean?' he said, pointing at it.

'It means the ground lines are clear and we can get going. Grab that handle to your right and pull it *really* hard.'

Andris took hold of the large handle and pulled for all he was worth. The handle suddenly moved in a short, sharp motion after resisting his initial heave. They felt a loud *clunk* as the docking clamp was released in the nose section and they floated free. Benjamin increased their buoyancy, dropped some ballast and engaged the engines. He oriented the propellers to give them lift to clear the tower and buildings. After about a minute, he adjusted them again to drive them on their way.

The compass reading indicated they were on a ninety-five degree heading and their altitude was gradually increasing. The night was clear and the normal flight plan called for an altitude of about one thousand feet, so Benjamin headed for two hundred feet above that. The larger airship would probably not go much higher than the flight plan called for, so being higher would make it easier to spot them.

The smaller class of airship was designed to be flown by two pilots, or in the case of an emergency, just one pilot. Most of the systems were available to the pilot and some of the secondary indicators and controls available to the co-pilot, which was now Andris' role in the expedition. After about ten more minutes, they reached their cruising altitude and Benjamin levelled their flight profile.

'We should be travelling faster than them, so I estimate we should catch up to them in about half an hour. Keep your eyes open; we should be well above them when you see them.'

Benjamin twiddled some knobs and pressed some buttons — at least that was what it looked like to Andris. He was really setting the autopilot to keep them on this heading and maintain their current speed, so that he didn't have to worry about it for now. Generally, on flights where the weather was calm and still, the gyroscopic autopilot saved the pilot from the mundane job of flying in a straight line — it often did a better job anyway. He explained most of this to Andris, as he was looking worried now that Benjamin wasn't *flying* the ship.

'How long will it take us to get to Nartill?' Andris asked.

Benjamin grabbed one of the books from the storage alongside his seat and flipped through the pages to find the flight timetable. 'According to the charts, at our current speed and head wind, it should take — about fifteen hours.'

'Wish we'd stopped at that bakery we passed on the way to the aerodrome,' Andris said, suddenly feeling hungry. He realised he had not had dinner earlier, what with the house burning down and them almost being killed.

'Check that locker over there,' Benjamin said, pointing over his shoulder to one of the knee-high storage lockers that doubled as a bench. 'The pilots would have some provisions for flights like this. If they were destined for Arendale or Torke, they may have as much as three days' worth of supplies in there.'

Andris suddenly looked hopeful and sprang out of his seat, heading for the locker. It had a padded cushion on top and seemed to double as a bunk, where the pilot or co-pilot could sleep during extended flights. Andris lifted the lid and found two leather holdalls, a metal box with a lid, what seemed to be survival gear and a flask that was hot to the touch.

Opening the metal box, Andris found a feast of various foods, neatly wrapped up in paper. Sandwiches, cold meats and fruit — they had it all. The holdalls contained a change of clothes, extra jumpers and basic toiletries for freshening up en route.

'Seems like we'll be alright for supplies. There's enough to last several days in here.'

'Good. Take only what you need for now, we'll do an inventory later,' Benjamin said.

'Do you want anything?'

'No thanks. I'll have something later. I need to send a message to the Society. They need to know what we're getting into.'

Andris nodded at the back of Benjamin's head as he grabbed a sandwich from the box and closed the lid. 'So, you're an agent? I guess that explains a lot.'

'I'll explain everything,' Benjamin said.

Sitting back in the co-pilot's seat, Andris unwrapped the sandwich and found that it was chunky, filled with chicken, lettuce and some kind of spicy relish. He wasted no time and took a large bite. 'Mmm, that's a good sandwich,' he said through an overflowing mouthful.

Benjamin smiled. He had opened the coded transmitter panel to the right of the flight control stick and was setting the dials to the correct frequency. He changed a row of dials to set the transmission code to one that would get his message through to Kodey and began tapping out the message. 'So,' he said, turning to Andris. He wanted to make sure Andris knew enough, but not too much, so began to explain his job as an agent for the Society.

Chapter Nineteen

Borell could see from his position behind a wall that Benjamin was indeed planning to take the airship. The gun pointed at the ground crew confirmed that much. Now that the ship had stopped moving along the apron, he saw his opportunity and headed for the rear storage cabin. It was almost as far to the rear of the ship as you could get, and was used for storing passenger luggage and supplies. All the crew's attention was focused on Benjamin and his partner, and Benjamin's attention was focused on taking the ship.

Borell took advantage of this and kept low and quiet as he ran around to the rear loading ladder. His bruised ribs gave him a great deal of pain, but he knew that he could take it easy once on board. As he reached the ladder, he climbed it cautiously. As he expected, he found a crewmember organising supplies in the hold; he rushed in and snapped his neck before he could make a sound.

He pulled the ladder up into the hold, wedged a piece of paper in the door switch and closed the rear hatch quietly. The pilot should see that it was closed from the flight console and not worry about it. Hopefully the ground crew would see the same, if they were at all interested after their ship had been taken. He would be able to open the door inflight without the alarm sounding in the cockpit and dump the body.

A low powered light illuminated the hold and only a single tiny window at the front provided any view to the outside. Borell covered the window with a sheet that was laying on the floor and settled down for the duration. It looked to him like the airship had been providing supplies to a mining facility. There were crates of explosives, food and other essential supplies. Moving some bundles of clothing, he fashioned himself a bed.

He turned out the light and fell asleep.

Chapter Twenty

'Come in,' called Kodey to the person knocking at his closed door.

'An urgent message for you, sir,' said the girl, who brought the message directly from the communications room.

Kodey opened the envelope and saw that it was from Benjamin. 'Has this been verified?' he asked her.

'Yes sir.'

'Thank you, that will be all,' he said, and the girl left, closing the door behind her.

A moment of silence.

'He what?!' Kodey shouted, making the girl stop halfway down the hallway and giggle. He read the message again to make sure he had understood it correctly the first time.

> *Kodey.*
> *Bought/stole airship at east dock.*
> *Please pay for and collect Fortworth.*
> *Headed to Nartill in pursuit of device on the Nightstar.*
> *Run checks on Andris Tar, Student Uni. of Browne.*
> *Sorry.*
> *Benjamin.*

He laughed with disbelief at Benjamin's antics.

'What the hell are we going to do with an airship?' he asked himself aloud. He folded the message and put it in his pocket before walking over to a cabinet on the other side of his office and unlocking it. Inside was a smaller locked cupboard that required another key. Upon opening this lock he stood facing his Society issued pistol and ammunition. He took the revolver from its mount and loaded it with bullets from a box next to it. Spinning the cylinder a couple of rotations, he pushed it back into the frame with a satisfying click. He grabbed his shoulder holster from the larger cabinet, put it on, slotted his pistol into it and closed the cabinet.

'I just hope he doesn't destroy it,' he said to himself, knowing that the odds of Benjamin bringing the airship home in one piece were slim.

He headed for the intelligence team, to pass on the request from Benjamin about Andris. It would take them a little time to dig up any information, if there was any to find. Kodey estimated that it would take Benjamin the best part of a day to get to Nartill, so he had some time to let his people work.

His next stop was the aerodrome to find out how much this airship was going to cost him.

Chapter Twenty-One

'So tell me about yourself, Andris,' Benjamin asked as the airship flew its own dead straight and level course. 'I've seen you are pretty keen to help rescue Lilly. Are you two —?'

'No, oh no. We're just friends, I mean.' Andris suddenly felt flustered, like he was being quizzed by a daughter's father with a large shotgun pointed at his head.

'What happened at Browne that made you two come all the way to Trellern?'

Andris took a breath. 'Well, I saw Lilly running from a man through the back streets. It looked like she'd been running for a bit, looking tired. I managed to get her to safety. Anyway, I helped her take a more scenic route back to the university, but we found her friend Mia stabbed in an alleyway. By the other man chasing them. After going to the hospital, we were found by the same men and chased by two constables. We hatched a plan to come here, as I was about the only person she thought she could trust. Honestly, she didn't really want to involve any of her friends, so I'm not sure what that makes me, actually.' Andris took another breath.

'It makes you someone who put his own life at risk for someone else. It takes a special kind of person to do that,' Benjamin said.

Andris' face lit up a little at the compliment, but it soon faded as he continued the story. 'Then we got a train to Trellern to find her grandfather. We ended up at your house after we couldn't get in to Mr Burns' shop.'

'Did you find out anything more about the men that chased you? Did you report it to anyone at all?'

'Lilly didn't want to risk it, she didn't know who to trust. She said we'd be safer in Trellern with family. I had to come with her really. I knew I'd be in danger too, now that the men had seen my face and knew I was somehow involved with Lilly.'

'You two did the right thing. I'm just sorry things turned out this way.' Benjamin sighed. 'We *will* get Lilly and Jackson back, but you'll be risking your life again if you stay with me. There's no shame in staying out of the way when we get to Nartill. Things will get bloody and you may have to pull a trigger for real next time.' Benjamin could see Andris was starting to contemplate the wisdom of tagging along with him.

Andris took another bite of the sandwich he had been eating, chewed for a good minute, then swallowed and said, 'Oh, I'm with you.'

Benjamin smiled. 'I've been to Nartill a few times, so I know the lay of the land somewhat. As to where in Nartill we are heading I have no idea. The island is quite large but not densely populated. The capital city of Anundale wouldn't be where I'd expect them to dock. Most probably one of the independent towns or private estates. We'll need to do a bit of walking once we land, I can't risk putting this thing down too close. If they see us coming, our rescue is over before it begins.'

'Walking I can do,' said Andris. 'These shoes have seen plenty of miles. They're as comfortable as the skin on my own feet.'

'Good. We'll have to raid the ship for supplies and equipment. You have the consumables in hand, literally,' Benjamin joked, 'so we just need to get all of that out and pack only what we can carry. You said there were enough supplies for several days?'

'Yeah.'

'Four days? Five days?'

'Easily, for two people,' Andris said, looking back at the cache of food he'd taken out of the storage locker earlier.

'I've been looking at the flight plan that the pilot had stowed for their trip. It looks like they were going to carry miners and supplies to the Alexton Mines, north-east of Trellern, on the border with Torke. There's no manifest though — I suspect we interrupted their usual procedures slightly, so we'll have to go back and take a look in the hold.'

'We can get to the other parts of the ship from here?' Andris asked, having never been inside an airship before.

Benjamin indicated to a hatch above the rear section of the cockpit. 'There's a service crawlspace through the balloon that links the three gondolas. It also provides access to the engines, buoyancy and control systems. I'll go check the hold; you can keep your eyes peeled for the *Nightstar*.'

Andris was excited to be on an airship, let alone in the cockpit with all the workings therein. He tried to hide the excitement from his face, but managed it barely; Benjamin spotted this.

'Whilst I'm gone, don't touch anything. If there are any alarms, shout into these voicepipes,' Benjamin said, pointing to the brass contraptions on the wall. 'They go to the main cabin and the hold.'

Andris nodded.

A simple and reliable means of communicating between the gondolas, the two brass mouthpieces were mounted on the cockpit wall, just behind the co-pilot and connected to a similar mouthpiece on the other end by a simple tube. It was a low-tech solution that had worked for many decades and was favoured in the smaller craft. Larger craft used new electrical intercoms, but they were far more complex and frequently went wrong, meaning someone had to run a message to the other person until they were repaired; they carried someone specifically for this job, as they failed so often.

Andris turned round in his chair and looked at the elaborately engraved brass cones protruding from the wall. He noticed that there were engraved plaques beneath each one, saying *'Hold'* and *'Cabin'*. There were lots of other dials and indicators on this side of the co-pilot's seat, in which Andris took an interest. There were dials for various pressures in the main and reserve hydrogen tanks; pressures in the numerous balloon bladders, with red warning markings telling you when a bladder was leaking; fuel gauges for the mechanical engines propelling the ship; temperatures for each of the engines and for the hydrogen compression systems. He would have to remember to look outside the ship occasionally too.

'I will be back in a little while,' Benjamin said as he walked to the rear of the cockpit, reached up and pulled open the crawlspace hatch. The noise in the cockpit increased substantially with the sounds coming from the bowels of the balloon envelope. Benjamin climbed the ladder built into the back wall and up into the hatch, disappearing from view, closing the hatch behind him.

The inside of the crawlspace was not cramped or claustrophobic in any way. Above and to the side of him, Benjamin could access the engines and various systems he had described to Andris earlier. Hopefully this ship had been well maintained and he wouldn't have to go near them. As he made his way along the crawlspace, he came to the hatch that opened into the passenger cabin. Benjamin thought it would be worth checking to see if there were any items of use in here too. Although passengers had not boarded, it may have been stocked for their journey.

He sat with his feet inside the hatch space, leant down and turned the handle. The hatch dropped open and he slid a ladder down that was stowed to his left. Once it was extended, he climbed down.

The passenger cabin was comfortable, but not luxurious, not by the standards of some of the larger vessels. This was a working class transport. It provided comfortable chairs; a bar for those who could afford a drink; bunks towards the rear of the cabin for those that needed some sleep en route and tables that provided somewhere to sit and play cards to gamble their earnings away.

As he had suspected, the cabin was mostly empty. The bunks were made, the bar stocked, but nothing else of any use. He climbed back up the ladder back into the crawlspace. Continuing along the smooth boards, the noise from the outboard engines grew louder. They were physically mounted outside the balloon's envelope for safety, but they still made an impressive rumbling sound he could hear from inside.

The crawlspace ahead of him didn't continue much farther and it soon changed direction to become a ladder providing access to the levels above him. The hatch into the hold was just before the end of the crawlspace. There was no ladder this time, but the shelving below him inside the hold provided a means to climb down.

It was dark inside. Benjamin felt along the wall for a switch for a few moments before — *click* — he found it and turned the lights on. He span around, cocked his pistol and had it trained on the man laying asleep on the makeshift bed along one shelf. The man appeared to be fast asleep, or at least pretending to be.

'Don't move, fella, or it'll be your last,' Benjamin said, training his pistol on the man.

'We both know you're not going to risk shooting that in here,' he said from underneath the covers. Slowly the man pulled the blanket from his face and looked Benjamin in the eyes. 'You got me, Sorrow,' he said.

'And you have me at a disadvantage.'

'My name is Borell. And you are the famous Benjamin Sorrow, pride of the Society's agent program. Retired, I thought,' Borell said.

'Show me your hands slowly. I can shoot you without going anywhere near the balloon.'

'Easy, easy,' Borell said as he lifted his hands above the blanket and raised them slightly above his head. 'I'm not armed.'

'Remove the blanket slowly and sit upon your hands,' Benjamin instructed. Borell did as he was told; there was no fight in him at the moment and he ached too much. Besides, there was nowhere to go when you are in the air except down, and he didn't fancy learning to fly today.

'So, introductions out of the way, who are you and what are you doing in the hold of this ship?' Benjamin asked.

'Borell is no one you know. You, on the other hand, I know well.' He looked at Benjamin and cocked his head a little. 'You are the man who takes down secret organisations. The man who kills for the *good* of society. A man who enjoys bending the rules to get the job done.' Borell smiled.

'Okay, you know who I am, but that still doesn't answer my question.'

'Come on, Benjie, you know more about me than you think you do.'

'No one's called me that since I was a kid. And even then, there was only one person who...' Benjamin fixed Borell with a long stare.

'Ah, the penny has dropped. I said I am no one you *know*.'

'The only person to call me by that name died many years ago. You're just someone who heard that name in whatever public house you frequent or just guessed at a childhood nickname.'

'Maybe so, but you know there is more to it than that.'

Benjamin stared at Borell, a flicker of recognition in his weathered features, 'You can't be —?'

'Be who, Benjie?'

'Jadon?' Benjamin said with a face of disbelief. 'But you died when we were at the academy. I saw your body.'

'You saw some poor sod's body. We work for the

Society remember. Don't you think they can orchestrate the death of a student?'

'Wait. So what, they arranged your death? Why?'

'We both have skills, Benjie. Mine just happened to be more colourful than yours were. You continued your training to become an agent, and so did I. I just belonged to a different programme to you. I still remember your eulogy at my funeral. Very touching.'

'You were there? At your own funeral?' Benjamin said in disbelief, still struggling to comprehend this turn of events.

'Well of course I was at my own funeral, I just wasn't in the casket as people expected,' Borell said with a chuckle. 'The programme required that I leave my old life behind. It wasn't something I was very attached to, if I'm honest. I only had one real friend and he needed to believe I was dead and buried.'

Benjamin's mind was starting to fill in the blanks and the story started making some sense.

'You haven't heard of the Pegasus Project, I presume?'

'Clearly not,' Benjamin said as he sat down on the stack of crates behind him. Borell lifted his shoulders in a gesture, asking permission to remove his hands. 'Just don't try anything. I'm still not sure I believe anything you're saying,' Benjamin said.

Borell removed each hand one at a time and gave them a rub. 'Thanks, they were starting to go a bit numb.'

'Okay, so you're part of something called Pegasus. What does Pegasus *do* exactly?'

'We were trained to become deep cover agents. To do the things you as an agent wouldn't be able to do. Sure, you go undercover and bring down the bad guys. We *became* the bad guys to bring down the *really* bad guys. There are some lines which have to be blurred, which is why my academy evaluations suggested I'd be better suited for this life than you.'

'You mean family?'

'Partly. Your family were well known and there was no way you could separate your life from them. I, on the other hand, had no family. Nothing to connect to me — no life, little history. I could become Borell and become an asset to whoever wanted to hire me. Sure, I've crossed the line plenty of times. Some days it's hard to remember who Jadon really is, if he's even still in here somewhere. I have become more Borell than Jadon now. Morals have something to do with it too, or the capability to be flexible with them.'

'How many Pegasus agents are there?' Benjamin asked.

'Don't know. I was trained away from everyone else, as I suspect any others were. I spent many years in a town near Torke, with my mentor. I learned over the years that he reported directly to a senior prefect, but I never met him. I heard his name — or at least a cover name — once: Treddan. My guess is that this prefect dreamt up the whole programme and kept it quiet from the others. You think the Society is secretive — you have no idea. I don't even think the principal knows the programme exists. Otherwise I don't see why he would have sent you to retrieve the device.'

Benjamin looked at him quizzically.

'Yeah, I heard that you were involved in this. I have been trying to stay out of your way.'

Benjamin lowered his gun slowly, a memory returning to him. 'If you really are Jadon, show me your side.'

'Ah, I wondered if you would remember,' said Borell, smiling. He slowly lifted his shirt, aware that Benjamin's pistol was still pointing in his direction, if not aimed.

'Son of a...' Benjamin saw the familiar scar along Borell's ribcage. 'How did you get that?'

'Like you don't remember. You sliced me open when we were sparring with swords in the academy gymnasium. I spent two weeks in the infirmary with an infection thanks to you, not to mention the reprimand we both got. Got a nice scar out of it though, it's provided plenty of nice backstories in my new life.'

'Jadon? It really is you?'

'Yes, Benjie, it really is.'

'Please stop calling me that,' Benjamin said with an irritated face.

Borell beamed a smile at his old friend. 'Sure, Ben.'

'Better. So why are you on my boat?' Benjamin asked as he eased the hammer on his pistol back into a safe position and put it back into the holster under his arm, still cautious.

'I've been trying to get inside the organisation that wants this device Jackson Burns created. We've been going at the same thing from different angles. I planned to get myself on their ship and infiltrate their headquarters. Things took a bit of a turn for the worse though,' he said feeling his ribs to make sure they still hurt. They did.

'You're lucky to be alive — at all.'

'Hey, no one's perfect. A miscalculation perhaps, but when I saw you were heading after them I thought I could tag along unseen and still do what I needed to. Hadn't counted on you finding me here though.'

'It really is you isn't it.'

'You'll get used to it. Who's the chap you boarded with? I didn't recognise him, another agent?'

'Not exactly.'

Benjamin proceeded to explain all about the kidnapping and the destruction of his house whilst they searched the hold for supplies. All the while, Benjamin kept a wary eye on his long lost *friend*. He knew the Society did indeed keep all manner of secrets, but there are also secrets available for a price, such as the death of an academy student, so he made sure not to divulge anything that was too sensitive.

At least whilst they were in the air it was unlikely that Borell would attempt anything; he would have to be able to fly the ship in that case.

'Mr Sorrow,' came Andris' voice from the pipe on the wall. 'I think I can see the other ship!'

'That was quick — come on.' Benjamin indicated towards the shelf-come-ladder. 'After you.'

'Still don't trust me?'

'Would you?'

Borell made a face, which conceded 'probably not', and started climbing into the crawlspace. Benjamin was close behind as they made their way forward to the cockpit. The thought of *Jadon* being alive kept running through Benjamin's mind.

***

'Your friend isn't going to shoot me, is he?' Borell asked as he sat on the edge of the hatch into the cockpit.

'I think you're safe.' Benjamin smiled, unseen.

Borell leant into the hatch and turned the handle. He looked in but couldn't see Andris, so started down the ladder. Andris was busy looking out of the front window of the cockpit using a pair of Stenner binoculars he'd found stowed in the console by the co-pilot's chair.

'They're below us like you said they would be,' Andris said.

'We'd better back off otherwise they are likely to spot us,' Borell said as he stepped off the bottom rung of the ladder. Andris whipped his head around in surprise and fumbled with the binoculars, almost dropping them in a comical show of flailing hands.

'Who the hell are you?' Andris said, now brandishing the binoculars in the most threatening way he could.

'Take it easy, son, no one needs to get hurt,' Borell said, smirking and feigning fear at the threat of Andris' binoculars.

Benjamin came through the hatch and down the ladder a moment later. 'You can put those down, Andris,' he said. 'This is Borell. Borell, Andris.'

'Nice to meet you, kid,' Borell said, stepping towards Andris with his hand outstretched. Andris looked at Borell's hand, then at Benjamin and back to Borell.

'It's okay,' Benjamin reassured Andris. 'I found him in the hold. We have a — history. He's going to be helping us.'

For a moment, Andris looked unsure, but lowered his weapon and shook Borell's hand.

'Attaboy,' Borell said, and made himself at home in the pilot's chair, taking the binoculars from Andris as he did so. 'Looks like we're gaining on them a little quick. If they've got any half decent watchmen on their aft quarters, we'll be spotted, if we haven't been already.'

'Then I'd appreciate the pilot's chair. This is my mission, as ad hoc as it is,' Benjamin said.

'Sure thing Benj — Ben.' Borell grinned a toothy apology for the name slip. He handed the binoculars over and sat down on the comfortable bench towards the rear of the cabin rubbing his sore ribs.

Benjamin looked at the *Nightstar* in the distance and knew Borell was right. He pulled back on the throttles, slowing them down. He would have to sight their speed for the next few minutes to maintain the distance. Leaning over to the centre of the console, he flipped a series of switches that turned out all the running lights and finally a switch to dim the cabin. They were now running dark, which would make them much harder to spot.

'Andris, keep an eye out for other airships too. They won't see us until it's too late, we're higher than I'd expect anyone else to be, but better to be safe than sorry,' Benjamin said.

He handed the binoculars over and told Andris to let him know if he saw any unusual activity from the *Nightstar*. He then turned back to the coded transmitter panel and started to send another message to Kodey. He noticed one of the dials was set in the wrong place, but assumed it had been knocked or moved whilst Andris was leaning against it looking out of the window. Resetting the dial, he sent another message:

Kodey.
Check Society Pegasus Project.
Jadon Tarren is alive and claims to be an agent in programme.
His cover name is Borell.
Prefect in charge was Treddan. Possible cover name.
Destination is still Nartill.
In sight of Nightstar.
Benjamin.

'Right,' Benjamin said, getting up and heading back to Borell, sitting opposite him on the other bench. 'We need to talk.'

Chapter Twenty-Two

Lilly put her hands to her head and rubbed her dry and sore eyes, her head pounding. She could barely see through her foggy vision, but after a few moments, the room became clearer. She was lying on her back looking up at a dull grey ceiling. The bed was comfortable. She lay still, listening for noises around her. The only one that she could focus on was a low droning noise.

Lilly gradually felt more aware of her surroundings, still sore, but able to attempt to sit up. Slowly rolling onto her side and pushing herself upright, she could see the rest of her room. The first thing that she saw that made her scramble backwards on the bed and push herself up against the wall was a large, heavyset man standing in the open doorway, watching her.

The man was staring impassively into the room. He was wearing dark leather clothing and was well armed, with a pistol visible on either side of his belt. When he didn't move, Lilly settled down a little and looked around. The windowless room was sparsely furnished, a cabin of some kind. The only things in it were her, the bed she sat on, a dressing table and a mirror.

'Where am I?' she asked feebly, her throat dry.

The guard didn't answer.

'Hello?' she tried getting his attention again. This time he simply looked at her, turned and closed the door behind him.

Lilly got off the bed and tried the door handle.

It was locked.

She banged on the door as hard as she could. 'Hey, let me out of here!' she shouted, her voice returning, listening for any kind of response. She tried again — nothing.

She walked over to the bed and sat down, hugging her knees for comfort. Resting her head on her arms stopped it from pounding but didn't do much to calm her down. Lilly listened to the noise she heard before and it began to sound like engines, constant and unchanging. She let herself get lost in the sound, focusing her mind and trying to ignore the pain in her head. Whomever her captors were, they would make themselves known soon enough.

A sound at the door woke Lilly from her deep focus as it opened to reveal a woman.

'Hello, Lilly,' she said. 'My name is Loren.'

If Lilly had any thoughts about escape, they were soon quashed when she saw the same hulk of a man that had stood in the doorway minutes before, arms folded with a serious look on his face, standing behind the woman.

'Where am I?' Lilly tried again.

'You are on an airship heading to your new home. How permanent that home is depends on your grandfather.'

'What have you done with him?' Lilly shouted, dropping her legs from the bed, making the hulking man step forward. He didn't have to say a word, Lilly got the message: don't move.

'He is fine for now. We don't want to harm him; he is far too valuable to us for that. No, he is sleeping off his unfortunate meeting with one of my colleagues. Not unlike yourself.' Loren indicated to the bed. 'May I?'

Lilly shuffled over and Loren sat next to her.

'Your grandfather has a very important role to play in our plans my dear. As will you.'

'Me? What can I possibly be of value for? I'm a student, for crying out loud!'

'You will be the one to encourage your grandfather to help us,' Loren said, smiling.

'Why would I do that? He won't help you and neither

will I,' said Lilly, folding her arms in defiance.

'Whether it is through your own actions or inactions, you *will* help us.'

'What do you mean, "inactions"?'

'If you don't want help us willingly, then there is someone you should meet.' Loren looked at the hulking man; he stepped aside and in walked a skinny, balding man wearing a pristine white suit and carrying a canvas bag. He was grinning from ear to ear, which lifted his little beady eyes and stretched his sagging skin.

'Oh, right,' Lilly said beginning to understand what was going to happen. 'So you torture me to get my grandfather to help you.'

'You are a bright girl. It must run in your family,' Loren said. 'This is Mr Frederic. He is very persuasive when it comes to helping us get what we want. But don't worry, there's no need to spoil your pretty face just yet. Your screams won't help us until your grandfather is awake.'

'Mr Frederic,' Loren said, looking at him, 'please let me know when Mr Burns has awakened.'

Mr Frederic, still grinning, walked back out of the room, leaving Loren to continue her talk.

'So you see, either way you will be helping us.' Loren looked at her pocket watch. 'We won't be arriving for several hours yet. You may as well get some rest.'

'I really don't think I'll be resting,' Lilly said.

'Entirely up to you, my dear. I will have food and water brought to you. You are of no use to us weak and fatigued.'

'Screw your food,' said Lilly, as viciously as she could. Although she knew she would probably eat if they did bring her anything, she wasn't about to concede that.

'Indeed. You have fire in you. Mr Frederic will be pleased.' Loren got up and walked over to the door. 'And don't think of going anywhere. Royston here will be just outside.' She closed the door behind her. Lilly returned to the bed, digesting the increasingly horrible events that were unfolding around her.

***

Loren walked along a corridor towards the aft of the main deck and then headed to a lounge on the port side. The *Nightstar* was a luxurious ship, worthy of the patronage the wealthy could afford to provide. At this moment, the *Nightstar* was being privately used by the Toren, which in itself was a testament to the influence and power they had gathered over the decades.

None of the patrons would have argued or objected to the private running of this ship today and the crew were loyal and well-paid members of the Toren.

'She won't be a problem,' Loren said as she walked into the lounge.

'I'm glad to hear it,' said a man standing in front of one of the large portside windows, looking down on the lands passing beneath them. 'And our special guest?'

'Still sleeping,'

'Very well. I have received word that preparations have been made for our arrival. Mr Frederic will have to wait until He has spoken to our guests.'

'Mr Frederic will be disappointed,' Loren said with a smile, lost to the back of the man's head.

'Let me make it perfectly clear, Loren. No harm will come to them yet,' said the man, turning to look at her directly. 'Please see that they are fed and watered and that any injuries are seen to.'

'Yes, sir,' said Loren, bowing her head.

'Bring Mr Burns to me when he has awoken,' said the man, turning to look out of the large window again. 'That will be all for now.'

Loren turned and walked out of the lounge. She knew better than disobey Durrant; his loyalty to Him was unfaltering.

Durrant was feared amongst the followers of the Toren as much as He himself.

Chapter Twenty-Three

Kodey pulled up in the underground lobby for the Society offices in the Fortworth, after retrieving it from the manager of the aerodrome and handing over a sizable payment for the airship Benjamin took.

'Lucky the old bird was being retired soon anyway. Bought y'self a bargain,' the man had said, and laughed heartily as he walked away with the money.

Kodey knew he would be getting it in the neck from the other prefects when they found out, but Benjamin's mission was too important to argue over money right now. With a bit of luck, they would get the airship back in one piece and sell it to someone who really wanted it.

He jumped out and headed for the security guards standing by the lobby door. He knew them both, which just made getting inside quicker. Prefects enjoyed more freedom and less restrictions than others; less time spent being searched and more time working was how they looked at it — sometimes. It still took him a few minutes to pass the security checkpoint before getting into the garage though.

'Gentlemen,' he said as he approached them.

'Prefect Twill,' the two men said in unison.

Kodey opened the door to an anteroom with a desk, and a security officer sat behind it. He went through the usual signing in procedure, but didn't need to check his weapon — another benefit of being a prefect. Once signed in, he pressed the call button for the lift and waited for the doors to open. It took him up the opposite side of the building, so it was a short walk to his office. His first port of call was the communications room, to see if there were any more messages from Benjamin.

Ping.

He walked along the corridor, past four office doors until he reached the room he wanted and went in. Opening the door, he was awash with the familiar chaotic sound of message machines typing, and raised voices trying to be heard above the mechanical chorus. There were two rows of desks with an operator sitting at each, in front of various wireless receivers; the machines were clattering out messages onto strips of paper on one row. As a message was received, it was decoded by the machines, and then the message would be handed to someone sat on the desk opposite for verification and then passed to a runner for delivery. Some messages were simple updates that would be logged in daily files; others, such as the one for Kodey, were delivered directly.

Kodey walked up to the front desk and asked Karen, the woman sat there, if he had any messages.

'As a matter of fact you do. This came in a little while ago, but it was returned because you were out of the building,' she said.

He took the envelope containing the message and thanked her.

Reading through the message inside, he looked bemused at the Pegasus Project question; he clearly had not heard of it either. He headed back towards the lift. He did recognise the cover name of Treddan though — it had belonged to a retired senior prefect by the name of Tarborthian. If this project was still running, then he needed to find out who was masterminding it now. Kodey would need to go to the records room and get a current address for Tarborthian to find out more about Pegasus. Prefect or not, he wouldn't be allowed to the sub-levels with a firearm on his person, so headed back to his office first to lock it away.

A quick trip up two more floors by another lift brought him to the prefect floor and his office. As soon as the lift doors opened, Kodey saw Senior Prefect Hoyt pacing impatiently up and down the hallway outside Kodey's office.

'Prefect Hoyt,' Kodey said, acknowledging him as he walked towards him.

'Prefect Twill, may I have a word?' Hoyt asked in a rather pensive voice.

'With all due respect, sir, now is not a good time. I need to be somewhere else urgently.'

'I appreciate your candour, but I think we need to have a conversation, Kodey.'

Kodey knew something was wrong when Hoyt used his first name. 'Is everything alright, sir?'

'Can we talk in your office?'

Now Kodey was intrigued, but still had his mission foremost in his mind. 'Yes, sir, but I can only give you a few minutes.'

'Understood. I think you may have more time to give me when you hear what I have to say.'

Kodey unlocked his office door and extended his arm for Prefect Hoyt to enter first, and followed close behind. He offered Hoyt a seat and began disarming himself and locking his pistol away. Hoyt didn't sit down, but walked over to the large window and looked out across the city. Everyone seemed to appreciate the view from Kodey's office.

'Kodey, everything I am about to tell you must remain in the highest confidence. This day has been coming for some time, but current events have brought my timetable forwards a little.'

Kodey sat down and looked at Hoyt.

'Your assignment from the principal this morning involving Agent Sorrow crosses directly with a major undercover operation I have been working on for the best part of two years.'

Hoyt continued to explain to Kodey about the operation. About how he had orchestrated the leak of information about a fake energy device as a trap, but that a mole within the society had since sold real information that compromised an actual device. Hoyt was avoiding telling Kodey the truth about the secret programme he was running, but only because the act of divulging the details was personally hard for him.

'Sir, why has none of this been included in my mission briefing from the principal? If Agent Sorrow has encroached on a larger operation, we should have been told.'

'You are correct.' Hoyt turned and stared out of the window again.

'Sir, if you have pertinent information that could assist Agent Sorrow, then I think you should just tell me.'

Hoyt turned and looked at him, then quietly sat in the chair opposite. 'Your message from Agent Sorrow, enquiring about Borell and the Pegasus Project —'

'Wait a minute,' Kodey said, leaning forward, resting his arms on the table. 'How do you know about Benjamin's message?'

'Even as a prefect, there is much you do not know. Secure messages aren't as secure as you think.'

Hoyt reluctantly told Kodey about the Pegasus Project and how it was founded by his mentor, retired Senior Prefect Tarborthian, whose codename was Treddan, as Kodey already knew. Hoyt was brought in to run the program two years before Tarborthian retired and has been managing it since. He explained that Pegasus operated covertly within the Society, unknown to the incumbent principal.

Kodey sat and listened to what Hoyt had to say, not really believing his own ears.

'Tarborthian saw that some endeavours undertaken by our agents were not attaining the levels of success that we needed. The programme was created to address this.

Invisible agents, who don't exist, make certain goals more achievable.'

'So, this Borell is one of yours then?'

'Yes, and as Agent Sorrow has a long lost connection with him already, it has only made hiding this project from you counterproductive.'

'How have you managed to keep this from the principal all these years? Can I assume the methods they employ are less than moral?'

'Indeed they are. Agents like your friend Sorrow are fine men, but they obey the rules, with a little bending of them here and there. Agents like Borell follow no such rules to attain their objectives. They make very valuable assets to our cause. Many of the successes our agents have had over the years have been because of the Pegasus Project. Without their undercover work, we would be mourning many more agents than we have. Unfortunately, in this operation, things didn't go quite to plan.'

'You mean Jacob Abner,' Kodey said.

'Very astute. Abner was charged with leaking the information about a fake device, but took the opportunity to orchestrate the theft of the real device when he discovered its existence in Special Projects. I received word that he has been *eliminated* from the equation earlier today.'

'What? You had a prefect, one of our own, killed?'

'Indeed I did. But he stopped being one of us when he sold out his own people for money. Like I said, this program doesn't exist and if pressed I will deny any knowledge of it or anything that may or may not of happened because of it.'

'So Benjamin was brought in to recover the device on a directive straight from the top, but you kept your involvement quiet?' Kodey asked.

'Correct.'

'And who has the device now?'

'The Toren. Thanks to Abner's efforts, once the real

device was in circulation, we took the opportunity to infiltrate them and take them apart from the inside. Borell was our man on the ground. He recovered the device and —'

'Hold on.' Kodey put up a hand to cut Hoyt off. 'You had the device in your custody, but then used it as bait — and lost it?'

'Look at the bigger picture, Prefect Twill,' Hoyt said, not liking the change in Kodey's tone.

'The bigger picture can go to hell. You deliberately let a faction that opposes our very way of life obtain a device that, by all accounts, is nothing short of absolute power! Not to mention the man who created the device has also been taken, so who knows how many more of these devices they will be able to create.'

'An unfortunate turn of events —'

'"*An unfortunate turn of events*"?' Kodey echoed, shocked at the coldness now exuding from Hoyt.

'Clearly the Toren found out about the missing piece of the device and acquired Mr Burns for his ability complete it for them.'

'So Benjamin is cleaning up after you, but has no idea that his own organisation orchestrated this whole mess in the first place. Right now he's chasing the missing device and his friends all because of your incompetence!'

'Kodey, please calm down.'

'The hell I will!' Kodey shouted as he leapt up out of his chair.

'Matters are out of our hands, so to speak. Agents Sorrow and Borell are the only hope we have of returning the device.' Hoyt was already questioning his decision to bring Kodey on board. He could see that Benjamin's involvement was striking a personal chord with him.

'And Jackson Burns is what, expendable?'

'I am sure Agent Sorrow will recover the device and his friend,' Hoyt said calmly. 'I have every confidence in Borell that he will assist Agent Sorrow and complete his original mission to recover the device and infiltrate the Toren. I need your absolute confidence on this Kodey. We cannot afford to fight amongst ourselves — let Agents Sorrow and Borell do their jobs.'

Kodey got up and paced back and forth, thinking matters through. He realised that there was little point exposing the Pegasus Project at the moment; that could only hinder the recovery of the device and Jackson. Finally, he said, 'Agreed — for now. We need to get this device back and stop the Toren. Do you have any information on what they are planning on doing once they have the device?'

'Some,' Hoyt said. He placed a large leather-bound folder on the desk in front of Kodey. 'This is information obtained from one of our agents two weeks ago,' he said, removing the leather tie from the folder and pulling out a stack of pages. Amongst them were a dozen photographs, blurry in some cases but unmistakable in what they showed. He spread them on the desk for Kodey to see.

The grainy and blurred photographs showed ranks of what could only be described as mechanical warriors, standing what looked like twenty feet tall based on their surroundings and armed to the teeth; an army amassed for only one purpose.

'What the hell are they?' Kodey asked, standing over them.

'We are not entirely sure. They have been amassing an army of these machines, according to one of our agents. Numbering in the hundreds, apparently. He also said that he saw prototypes of these warrior-machines being tested in part of the facility, but that they were incomplete. They were tethered to huge generators and several experienced catastrophic failures whilst being tested.'

'So a small power source such as Jackson's device would be critical to their deployment. Do we know who they are planning on using them against?' Kodey asked.

'Does it matter? They have the means to subdue any kingdom they choose, whether it is our allies or ours. But they are just piles of metal without Burns and his power source.'

'Why haven't we mobilised more agents to this?'

'As of now, there are only a handful of people who are even aware this is taking place. There is no way we can prepare for an invasion of this scale; it would only cause panic if this information were public. And I have no doubts that it would become public with more of our organisation involved. The case in point would be Jacob Abner. I have already had his brother, Dunstan, detained for some fabricated felony, just in case he is involved in some way.'

'And if he's not?' Kodey asked.

'Once this is all over, we'll apologise and he will return to his post,' Hoyt said with a calculated smile.

'What about our allies and neighbours?'

'We have agreed that none of them would stand a chance of repelling this kind of technology, so we decided that it would be best they didn't know.'

'Very magnanimous of you,' Kodey said sarcastically.

'Kodey, please understand. At this moment there are only two agents that can prevent an invasion from happening and they need us in their corner,' Hoyt said, losing his temper at Kodey's quip. 'Borell has all the current information that is available to him and I reiterate my confidence in his abilities.'

Kodey realised that Hoyt was serious about his request for confidentiality so decided it was best not to push him too far. 'And there's no way we can launch an offensive against them? A pre-emptive strike against this facility?' he asked.

'Unfortunately not. We have lost several agents who have been there just to scout and obtain intelligence. Their position is too heavily fortified to allow an assault. Believe me, we have discussed this at length with the intelligence we already have.'

'And what are these?' Kodey said, moving some of the

photographs around and revealing two airships of huge proportions, the like of which he had not seen before. The photograph was a little out of focus and distant, but showed airships, which looked very much like two airships side by side joined together. A large gondola fixed to the belly looked like a fortress, whilst there was a large platform on top of the envelope that seemed to have aircraft performing manoeuvres.

'Another problem, one I fear will not require the device, but will be all the more horrifying with it.'

'With an air presence like this, we really wouldn't stand a chance. Can I speak to the agent who took these?' Kodey asked.

'I'm afraid not. He was killed not long after getting these to us. It appears our internal security issues are widespread.' Hoyt rubbed his tired eyes.

Kodey picked up the photograph of the mammoth airships and studied it closely for a moment. 'I need to get a message to Agent Sorrow. You have my word that we are working for a common purpose for now, Prefect Hoyt.'

'I would appreciate you updating me with any developments from your agent. If they are unable to obtain the device before it has been duplicated or used for whatever purpose, we will need to mobilise whatever we can to stop any advance of their army.'

'Too little too late,' Kodey said.

'That as may be, but acting too soon could have just as dire a consequence for us.'

Chapter Twenty-Four

'That's not something I want to do again,' said Andris as he buttoned the fly on his trousers and closed the flap on the tube at the rear of the cockpit. 'What do you do if you need to — you know,' he said, trying to gesticulate another bodily function.

Borell laughed. 'You bag it or hold it inside ya, son.'

'Or you could just go back and use the passenger toilets,' Benjamin said with a chuckle.

'So I didn't need to —? Thanks for telling me!'

Benjamin and Borell smiled at each other as if they were back in their academy days.

Andris sat opposite Borell and looked at him. Borell had told him a little about himself, but just enough to sate Andris' curiosity. Just because Benjamin trusted Andris, Borell saw no reason why he should.

'So didn't you miss anything from your old life? It sounds like you and Benjamin would have made a great team.'

'You don't know what kind of freedom you have when you don't need to follow the rules of society, kid,' Borell explained.

'But you are just a criminal now. Sure you have a purpose beneath all of that, but how blurred have the lines become between Borell and your old life?'

'Blurred?' Borell laughed. 'There is no line *to* blur. If I die now, I die as Borell. If I give up this life, there will be another name waiting for me.'

'So it's something you would give up?'

'Perhaps,' he said. 'Borell doesn't need to keep a track of finances, so when he dies you would only need to know where his money was stashed to live a long and comfortable life.'

'So you've been profiteering from your life as Borell too?' Andris asked, clearly intrigued by Borell's lack of morals.

'Look, kid, I gave up my life because I was good at something — something bad. When I retire, do you think the Society will give a damn about me?'

'Well, erm...'

'They won't, I'll be forgotten quicker than a lanced boil. That doesn't bother me; I came to terms with that long ago. Which is why, as you put it, I profit from my life as Borell for my own future. I am expendable to them.'

'And that really doesn't bother you, does it?' Andris pressed.

'Not at all. To be brutally honest —' Borell leaned across the gap between him and Andris '— I enjoy it,' he said with a wink.

Andris looked into Borell's cold eyes and he could see that he meant it.

'Besides, tell me your little escapade at the aerodrome didn't excite you just a little, and leave you wondering why you spent all day in classes being taught by stuffy old men?'

Andris was a little taken back by this, but thought honestly about it for a moment before replying.

'It was the most exciting thing that has ever happened to me.'

'Imagine that as your day — everyday. Exciting, rewarding and dangerous.'

'Easy, old friend, don't go recruiting him just yet,' Benjamin said from the pilot's chair.

Borell smiled. 'We could do with a few more men with bottle, like the kid here.'

Andris grinned and sat up straight, feeling his ego

inflating a little. Borell gave Benjamin a sly wink when Andris couldn't see and Benjamin realised that he was just building Andris' confidence. It was well justified, as they had no idea what they were walking into.

The wind had picked up a little in the last hour or so, and the ship wasn't as steady as it was when they had left port. The autopilot was doing a fine job of keeping them pointing in the right direction, but Benjamin was making more corrections as the weather deteriorated and their speed had slowed, making the engines work harder. Benjamin was having to ease back on the throttles so the engines didn't burn up. The starboard side engine was running very hot already.

A light on the coded transceiver started to blink and a message printed out onto a paper tape as it was decoded. Benjamin waited for the message to be printed out and tore it from the machine. Still unsure of his associates, he read the message to himself.

> *Benjamin, Pegasus Project is Society.*
> *Classified.*
> *Borell is an active agent, knows details of Toren threat.*
> *SP Hoyt read me into project.*
> *Work with him if you can, trust at your discretion.*
> *No details about Andris Tar available.*
> *Will update when further checks are complete.*
> *Likely heading for S.E. Nartill mountain range.*
> *Authorised to take any action to neutralise Toren threats.*
> *Kodey.*
> *WFR.*

'Well it looks like we're officially working together on this now, old friend,' Benjamin said. 'Hoyt sends his regards.'

'So that's who's running the show?'

'Looks like it,' Benjamin said.

'If he really is who he says he is then, what do you need me for?' Andris asked, looking a little worried.

'You might make all the difference, Andris; three men are better than two,' Benjamin said reassuringly.

'You should probably stay behind us though, just to be sure you don't get killed before we get you home,' offered Borell.

'Touching,' Benjamin said.

Borell chuckled. 'Hey, I'm all heart.'

This made Andris relax again; he was still unsure what he was getting into, but had decided that worrying wasn't going to get Lilly and her grandfather home. Right now, that was all he was concerned with — that and not being killed. Besides, he was with two experienced Society agents who would look after him.

'What else did your man say?' Borell asked.

'He said that the Toren are behind all this, but you already knew that, didn't you. We have authority to do whatever is necessary to stop the threat — whatever the threat is. I am assuming that the device being in their hands is just the tip of the iceberg?'

'Yeah, about that. I should probably tell you what I know about the Toren.'

With that, Borell started to explain the threat as he knew it; mechanised warriors, land ships, the behemoth airships and the requirement for masses of power.

'We have nothing that could repel an invasion of that magnitude,' Benjamin said. 'How credible is the threat of an invasion?'

'At the moment, we don't really know. We do know that the Toren have been amassing an army of men and machinery, but we have little intelligence as to what they plan to do with it all. There have been some rumours of a full-scale invasion of the mainland, but nothing substantial. We don't even know what their target would be,' Borell explained.

'You don't know an awful lot about this then, do you?' Benjamin chuckled.

'That's not the worst of it. The intelligence we do have about the Toren suggests that they have many loyal followers deep inside our borders. Our allies' borders too. Even if we prevent them from making use of this device, I doubt very much if the threat from the Toren will be over.'

'Another problem for another day,' Benjamin conceded. 'Right now, our main objective has to be getting Jackson's device back — destroying it, if need be.'

'Putting the mission before your friends — *now* you're sounding like me.' Borell smirked.

'Don't mistake my intentions, *Borell*. We will get Jackson and Lilly back or die trying.'

'Wherever the device is, you can be sure they won't be far away. The only reason I can see they have Lilly is for leverage. She will be close by; Burns will need to be able to hear her scream.'

'Stop it!' Andris shouted, suddenly feeling both Benjamin's and Borell's eyes turning to him. 'They won't really torture her, will they?' he heard himself plead.

'What did you think they were going to do to her, kid?' Borell said. 'Buy her a pretty dress and put her up in a fancy lodge?'

Andris looked horrified at the new thoughts running through his head. He realised that he may have more feelings for Lilly than he had first thought.

'Look, they won't kill her until they have what they want from Burns. But she may be a little bruised — maybe missing a limb or two —'

Andris lunged at Borell, catching him off guard with a blow to the side of his face. Benjamin grabbed hold of Andris and pushed him back onto his seat, hard.

'That was stupid, Andris. Borell wouldn't think twice about killing you, you do know that, don't you?'

Borell started laughing loudly, holding his stinging jaw, moving it from side to side.

'You've got some fight in you, kid. Remember that feeling. When you need to make a hard choice, that anger will give you the strength you need to follow through with your actions.'

Andris looked at him with a rage inside him that even he didn't know he possessed. Benjamin let go of him and stepped aside.

'But,' Borell said, the laughter gone now, 'strike me again, and you better make sure you finish the job. That one was for free. You won't get a second.'

Bemused, Andris looked at Benjamin, who knew exactly what Borell was trying to do. He realised his old friend was indeed clever and manipulative — something that clearly made him a good recruit for Pegasus.

'Listen to him, Andris. You'll need to use those feelings when we get to Nartill. They won't give you the benefit of a second chance; make them count.'

'But I'm not an agent like you. I don't have any training — I've never killed anyone!'

'Kid, if you *need* to kill someone you *will* kill them. When it comes down to it, if you think someone is going to kill you, you get in there first. Better to be alive and wrong than dead,' Borell said. 'Besides, where we're going everyone will be trying to kill us. You can worry about the moral dilemma later.'

'I thought you were trying to give him confidence,' Benjamin whispered to Borell.

'Confidence, yes. Disillusion him, no.'

'I get what you are saying, I really do,' Andris said, calming down again, 'I just don't know if I can kill someone.'

'You will know if you can do it when the time comes. If you don't, then it was nice knowing you.'

'Okay, enough talk about getting killed,' Benjamin interjected. 'As we're officially working together now, you can go back to the hold and get an idea of what provisions we have.'

'Fine, but only because I don't know how to fly this thing,' Borell said. 'Andris, how about you and I go back and see what we can find?'

'Promise you won't kill me?' Andris said, half joking.

'Sure, why not,' Borell said, returning the sentiment.

'Oh — one more thing,' Borell said to Benjamin. 'We won't be heading for Nartill. Our intelligence tells us that their base is in the impenetrable mountain range, South East of the island.'

'So I've been told,' Benjamin replied, waving the communique. 'We'll need to come up with a plan to get inside their compound.'

'I have some thoughts on that, but we are going to need *a lot* of supplies.'

Chapter Twenty-Five

Durrant was sitting in a large leather wingback chair drinking a fine Nartillian brandy when Loren brought Jackson Burns into the portside lounge. 'Thank you, Loren, you may leave us,' he said.

'As you wish.'

'Please, sit down, Mr Burns,' Durrant said, pointing to an equally comfortable looking chair opposite him. Jackson sat gingerly, his bones aching from the manhandling he'd received earlier in the evening.

'Can I pour you a glass?' Durrant said, holding up his own glass to Jackson. 'A very fine vintage; I'm sure you will find it pleasurable.'

Jackson could think of many reasons why he should not, but shrugged and accepted anyway.

'Why am I here?' he asked.

Durrant finished pouring Jackson a drink and handed it to him. 'Your work more than interests us, Mr Burns. May I call you Jackson?'

'It is my name,' he said matter-of-factly.

'Thank you, Jackson. My name is Durrant. As I said, your work is of interest to us. We have followed your progress in various fields for many years now. But there is one that interests us more than the others.'

'My energy research,' Jackson said.

'Indeed. Our scientists have been building similar devices using your technology, but they have been unable to complete their work for various reasons.'

'How have you had access to my work?'

'Money makes a friend of many people. We have people within your own organisation working for us, feeding us details of your inventions and discoveries. Your energy storage technology has given us a great leap forward in our plans. We now need to perfect your energy source to attain our goals.'

'Goals? What goals?'

'You will see soon enough. But first I must express to you the urgency with which we need your assistance.'

'You expect me to help you build a working device?'

'No, Jackson, I expect you to help us build *many* such devices.'

'There's a simple answer to that.' He paused for effect. 'No.'

'I don't think I am making myself clear. If you help us, you will be richly rewarded, a hero to our people in the coming revolution.'

'And if I don't?' Jackson interrupted.

'If you choose to resist our efforts then certain pressures will be applied to persuade you otherwise.'

'What pressures?' Jackson asked, looking confused.

'Your granddaughter, for one. She is a beautiful young lady. I would hate to ruin what remains of her young life.'

'You're lying,' Jackson said, not convinced that he was.

'Come now, Mr Burns. If you need convincing — Loren,' Durrant called.

A moment later Loren appeared through the door to the lounge, 'Yes, sir?'

'Would you be so kind as to bring Ms Jansen in, please?'

'Yes, sir.' Loren disappeared through the door again.

'Please enjoy your brandy whilst we wait — it is most exquisite.' Durrant gestured his own glass as he took a sip himself.

Jackson looked nervously around the room, seeing that Durrant was watching him confidently.

'Grandfather!' Lilly shouted as Loren pushed her into the room. She ran across the lounge and hugged Jackson tightly.

'You monster,' Jackson spat at Durrant.

'That as may be, but you can now see that we are serious about needing your assistance. Help us willingly and Ms Jansen will be spared any pain or suffering. Cross us or refuse to help and you will see first-hand how well-trained and passionate our best surgeons are in inflicting pain.' Durrant took another sip of his brandy and smiled at them both. 'Loren, would you please remove Ms Jansen, they have seen quite enough of each other for now.'

Loren took hold of Lilly by her arm and dragged her to her feet.

'No, he's not well, can't you see?' Lilly lied, trying to stay with him.

'Come now, Ms Jansen. Your grandfather is in fine health.' Durrant nodded at Loren, who began dragging Lilly away shouting. Lilly felt a tiny lapse in Loren's grip and swung her arm around, intending it to connect with Loren's head. Unfortunately, Loren was also well trained and Lilly found herself staring at the floor with her arm bent awkwardly behind her.

'Please, I'll help you, just don't hurt her,' Jackson pleaded.

'No, Grandfather. Think of all the people who will die.'

Durrant held his hand up to Loren who waited for a moment.

'Your granddaughter is correct. Many people will die, but she doesn't have to be one of them. It is your choice, Mr Burns. You have several hours to make up your mind before we reach our destination. *He* wants to speak to you personally before you start work on the device.'

'*He?*' Lilly asked, slightly out of breath from struggling with Loren.

'Yes. *He*, our saviour, our noble leader — Shranlon.'

'Never heard of him,' Lilly said.

'But your grandfather has. Haven't you, Jackson?'

Jackson looked at Durrant, shocked at hearing a name he thought lost to history. 'He is alive?'

'Very much so. The news of his demise was greatly exaggerated I'm afraid. Many of your Society friends will be turning in their graves at this revelation, I'm sure.'

'Who is Shranlon, Grandfather?'

'He was a nightmare I once believed destroyed. How did he survive? He was killed —' Jackson searched his memory for the year '— thirty years ago.'

'All in good time, all in good time,' Durrant said, nodding to Loren once more, who obliged by removing Lilly from the room this time with some help from a guard.

'Think your options over, Mr Burns,' Durrant said, rising from his chair and walking to the portside windows. 'Help us, or your granddaughter suffers a pain you can only imagine. Help us and we spare you both. Although you will never set foot in your homeland again.'

'I... I...' Jackson fumbled for words. He never once thought that the dark soul that was Shranlon would be alive. His thoughts ran to Lilly and his promise to keep her safe, feeling the failure deep in his heart.

Durrant raised a hand. Two large men entered the lounge and lifted Jackson bodily from his chair, removing the brandy as they did.

'Why would you serve that monster?' Jackson asked as he was escorted from the lounge.

'Wait,' Durrant ordered his men. 'You call him a monster, yet everything depends on your point of view. Would your Society not be a collection of monsters from our perspective? They impose their interpretation of your kingdom's laws on others, and claim it for the security of your people. We have suffered at their hands for many decades, destroying any advances we make as a civilised people, because they believe we are a threat, forcing us into hiding. They have turned us into what we are today and the consequences of their interference will be felt across the entirety of your kingdom.'

Jackson couldn't hide his fear and this made Durrant smile as the two men took Jackson back to his room and stood guard outside.

Sitting on his bed, Jackson searched his mind for the events surrounding the demise of Shranlon. He was positive that he had been killed. There was an investigation, an autopsy. The corpse's identity had been confirmed by several senior agents and doctors. How could he have fooled so many people? They had lost many agents and good men during the Siege of Sorent — now, thirty years on, would they have to suffer greater losses, not just of men but civilisation and freedom?

Jackson held his head in his hands and wept. He was truly terrified for the first time in many years, both for Lilly's fate and what was to come.

Chapter Twenty-Six

Lilly balanced on the dressing table along one wall of her room. She had discovered that although the walls were solid, if not very thick, the ceiling was made of a stretched canvas over a steel framework. She supposed it was to save weight in the construction of the airship. She needed something sharp, something she could cut the canvas with; since the knife she had hidden back at Benjamin's house had been confiscated, the mirror was the obvious choice.

She climbed down from the dresser and started banging on the door. 'Hey, let me out, you bastards! You're gonna be sorry when my rescue gets here.' She wasn't sure what she should be shouting, but she only needed to get their attention.

She banged on the door some more and shouted more obscenities at the guard outside. Royston finally gave in and opened the door. 'What do you want?' he said in a cool, calm voice.

'To get out of here, for a start!' she shouted back.

'Well that ain't going to happen, is it.'

Lilly screamed and shouted in a rage that wasn't entirely fabricated, picked up the chair and threw it at the dresser, smashing the mirror in to a dozen or so pieces.

'Feel better?' said Royston with little care that the mirror was smashed.

Lilly panted for a moment. 'Actually yes, I do.'

Royston huffed at the mess and closed the door. Lilly wasted no time and found a piece of broken mirror that she could hold easily and wrapped it in a bit of sheet torn from her bedding. She climbed back onto the dresser, quietly moving bits of broken mirror as she did. The corner of the ceiling tore easily with the sharp edge of the mirror and she made a hole big enough, first to see beyond, then to fit through.

Climbing through the hole in the canvas and into the void above, Lilly took a moment for her eyes to adjust to the dark. She was now inside what looked like the envelope of the balloon. She could see lots of steel framework with large bladders of gas secured inside. There was a gantry to her right, which was easy to clamber onto, although she wasn't sure what she was going to do now she was free of her room. She hoped no one would check on her for a while. It was a big ship; there would be many places to hide in any case.

Slowly, she made her way along the gantry and could see the ceilings of all the other rooms below her. She wondered if she would even be able to find her grandfather and free him.

Lilly walked along the gantry until it joined another, heading lengthwise along the ship. It made sense that this ran above the corridor below her. She was near the rear of the accommodation block from what she could work out, based on the layout of the gantry and the spaces below, so she headed forward. Making sure she was making as little noise as possible and keeping her eyes open for any crew, she listened at the ceilings of each room by hanging over the side of the railings.

Twenty minutes passed as Lilly listened for her grandfather, slowly advancing along the rooms and back in the opposite direction when she realised there were two corridors and gantries to follow. Most of the rooms appeared to be unoccupied; some had voices that she didn't recognise. She continued along the gantry until a faint voice made her stop and listen again. Lilly recognised the mumblings of her grandfather in an instant.

She climbed over the railings and carefully balanced on the steel structure above the ceiling to Jackson's room — not an easy feat when aboard an airship in flight. Lilly made her way to a corner that would be furthest away from the door, then crouched and used the broken mirror to make a small slit in the canvas. She peered inside.

'Grandfather,' she whispered.

'Lilly?' Jackson replied in a loud whisper. 'Is that you, dear?' Jackson looked around but couldn't work out where the voice was coming from. 'Where are you?'

'Up here, in the ceiling.'

Jackson looked up and his eyes wandered across the canvas until he saw the tear. 'Lilly? How did you get up there?'

'I'll explain later. I'm going to get you out of there,' she said with confidence.

Lilly used the mirror to cut a larger section of the canvas and let the flap hang against the wall. Jackson saw her and his face brightened.

'Oh, my dear, I feared the worst.'

'I'm fine for now, but *we* won't be if we don't get out of here,' she said, offering Jackson her hand. 'Use the chair to climb up.'

Jackson sprang off the bed, the sight of Lilly giving him renewed energy. He quietly moved the chair to the corner of the room and carefully climbed up, his numerous years and many aches making themselves felt again.

'Take my hand.'

Jackson gave a quiet chuckle. 'I've not climbed anything in years — this will be interesting.' He took hold of her hand and reached up to grab the edge of the exposed ceiling, putting his foot on the back of the chair and pulling himself up. Despite his advanced years, he felt like a child again and actually enjoyed the climb, if not the subsequent pain in his joints.

Once into the ceiling void and on the gantry above, Lilly hugged her grandfather tightly.

'What do we do now?' she asked him.

'I thought you had the plan?' Jackson laughed.

'Well, my plan extended as far as finding you. After that — well I'd not thought that far ahead. How do we get off this ship?'

'Big airships like this are all equipped with one or more aeroplanes for emergencies or —' He stopped and looked over Lilly's shoulder. 'Oh dear,' he said, deflated.

'Oh dear indeed,' Loren said, standing behind Lilly, backed up by several guards. 'I see we will have to find you alternative accommodation.'

The guards moved to surround Lilly and Jackson.

'A very valiant attempt at a rescue, Ms Jansen. Please take that as a compliment — I don't make them often,' Loren said as she escorted Lilly and Jackson to the ladder at the end of the gantry that took them back into the upper deck.

'How did you know where we were?' Jackson asked.

'We found the hole in Ms Jansen's accommodation and it wasn't a great leap to work out where she would be going. A very clever diversion, I have to say. Royston was most annoyed.'

They climbed down the ladder and into a corridor of the upper deck, where Royston and several more guards were waiting to take them to the starboard lounge. Once Lilly and Jackson were inside, the doors were left open and manned by Royston and another guard.

'Make yourselves comfortable,' Loren told them. 'Despite being an inconvenience, He still wants you to be looked after.'

'Why don't you just use his name? Shranlon. His name is Shranlon,' Jackson said.

Loren smiled and left, her guards standing firm at the door watching them with eagle eyes.

'I'm sorry, grandfather.'

'Don't be silly, dear. We are together for now, that is all that matters to me at the moment.'

Lilly smiled and hugged her grandfather again.

Chapter Twenty-Seven

Benjamin looked at the *Nightstar* several hundred feet in front of them through the binoculars. They had not changed their course or speed and despite the changing weather conditions giving their smaller ship a bit of buffeting, the *Nightstar* seemed markedly stable.

He adjusted the ship's speed to keep their distance and as yet, it appeared that they had not been spotted. The night sky was clear for the most part, but dark clouds loomed ahead of them in an eerie patchwork that was contributing to the changing conditions.

The trapdoor in the rear of the cabin dropped open and Andris climbed down the ladder.

'Where's Borell?' Benjamin asked.

'He's coming,' Andris said as he dusted himself off.

'Nice clothes.'

'My shirt was a bit singed, so I took advantage of the mining supplies,' he said, holding the lapels of his new jacket and showing it off proudly.

'Only two days away from home and already thieving,' Benjamin joked.

Andris smiled. 'You should see what Borell has found.'

Moments later a large canvas sack dropped through the hatch and landed with a loud thud, closely followed by Borell.

'Well,' he said as he closed the hatch above him. 'We will be good for a while. Lots of explosives, tools and clothing. I've packed us enough to use and to trade.'

'Good,' said Benjamin. 'I've been looking at the charts.

We have about seven hours before we get to Nartill. Andris, you may as well get some sleep in the main cabin if you can. Borell, you have just been promoted to co-pilot.'

'Aye, captain,' Borell said, sitting down in the chair next to Benjamin and putting his hands behind his head. 'Just don't ask me to fly her.'

Andris climbed the ladder and opened the hatch, not entirely confident that he wanted or needed sleep, but as he didn't know when he might next have the chance, he thought it foolish to pass up the opportunity.

'So what do you think our chances are?' Benjamin said as soon as the hatch closed.

'Oh, we'll probably be killed before we get anywhere near their base to do anything.'

'So pretty confident then.'

'Well, it's the two of us against an army, not counting pretty boy. If we're smart, we'll turn this thing around now and find a nice place to retire with lots of sun and plenty of women.'

'Same old sarcasm, I see.'

Borell grinned. 'I still don't rate our chances though.'

Benjamin stared out of the cockpit window at the night sky. 'We should be alright on this heading for a while. Keep an eye on the *Nightstar*; when they change course, wake me up,' he instructed.

'I'll give you two hours. Then we swap.'

'Fine.'

Benjamin headed for the benches that doubled as bunks behind them. He put his gun under the cushion, stretched out and promptly fell asleep. That was something he was always able to do — catch sleep whenever he needed it.

Andris finally realised what his body already knew, that he was in fact exhausted, physically and emotionally, and he passed out the moment his head hit the pillow on his bunk.

Borell put his feet up on the main console and stared off into the night.

***

The sky had cleared again as the sun started to peak its head over the horizon to their port side. The morning light was a welcome sight, but meant that it would be far easier for the *Nightstar* to see them now. It also meant that Benjamin could drop the ship further back. He reduced their forward speed to put more distance between them and adjusted the autopilot to lower their altitude a little.

'Wake up,' Benjamin said as he took a small binder from the console next to him, threw it over his shoulder and landed it expertly on Borell's stomach as he slept.

'You bastard, I was enjoying that dream,' Borell groaned as he rubbed at his stomach and sat up.

'Back to reality — I can see Nartill in the distance.'

Benjamin turned on their running lights, so they looked less like a ghost ship and more like they were heading to Nartill.

'They still haven't seen us yet?' Borell said, dropping the binder on Benjamin's lap as he sat in the co-pilot's chair.

'Not yet, but it won't be long. They've changed course, heading away from the capital towards the South East.'

'The kid still asleep?' Borell said, rubbing his face with his hands.

'Didn't see any point in waking him yet. He may as well rest.'

'She is a beauty, isn't she?' Borell said as he looked through the binoculars at the *Nightstar*.

'And deadly. She's one of the new class of airship, equipped with anti-piracy armaments. Their canons and repeating guns could knock us out of the sky in an instant.'

'So what's your plan then?' Borell asked.

'We keep our distance for now. They'll know we're following them as soon as I match their heading. I'm going to keep us as far away from them as I can; it will at least reduce their accuracy if they start shooting.'

'What about their aeroplanes?' Borell asked.

'That *will* be a problem.'

'Okay, I'm glad we agree on that.'

'We know roughly where they are heading, so if we keep low and distant, their watch crew may not notice us. It's a big ask,' Benjamin said.

'We'll have to put down outside the mountain range, somewhere that we can acquire some horses. Maybe a local guide.'

'You think anyone will be willing to take us into the mountains? If it's as well protected as you say, there can't be many that would risk it.'

'Depends if they are properly motivated.' Borell smiled. 'Besides, I have the intel from one of our agents who made it out alive,' he said, tapping his temple. 'I can follow his route back inside.'

'It's likely they'll have that covered now. Remove any vulnerabilities.'

'What choice do we have?' Borell said.

'True. Better wake Andris, we should brief him on our "plan".'

Borell shouted into the voice pipe connected to the main passenger cabin. 'WAKE UP, KID!' He only heard moans in the distance.

'You'd better get back there and wake him up. Get the rest of the supplies together whilst you're there.'

Chapter Twenty-Eight

'They have moved out of weapons range, sir, and have adjusted their course to match ours,' said gunner First Class Warren.

'Inform me if there is any change in their heading,' said his gunnery officer, who picked up an intercom handset and made a call to the port side lounge. 'Sir, the ship you requested us to observe has altered her course and is now line astern again. What are your orders?'

'Maintain observations for now. Inform me the moment their course changes, or they break off their pursuit,' Durrant replied down the intercom.

'Aye, sir,' said the gunnery officer, and replaced the handset on the intercom. 'Maintain observations and report any changes directly to me,' he said to gunner Warren.

'Aye aye, sir.'

***

'They are following us as He said they would,' Durrant said.

'I know he has always had a plan, but isn't this just madness?' Loren asked.

'Be careful, Loren,' Durrant warned her.

'I am sorry, Durrant,' she said. 'I know Shranlon has orchestrated everything according to his master plan, but sometimes you must think that his methods are abstract to say the least.'

'I will admit they are not always clear, but he has

never failed us,' Durrant said, starting to become annoyed by Loren's questions.

'No. You are right. Forgive me,' she said, not wanting to push him.

'Please inform our guests that we will be arriving in two hours.'

'Yes, sir,' Loren said, and walked across the lounge to the door. She followed the corridor of the upper deck forward, and then across to the starboard lounge. The guards had changed since Lilly and Jackson were originally incarcerated here several hours ago, but they stood to attention and moved aside when she approached.

'Two hours, gentlemen,' she said to them.

The guards nodded in response.

'Ms Jansen, Mr Burns,' she said as she walked into the lounge. 'I have been asked to inform you that we are about two hours away from our destination.'

'Is that supposed to make us feel better?' Lilly asked.

'Does it make you feel better?'

'No.'

'Then the answer to your question is no, it wasn't meant to make you feel better.' Loren smiled.

'Why do you follow Shranlon?' Jackson asked.

'He is a true visionary. He sees a better future for everyone. A future that we can all share if you are willing to help us.'

'I'll never help you,' Jackson said, standing to face Loren. 'He is the embodiment of evil and I will do everything I can to see that this madness is stopped.'

Loren laughed. 'You believed for thirty years that you had put an end to His grand plan. All you achieved was a brief stay of execution. His vision will endure, with or without your help.'

'Certain of this, are you?' Jackson asked.

'It is an absolute,' Loren replied directly.

'Then he *has* grown stronger over the years.' Jackson sighed.

'What do you mean, Grandfather?'

'Shranlon was the leader of a cult that professed to have abilities beyond that of normal men. He claimed to see the future — "precognition", he called it. There was no evidence to support his claims in the beginning, but after the Society became aware of him, we performed our own tests in a controlled environment with one of his followers.'

Loren huffed audibly but let Jackson continue his recount of events.

'One man, Henry, had decided that his ability wasn't something he wanted Shranlon controlling and came to us for help. The Society agreed to help him if he helped us understand his — ability. About two days after Henry had come to us, he died. A post-mortem indicated a massive rupture of blood vessels in his brain. We couldn't prove otherwise, but Shranlon claimed to have killed him to protect his cause.'

'He was a traitor to his calling,' Loren said.

'Maybe he was just misguided and realised too late that Shranlon was taking him somewhere he didn't want to go. When Shranlon was finally apprehended and killed, or at least we were led to believe, he used his precognition ability to kill all of his followers, in the same way as he killed Henry. The ones without this ability disappeared, or were incarcerated later.'

'Some idol to worship,' Lilly said to Loren with disdain. Loren didn't rise to this.

'We concluded after Shranlon's death that his ability was flawed. He couldn't see the future for what it really was, otherwise we wouldn't have been able to kill him.'

'But you didn't kill him. He saw what you were planning, so orchestrated his death and the death of some of his peers. You only played your part in his grand design.'

'If he is really alive, I fear she is right,' Jackson said to Lilly as he sat down again. 'If he truly is gifted with the ability to see the future, how can we possibly win? He will be a step ahead the whole time.'

'And there is your answer. I *follow* him because it is my destiny to.'

'In his *new* gullible brainwashed cult!' Lilly said.

'Call us what you will. When all is said and done, the new world that will arise from the ashes of old will be a much better place for all. Now, if you will excuse me, I have neglected my duties for long enough.'

Lilly folded her arms in disgust and looked out of the window as Loren left. 'You don't really believe that this Shranlon has the power to see the future do you, Grandfather? It's absurd to even think that a person could do such a thing.'

'I honestly don't know, my dear. A man I believed to be dead is suddenly back amongst the living. I'm struggling to comprehend the enormity of that alone.'

'Well I don't believe it. Knowing the future is a fantasy, pure and simple.'

'I hope you are right, my dear, I hope you are right.'

Chapter Twenty-Nine

Two more canvas sacks were lowered through the hatch in the cockpit, this time placed with a little more care.

'That one goes boom,' Borell said as he followed Andris down the ladder.

'Why does Andris have a cut on his forehead?' Benjamin said, directing the question to Borell.

'Why do you think it's anything to do with me?' he protested.

'Was it?'

'Maybe. Okay, but it *was* funny,' Borell insisted.

'What did he do, Andris?'

Andris had been quietly dabbing a piece of cloth to his cut and stabbed a look at Borell.

'I *may* have said that we were crashing and that we were all going to die,' Borell said jovially.

'Said? Said?! You shouted it in my ear whilst I was asleep!' Andris shouted, clearly in pain and not impressed.

'You really haven't changed, have you? Couldn't wake him up nicely, you had to scare the shit out of him,' Benjamin said, looking closer at the wound on Andris' forehead. 'You'll be fine, just a scratch.'

'Feels like a crevasse,' Andris said through gritted teeth as he dabbed at the wound again. 'Why are we flying so low?'

'It's just a precaution,' Benjamin reassured him.

'Against being shot at, right?'

'We should be too far away for them to hit us with any accuracy, but it's better to be closer to the ground — just in case.'

'Have they seen us then?'

'I don't know. I would have expected them to have noticed us by now. But I'm not sure why they haven't launched their planes to intercept us,' Benjamin said, helping Borell to pile the bags by the door.

'So, what? They know we're here, but are letting us follow them?'

'Could be,' said Borell.

'But why wouldn't they shoot us down as soon as they saw us?' Andris pressed.

'Look, kid. You're asking the right questions, but you're asking the wrong people,' Borell said.

'Something isn't right,' Benjamin admitted. 'We've been long out of the regular flight paths to Nartill; unless they're all asleep, they know we're here.'

Beneath them the countryside of Nartill whipped by, the keel of the airship occasionally brushing the tops of the tallest trees. Fortunately, the landscape on this side of Nartill was generally flat and level, arable and farmed for the most part. They were low enough to be able to see farmers tending their cattle, a look of confusion in their eyes at the sight of them floating by overhead, scaring herds of sheep and cows as they went.

'I've never been this far into Nartill before,' Benjamin said as he looked at the maps again. He pointed out the front windows at the mountain range that was starting to appear in the distance through the early morning mist. The map showed nothing beyond the mountains; it wasn't somewhere that had been charted for airships and the accepted route was around the coastline. The *Nightstar* had slowly begun to increase their altitude to clear a pass through the mountain range that was just becoming visible ahead.

Borell and Benjamin were looking around for somewhere suitable to put down. A cattle farm to their port side looked ideal.

'Erm, Benjamin...' said Andris from the rear of the cockpit. 'I would say it's a certainty that they know we're here.'

From where Andris was standing, looking out of the port side of the rear windows, he could see a smaller airship a few hundred feet behind them to their port stern.

Borell looked out of the starboard side. 'Got one over here too. They must have been following us since passing the aerodromes at Nartill.'

Benjamin hurried over to Borell and looked out to see for himself. 'They're fully armed. If they had wanted us shot down, we would be a fireball before we even knew it,' he said. 'It looks like we are now guests of the Toren.'

'You mean prisoners,' Andris said, sounding panicked.

'Pretty much, kid,' Borell said, slapping him on the back.

'How can you still be smiling?'

'This just means we get to have a clean fight, kid. They obviously want us alive for some reason, which just means there are opportunities for escape later. Right now, in this floating gas bag, we are sitting ducks.'

'Borell is right,' Benjamin said. 'We don't know why they want us or for what purpose, but there is always a way out.'

Andris didn't look reassured.

'We're not much of a threat at the moment,' Benjamin said.

'Time to ruin their day then. What do you say, old friend?' Borell said with a devious smile on his face.

Benjamin continued to watch their escort out of the rear windows.

Chapter Thirty

The intercom buzzed lazily and Durrant picked up the handset.

'Sir, they have adjusted their altitude and are maintaining a line astern course. Our escort is flanking them to their stern as requested.'

'Excellent. Instruct the escort to maintain their position until they have docked in the west bay.'

'Aye aye, sir,' said the gunnery officer, and rang off.

The *Nightstar* had climbed another one hundred and fifty feet to clear the mountains surrounding the Toren stronghold and was now entering a long passage through the mountain range. The natural passage had made it easy for the Toren to fortify their position and the mountain range surrounding them made uninvited visitors rare.

The sound of the engines echoed from the walls of the passage as they reduced their speed; snow was whipped up and blown around them with the change in air currents.

Permanent encampments, like tiny villages in the mountain pass, provided watchtowers and gun emplacements. The men living at these posts for months at a time were responsible for maintaining the security of the pass and deterring any visitors.

Occasionally, climbers would try to explore the mountains and mysteriously disappear, assumed to have been lost to the elements. The dormant volcano on the northern side of their corner of Nartill was the source of the Toren energy. Over the decades, steam turbine generators had been built to support the ever growing city, all drawing their power from the constant heat of the subterranean lava flows.

Durrant watched the mountains drift by as they slowly made their way through the pass.

'Nearly home, sir,' said Loren, walking into the lounge.

'Indeed. Are our guests ready to disembark?'

'Yes, sir. I have had them moved to the departure lounge.'

'Thank you, Loren. Have them escorted to the detention block when we arrive. Shranlon will call for them when he is ready. You will be personally overseeing their stay. I have been ordered to go directly to the *Ascension* upon our arrival.'

'Yes, sir, as you wish.'

The *Ascension*, one of the large behemoth floating platforms that had been secretly photographed by the Society agents, was recently completed and Durrant had been tasked with overseeing its final outfitting. This ship was something of a personal obsession of Durrant's over the many years of its construction. Its sister ship, the *Phoenix*, was missing from the bay next to the *Ascension*, as was shown in the agents' photographs.

Through the windows, Durrant saw the mountains give way to open space. The echo of the engines ceased and the low drone returned. The expanse of the Toren cityscape spread out below them.

They were home.

Chapter Thirty-One

Benjamin had taken over manual control of the airship whilst they followed the *Nightstar* into the passage through the mountains.

'This isn't the sort of place you would want to wander into,' Borell observed, using the binoculars to check out the artillery lining their way. 'They are massively armed. It's just as well we have an invitation.'

'The two ships following us are still there,' Andris said unhelpfully.

'They won't let us out of their sights until we have docked. Expect a welcoming party.'

'I guess we won't be needing our supplies then,' Borell said, playing with the strap of the binoculars.

'Check this out,' Benjamin said, throttling back on the engines as they cleared the pass and came out into the open air. Andris stood between Benjamin and Borell as they looked through the front window at the expansive hidden city below them.

'My god,' said Andris. 'This place is huge.'

Below them, they could see the city coming into full view. To their right they saw docking towers, with two airships already moored of a similar size to their own. Beyond this, an entire city with roads laid out like spokes on a wheel around a central domed building. To their left they could see an amassed army undertaking drills and training on various parade grounds and what looked like combat arenas. Some of the arenas were set out like little towns or villages.

'How the hell did we not know this was here?' Benjamin said.

'Look at that,' Andris said, pointing to the hulking form of the *Ascension* looming in the distance.

'That thing really is huge. The pictures didn't do it justice,' Borell said.

A green light at the top of one of the docking towers became illuminated, indicating where they should moor. Benjamin turned the ship towards the tower, adjusting their speed and altitude.

Around the base of the tower, they could clearly see a group of armed men waiting for them.

'Borell, can you hide yourself in the envelope somewhere where you won't be found?' Benjamin said.

'Sure. What are you thinking?'

'If they have any information from the ground crew in Trellern, they only saw Andris and I come aboard. They don't know you are here.'

'I get'cha. Then I sneak out later and come and find you.'

'No. You need to find the device and destroy it. If you do that and are still alive, *then* come and find us. We'll just have to take our chances. Maybe we'll find out why they want us alive too.'

Borell knew there would be little time to argue if he was to hide himself somewhere in the ship so he wouldn't be found. So, he grabbed the bag of supplies containing the explosives and made double time up the ladder and through the hatch.

'He was never here,' Benjamin said to Andris as the ship slowed to a standstill above the docking tower.

'Who?' Andris replied, feigning confusion.

As the ship dropped closer to the ground, some of the unarmed ground crew began scrambling for the ropes that hung from the gondolas. They wrapped them around huge cleats on the ground, each the size of a park bench, and began taking up the strain. They fed the ropes into large mechanical winches and slowly the ship descended until the nose docking clamp was in position.

'Hang on to something,' said Benjamin; he saw the light on the main console illuminate as the capture was lined up and ready.

Andris was just grabbing hold of the console when the *thump* of the docking clamp gripped them, shook them and held them fast.

'Well, that's that then,' Benjamin said. 'Whatever you do, don't piss them off. They may want us alive, but they probably won't think twice about beating on you for a while.'

Andris began to look a little pale.

Benjamin switched off the engines.

***

'Open the hatch and come down — slowly,' came a loud amplified voice from outside.

Benjamin lowered the ladder and opened the cockpit door. He looked out to see about a dozen armed men waiting for them, weapons drawn and pointing up at them. He thought it unlikely they would fire, but they gave Benjamin little choice about where to go.

'Come on,' Benjamin said as he turned around and started down the steps. 'Stay close.'

Andris nodded and followed him slowly, backwards down the ladder.

When Benjamin stepped onto the ground, he raised his hands, looking up to Andris to make sure he knew to do the same.

'Weapons,' one of the guards said as Andris stepped from the ladder and stood next to Benjamin, hands in the air.

Benjamin slowly removed his gun from inside his jacket and handed it to the guard.

'And the rest,' ordered the guard, indicating to the

other gun Benjamin kept in his ankle-holster. He bent down and removed it, handing it to the guard as well.

'You too, boy,' he said.

'He doesn't have any weapons, he's just a tag along,' Benjamin said. Clearly, the guards didn't care for this statement and proceeded to search them both regardless. They found a knife, ammunition and a toolset on Benjamin, which they confiscated, but nothing on Andris.

'I'll be wanting those back,' Benjamin said to the guard, 'Sentimental reasons, you understand.'

'You'll not be needing them again...' The guard smirked and sucker punched Benjamin in the stomach with the butt of his rifle. Benjamin bent forwards and put his hands on his knees, taking a few deep breaths to counter the pain.

'What happened to not pissing them off?' Andris said through gritted teeth, as Benjamin stood upright again.

'Quiet!' shouted the guard, who was clearly not in the mood for talking. 'Check the ship for anyone else,' he shouted at two of his men.

'Yes, sir,' they responded in unison.

'You two follow me,' the guard ordered. Benjamin followed him, with Andris keeping close behind. They noticed how warm the air was, their coats proving unnecessary.

The path they followed took them underneath the rear of the other docked airships and towards a monorail running alongside the major roads. A driver was sat in the seat at the front of the train, waiting for his passengers. The guard ordered Benjamin and Andris aboard.

'A pretty impressive set —'

'Shut up!' shouted the guard before Andris could finish his sentence.

Benjamin climbed the three steps up to the rear carriage and sat down. Andris took a moment to admire the engineering in the monorail before falling forwards onto the steps from the force of the guard's boot in his back.

'No more delays!' he said in an increasingly frustrated voice as Andris picked himself up and climbed into the carriage next to Benjamin, rubbing the small of his back as he sat down.

Benjamin sneaked a smile at Andris for being stupid and pushing the guard. Kind of an 'I told you so' and 'well done' at the same time. Three of the armed men climbed aboard and sat opposite Benjamin and Andris, not taking their eyes off them. The carriage slowly began to pull away from the platform and picked up speed until they were heading along at a sprint. The regular repeating *tat-tat* sound of the wheels as they sped along the monorail was almost hypnotic.

On their left, they passed men training in various combat disciplines out in the open. On the right, construction was taking place of vehicles and aircraft; function-first buildings bustling with activity and marked with only numbers on their front. Benjamin and Andris sat quietly, watching their new surroundings fly past. Benjamin didn't fancy being thrown from a moving vehicle, not today, so just took in as much as he could; anything that may prove useful in planning their escape later.

In front of them, the large domed building grew ever closer. They could see now that it wasn't a complete dome as it appeared from above, but more like a large dome roof covering a smaller maze of buildings underneath. The sides were open to allow the roads and monorail's access and a large cylindrical building stood directly in the middle of it all. As they drew closer, the monorail began to climb gradually until they were about thirty feet from the ground and then levelled off again.

Benjamin now had a view of the fertile fields beyond the dome, neatly laid out and precisely maintained. He could see various types of crops, but couldn't make out what they were from this distance. He guessed that this isolated city was mostly self-sufficient and probably didn't require many supplies from outside.

Moments later, the view of the fields was blocked as the outer curved leg of the dome moved in between them. The sight under the dome was just as remarkable, hiding an array of buildings surrounding the central cylindrical building.

'Impressive,' Benjamin said. The guard let this compliment pass by.

Their monorail carriages pulled up to an elevated platform close by the central building.

'Out,' said one of the guards, indicating to the platform with his gun.

Benjamin and Andris stepped onto the platform, followed by the other guards.

'Follow me,' barked the guard.

They walked along the platform towards the central building and an oversized arched doorway. Walls with basic decoration lined the hallways, an off-white colour on the top half and a deep red on the bottom. The guard stopped outside a lift and pressed the call button. The lift arrived moments later and they were ushered inside, followed by the guards. One of the lower buttons was pressed, but Benjamin couldn't see which one as the lift was crammed with people; they started to descend.

A dial above the doors stopped moving and showed that they had stopped at the third subterranean level. The doors opened and two guards stepped out, standing either side of the door. The main guard who had been ordering Benjamin and Andris about stepped out and told them to follow him. The two other guards filed in behind as the line proceeded towards the cells.

'Holy crap!' exclaimed Andris as they stepped into the hot, dusty air. They had descended a few hundred feet below ground into a massive natural cave and he could see men working the face with mechanical tools, extracting minerals and ore.

The light in the cave was poor. It seemed to be a combination of light from the surface channelled through light tubes, electric lamps hanging from the walls and a warm orange glow coming from somewhere below that they couldn't see. The corridor they were walking along had a drop straight to the cave floor many hundreds of feet below them, just the other side of the railings. Andris gritted his teeth and moved closer to the wall when he saw this.

'Quite a set up you have here,' Benjamin chanced.

The guard stopped and put up his hand, indicating everyone else to do the same. Andris was so busy hugging the wall that he didn't see Benjamin stop in front of him and walked bodily into him.

'You should be impressed,' said the guard. 'This is the detention mine, your new home. You will work here for the remainder of your natural lives. Criminals, traitors and those who trespass on our lands find themselves here, paying their debt.'

'I can't imagine one's natural life being very long down here,' Andris said.

'That depends on your attitude. Work hard and cause us no trouble and you will be fed, watered and protected from unnecessary beatings.' The guard stepped close to Benjamin and looked him firmly in the eye, smiling just a little. 'I encourage you to slack off and cause trouble — at least to start with. It makes our days so much more interesting, teaching people like you how to behave.'

Benjamin smiled back, not breaking his stare.

'Move on!' shouted the guard, still staring Benjamin in the face before turning and continuing down the corridor. They passed cramped cells built into the cave face, with nothing more than a bench and bucket inside. Several cells had men huddled in corners or pleading with the guards to set them free through the bars as they walked by.

One of the guards behind Andris smashed his baton against the bars, catching one of the men on the fingers with an audible crunch followed by a scream. The guards clearly enjoyed their jobs.

'These will be your *rooms*,' said the lead guard, pointing to an adjacent pair of open cell doors. 'You will be processed in a day or two.' Benjamin and Andris were pushed into the cells by the two guards.

'If you need anything — newspapers, food, water — please just ring the bell and we'll send a maid along promptly,' the guard said, erupting into fits of laughter, making the other guards laugh too.

The cell doors were slammed shut and the guards headed off back towards the lift.

'We're dead,' said Andris as he looked around his cell cut from the rock face, trying out the bench for comfort; there was none.

'We're fine,' said Benjamin calmly, watching the activities of the mine outside.

Chapter Thirty-Two

Lilly sat in her solid stone cell, realising that she would need more than a broken mirror to escape this time. Loren had escorted both her and Jackson to their temporary accommodation. She sat on the bed and began to cry. She had held her composure for as long as she could, but being in a cell on her own again gave her mind time to process what was happening and it was just too much to hold back.

'Now, now,' said Loren, as she appeared at the bars of the cell door a few minutes later, smiling.

'What do you want now?' Lilly said.

'Shranlon wants to see you and your grandfather.'

'Good, let's get this over with,' Lilly said, standing up, straightening her clothes and wiping the tears from her eyes.

A guard opened the cell door with a large bunch of noisy keys. Lilly followed Loren down the hallway to where her grandfather was waiting with another guard, looking tired and pale; she held his hand tightly when they were close enough. Her grandfather smiled and patted her hand as best he could in a comforting sort of way.

They continued down the corridor, past other empty cells, and into a waiting lift. Loren pressed the topmost button; the doors closed and the carriage quickly ascended. After about thirty seconds, the lift slowed and came to a stop, the doors opening.

They all stepped out, Loren leading, and the two

guards bringing up the rear. Peering around at the size of the room they had arrived in, it seemed that Shranlon occupied the top level of the building at the centre of the dome structure. A large glass window covered the middle of the ceiling, affording a view of the mountains and sky outside in the early morning light.

Although the colours in the room were warm and red, the temperature in the air was noticeably cooler than the rest of the building. There was little to speak of in the room; the floor smooth and clear of clutter, the walls free of any adornments, the only thing they could see was a shadowy plinth under the skylight that was hard to make out in the dim lighting.

A low, aged, confident voice sounded from across the room. 'It is agreeable to see you again, Jackson Burns.'

Jackson had no doubts as to who was speaking, even if the voice was older. 'Shranlon, I had rather hoped you were dead.'

'You may leave us, Loren,' the voice continued from the shadows.

Loren turned on her heels and walked back to the lift. The two masked guards standing either side of the door remained as she disappeared behind the closing doors.

'Why am I sitting in the dark, my dear?' Shranlon said.

'What? I wasn't thinking that,' Lilly stammered.

'Of course you were, my dear. An obvious question, perhaps, but one that I knew you would ask. Just like I know your grandfather wants to ask me how I am still alive after all these years. Isn't that correct?'

Jackson didn't say anything but stared into the darkness ahead of them.

'The darkness serves many purposes, but not for this reunion.' As Shranlon said this, the lights around the room slowly grew brighter, illuminating the large chair upon which he sat. He wore red and black robes and a dark shroud that hid his face, even in the now enlightened room. Lilly noticed that Shranlon only had one hand on the arm of his chair; she quickly realised he was missing the arm entirely.

'A gift from your grandfather and — friends,' he said to her, making Lilly feel uncomfortable in her own mind. 'I may not have died that day, Jackson, but it wasn't without a great deal of pain and suffering that I survived.'

Jackson still said nothing. He was in shock as much as anything else, and suddenly looked frailer than ever.

'Come now. Do you have nothing to say to me after all this time?'

'Nothing that wasn't said a long time ago,' he said finally.

'Indeed.' Shranlon stood slowly, revealing his tall six-foot frame. 'Fortunately my allies were able to save the leg. Although it took me many months before I could walk properly again,' he said, rubbing his thigh with his remaining hand.

'How *did* you escape?' Jackson finally asked, curiosity getting the better of him.

'Ah, we get to the burning question at last.' Shranlon slowly stepped down from the plinth his chair perched upon, clearly still affected by his injuries. 'Through a combination of a perfectly planned diversion, some well-paid loyal followers, the Society's overconfidence in their abilities and my knowledge of events to come. Even the best laid plans encounter some — *difficulties*, but the end result was acceptable.'

'Clearly your knowledge of how events would turn out was as fraudulent as you were. Otherwise there would be more of you left than there is today,' Jackson said scathingly.

Shranlon chuckled under his shroud, slowly walking closer to Jackson. 'Limbs are merely a physical manifestation of the whole. My mind has grown even stronger than you could possibly imagine over the years, although you never believed in all of that "hocus pocus mind stuff", did you? I believe that's what you called it, wasn't it?'

Jackson ignored his comment and Shranlon continued. 'Of all the tests and experiments you ran, did you never believe in the abilities we demonstrated? Never for a moment think that this mere shell of a body was a poor container for the human soul?'

'What does it matter what I believe? You still wanted to subvert our way of life, killing all those people, your followers.'

'They were not true followers,' Shranlon said dismissively, 'merely a means to an end.' He sighed and walked away from Jackson. 'Those men believed that their gifts would bring *them* wealth and power, but they couldn't see the bigger picture.'

'So you killed them all? Eighty-four deluded men and women who you made believe they were gifted beyond this world?'

'*Made* believe? Each and every one of those men and women *wanted* to believe in their "powers", as they called them. Some genuinely had abilities, some which rivalled mine at the time. Others wanted so much to believe that they were gifted, they created a delusional state of mind that needed to be quashed. They served their purpose, and then they were eliminated.'

'So you just used those poor people? For what?' Lilly asked.

Shranlon walked behind Lilly and Jackson and completed a full circle, coming to a standstill in front of them both.

'To understand, my dear, to understand. Knowledge is power, in this land or any other. Power can change the world, remove corrupt governments, unseat royalty that does not deserve to rule... It can free the people from their enslaved lives.'

Lilly gripped her grandfather's hand tightly again. Shranlon was an imposing figure standing before them, his conviction in what he said sent chills down her spine.

'As with any change,' Shranlon continued, 'there were

those who feared it. Your grandfather here was part of the plan to capture me thirty years ago, after it was decided that I should not be allowed to exist freely or otherwise within the Eight Kingdoms. I believe I was the first person in history to have a signed royal, government *and* Society warrant issued for my incarceration.'

'An accolade to be proud of,' Jackson said sarcastically.

'Quite. Even now, my allies work within your kingdom and others, preparing for the day of the New Rule.'

'With you as what, their king, their god?' said Lilly. 'The people will fight back, they will —'

'Will what, my dear?' Shranlon turned to look at Lilly, making her freeze. 'People are like sheep. Feed them, keep them warm, provide for them and they will follow those comforts to their end.'

'And those that don't follow you?' said Jackson.

'Even those men, women and children have their purpose in the New Rule. This time I cannot be stopped. I have seen this outcome many times over the years. Each time the image becomes clearer and more defined.' Shranlon turned to Jackson and stepped closer. 'You, my old friend, have the one final piece of the plan that I need. You will complete your device for me and I will spare your lives.' The arrogance was clear in his voice.

'I'll do no such thing,' Jackson said defiantly.

Shranlon began chuckling under his shroud again. After a moment, he said, 'Of course you will, you already know you have to.'

Jackson looked at Lilly, knowing that she would be the leverage used. Tears began to well up in his eyes. 'You bastard. She's an innocent in all this.' Jackson hoped a sincere capitulation to Shranlon's request would buy them both time and spare Lilly any harm. He prayed some form of rescue was underway. 'I'll do what you want, but please, I beg of you, leave her be.'

'No, grandfather. I'd rather die!'

'Who said anything about *killing* you, my dear? A body

can live for a long time if properly...maintained. Wounds can be inflicted time and time again with proper care. We don't *need* to kill you.'

Although they couldn't see his face, they could hear him smiling as he said this.

'Then I have your agreement, Jackson: your work for her life?'

Jackson looked away from Lilly, feeling her holding his hand tight. 'Yes,' he said in a whisper.

'I'm sorry?'

'Yes, damn it, I'll help you!' he shouted. Lilly threw her arms around him and began to cry.

'Good. And speaking of family...' Shranlon said as he turned back towards his chair. 'You never did tell him, did you?'

Jackson was sobbing, tears running down his face and onto Lilly's shoulder as he hugged her. He managed to lift his head and look towards Shranlon, who still had his back to them.

'As I thought,' Shranlon said without looking back. 'A promise to keep until your deathbed.'

'No words on the matter will come from me, that I assure you,' Jackson said with a sniff here and there.

'Be that as it may. He will know the truth soon enough.'

Jackson let go of Lilly and looked at Shranlon, who was now sitting down again. 'He will fight you, as did his father,' he said defiantly. 'He is a much stronger man than Drummond Sorrow and he alone will be your undoing.'

'Such confidence in him, but I think, on this occasion, I have the upper hand.'

'We will see.'

'Maybe sooner than you think, old friend,' Shranlon said. 'For now, you have work to do for me. My guards will escort you to our engineers. They need your help with a small piece of the puzzle, and then you will remain here as our guest — indefinitely.'

'You have built more of my devices?' Jackson asked.

'Many such devices, yes. An incredible piece of engineering. Far more power than I had required, but power can always be put to good use.' Shranlon sighed; clearly, the conversation was turning away from entertaining, becoming tiresome.

Shranlon indicated to his guards, who took hold of Jackson and Lilly by the arms and escorted them to the lift, which opened almost on cue. They were encouraged inside with a shove and the two guards followed them in, standing behind them.

All Jackson and Lilly heard as they looked at the closing doors was the sound of the lift moving — then a weak choking sound and a quiet thud as one of the guards slumped to the floor. Neither wanted to turn around, but they couldn't help themselves.

***

'What's going on?!' Lilly shouted.

'Easy, keep your voice down,' said the one remaining guard as he checked the guard lying on the floor.

'Is he dead?' Jackson said.

'Yup,' he said, removing his helmet and standing up again.

'Who are you?' asked Jackson.

'A friend of Benjie's. I'm half of his plan to get you two out of here.'

'Do I know you?' Jackson asked again. 'Your face seems...familiar.'

'You might do,' Borell said. 'We don't have time to reminisce right now. Put your hands on the wall and look at them.'

'What?' Lilly said.

'Just do it, we're almost out of the lift shaft,' Borell said, putting his helmet back on and drawing his stun-stick.

Lilly and Jackson did as they were told, not sure whether they should still be frightened of this man or not. A moment later, the lift doors opened and two guards standing outside turned to face them.

'What the hell's going on?' one of the guards said.

Borell knelt with his stun-stick pointed at his prisoners and one hand on the dead guard's wrist. 'He complained about feeling ill and passed out. Are you two the only ones down here?'

'Well, yeah,' the other guard said.

'Good,' said Borell.

He grabbed the fallen guard's stun-stick in his free hand and spun around, coming to his feet in one smooth motion. Both weapons were lodged under the chins of the two guards before they could draw their own weapons. Their bodies spasmed as Borell kept the triggers depressed for longer than he needed to.

'Isn't that enough?' Lilly shouted behind him.

Borell released the triggers and the two guards fell heavily to the floor. 'Better to be safe than sorry,' he said. 'Give me a hand to get these guys out of sight.'

The three of them began dragging the bodies of the guards into a storeroom just along the corridor.

'Help me get the uniforms off these two,' Borell said as he started undoing the boots on one of the guards.

They quickly stripped the men and Jackson and Lilly put their uniforms on. They were a close fit. A bit of cuff-rolling and belt-tightening here and there and they could pass for guards. They hid the bodies as well as they could inside the storeroom and went back into the corridor, looking as guard-like as they could. Borell took his helmet off and threw it in the storeroom. His worn and beaten face would pass fine for a guard and the helmet just obscured his vision too much.

Consulting a map on the wall, they worked out how to get to the sub-levels and the mines.

'We need to get here. Benjie and your friend are down there somewhere,' Borell said, pointing at the map.

'What friend?' Lilly asked.

'A fella named Andris. Risked his life to help rescue you, the daft bugger.'

Lilly smiled shyly and flushed a little pink around the cheeks.

'Yeah, he's a bit like that when we mention you too,' Borell said with a smile. 'Whatever you do between here and there, try and look like guards — and for god's sake, let me do the talking.'

Jackson did his best to stand up straight and walk proudly when they encountered anyone, which didn't take long.

'What happened to yer helmet?' asked one guard they walked by.

'Someone thought it would be funny to take a shit in it last night. Waiting for a new one,' said Borell, which made the other guard laugh. 'He's a dead man when I catch him.'

'I bet he is!'

So far so good, the guards were not overly concerned with them walking about and didn't seem at all bothered by the weathered looking face of Borell.

'Right, down here then we should find a lift to the mines,' Borell said, taking the lead and checking for any potential problems up ahead. Security was light, it seemed — unsurprising really, considering how hard it was to get into this place.

Sure enough, at the end of the corridor was an unguarded lift. They quickly bundled inside, pressed a button and closed the doors. Jackson relaxed, and his back thanked him.

'You're doing fine. We'll probably find lots more guards down here, so let me go first. You two just stand to attention behind me and act like you're there on orders,' Borell said. Neither Jackson nor Lilly could argue with that; they were still alive, even if they were walking into more danger.

The doors opened and the heat from the mines hit them like a hot summer's day. Borell stepped out with purpose and the three of them headed along the walkway towards the holding cells. A guard station just up ahead, cut into the rock, echoed with voices. He couldn't see how many men were inside, but immediately Borell could see a problem. 'Okay, stay back a bit, let me deal with this,' he muttered over his shoulder.

Lilly and Jackson slowed down and stayed out of view of the men inside.

'Fellas,' Borell said, walking up to the door of the guard station.

'Who are you?' a sergeant sitting at the table said. 'And where's ya helmet? And why the hell aren't you saluting an officer?!' He was yelling now. The two guards of lower rank sat next to him started to giggle under their breath.

Borell resisted the urge to kill him there and then, and saluted him instead. As he withdrew his hand, he changed his mind and muscle memory took his hand straight for his gun.

'Fish in a barrel,' he said to himself as he put the now smoking pistol back in its holster. The sergeant and one of the guards had been unable to get to their weapons in time, and were now slumped against the bloodstained whitewashed rocky walls of their alcove. The third guard managed to get a shot off, clipping Borell's arm. This guard had a couple of additional holes in him now.

Borell unclipped a bunch of keys hanging from the sergeant's belt and swung the loop around his finger, jangling the keys.

'Hell's teeth, the whole cave must have heard that!' Jackson said as Borell emerged from the station with a stone cold expression on his face.

'They won't know where it came from. Echoes are great that way,' he said. 'Come on.'

Borell quickened the pace a little, just in case anyone had heard him and came to investigate. They passed numerous empty cells, a few with starved occupants and then stopped outside Benjamin's cell.

'I thought I heard your handiwork. Took your time, didn't you?' Benjamin said as he picked himself up and dusted off his trousers in an overly dramatic way.

'Well you know, people to rescue, people to kill. It takes it out of a man,' Borell joked as he found a key in the bunch that unlocked the cell.

'Uncle Ben,' Lilly shouted as he stepped out onto the walkway.

'Thank the gods,' Benjamin said as she ran over and put her arms around him.

'God is a little lofty for me, but I'll take it,' said Borell.

'I owe you.'

'Let's just get the hell out of here. From what I heard upstairs, we've got some work to do.'

'Hello?' came a voice from the next cell. 'Would anyone like to let me out as well?'

'Andris!' Lilly cried with relief. She let go of her uncle and ran over to the cell bars. 'What the *hell* are you doing here, you could have got yourself killed!' she screamed at him. Andris couldn't work out whether he was in trouble or not.

'Erm,' he stumbled.

Fortunately, Borell unlocked the door and Lilly answered the question for him. She threw her arms around him and gave him a long, hard hug.

'Well, now the kids are back together, can we *please* get the hell out of here,' Borell said with some frustration showing.

'Did you find the device?' Benjamin said, taking a pistol offered by Borell.

'Yeah, about that. Turns out they have *lots* of these things, but only one that actually works. Looks like we're going hunting.'

'They found the initiator at the house, didn't they?' Benjamin said.

'It would seem so,' said Jackson, who was steadying himself against the railing. 'They took it when they kidnapped us, but it would seem they have been building the devices for a while.'

'So at the moment we have to find and destroy one; that's our immediate problem.'

'Not exactly our immediate problem,' Borell said as an alarm claxon sounded in the mine below them. Several bullets ricocheted from the cave walls around them as he looked over into the murky depths below. Everyone ducked down inside the walkway for cover.

'We won't last long out here,' said Benjamin. 'They're firing at us from the opposite side, but they're too far away to be accurate. Stray shots, on the other hand...'

'So what's the plan, chief?' Borell said to Benjamin as he returned fire blindly over the side of the railings.

'Save your rounds, for a start.' He turned to Andris. 'Time to step up, kid. We'll distract them and head for the device. You're gonna have to get these two to the surface. If you have to shoot people, make it count, like we said. There's no time for second thoughts from here on out. Shoot or be shot. Got it?'

Andris nodded his head, remembering what Benjamin had told him earlier and pulled the pistol from the holster on Jackson's belt.

'Try and get back to the airship; we'll meet you there as soon as we can. Use your uniforms to your advantage.'

More bullets bounced around above them; it was time to go. Lilly removed and cocked the pistol that was in the holster around her waist.

'What are you doing?' Andris shouted.

'I'm not going down without a fight,' she said.

'Head down that corridor and use the stairs to get to the surface — avoid the lifts or you'll be sitting ducks. You three will have to work together to get out of here. Do whatever you can to get back to that airship,' Benjamin said.

'Time to go!' Borell shouted over the sound of the claxon.

'Go on three,' Benjamin shouted, cocking his pistol and taking a breath. 'One — two — three.'

Benjamin and Borell both stood up and returned fire towards the opposite side of the cave to give the others cover for a few moments. It took only seconds for them to be hidden by the rock face and out of the line of fire.

'Coming?' shouted Benjamin.

'Hell yes!'

They both ran at full speed towards the lift that Borell had come down in. Ahead of them, the doors opened and four guards exited, weapons drawn. Benjamin and Borell were already firing as soon as the doors opened and the four guards soon lay in a heap just outside.

'Hang on,' Benjamin said as he dipped into the security station Borell had cleared earlier.

'Got it,' he said as he ran back out, wearing his ammo belt, holding up his own gun and tucking other items into his pockets. Borell was waiting in the open lift and holding the door for Benjamin with a huge grin on his face, clearly enjoying the chase.

'So we're ignoring our own advice on lifts then,' Borell said as Benjamin half ran, half fell into it at speed.

'We have an advantage,' Benjamin said, holding up his gun and one of the guns from a fallen guard.

Borell grabbed a second gun and wiped his brow. 'Let's head for the white coats, they'll be easier to get information about the operational device from. We might even get lucky and find it tucked away in a lab somewhere.' He stabbed at a button and the noise and heat from the mine ceased.

'You have high hopes,' Benjamin said as he reloaded his pistol. 'It's never *that* easy.'

'No, I know. But just once it would be nice, you know?'

The doors opened and in all the confusion, the two guards who had replaced the ones Borell killed earlier were taken by surprise. Borell and Benjamin rushed them before they had a chance to open fire and subdued them without letting a shot off.

They ran along the corridor looking for lab coats and it wasn't long before they passed a window into a room with a worried looking scientist hiding inside. Benjamin kicked open the door and grabbed the man by his collar, lifting him to his feet again.

'Tell me what I need to know and I promise you won't get hurt,' he said.

'Not even a little?' Borell questioned.

Benjamin ignored him and the scientist stood quivering in his grip. 'Just tell us where the operational device is, the one that was completed today.'

'W-wha —' the man cleared his throat '— what device?'

Borell pointed his gun at the man's head and cocked the trigger for effect.

'Okay, okay. It's not here.'

'We can see that. Where is it?'

'No I m-mean it's not been here since it started working. When the m-missing piece arrived. It's on board the *Ascension*. We've been working on it since we left Trellern.'

'What's the *Ascension*?' Borell asked, waving the pistol about in the man's face.

'The airship. The big one,' he said with his eyes closed so he couldn't see the gun.

'That's just great,' Borell said. 'I'd hoped we were done with airships.'

Borell struck the scientist across the side of the head with his gun and he slumped to the ground, sliding out of Benjamin's grasp.

'Did you need to do that?'

'No.'

'Thought so. Come on.'

All around them alarm bells were still ringing, but security was still lighter than they had expected.

'I thought there'd be more resistance than this,' Benjamin said as they returned fire to a handful of guards who had bundled into the corridor then wished they hadn't.

After a quick reload, the two of them tore down the corridor, stepping over bodies, and slid to a stop at the map showing them the layout of the buildings. A stairwell to their right led up to the surface and they decided to take their own advice this time, avoiding the lifts. It looked like the scientists and engineers had been instructed to lock themselves inside their labs if the alarms sounded, as they had not fallen over any in a mad rush to see what was going on.

Benjamin kicked the door open to the stairwell and Borell rushed inside, making sure no one was waiting for them.

'Still too quiet,' said Benjamin as they started up the stairs towards the surface.

'You won't be happy until we're surrounded, will you?' Borell said, grabbing at his bleeding arm as they ran up the stairs.

'It worries me that there aren't that many guards looking for us down here. It worries me more that they're waiting for us on the surface.'

'I see your point. Ideas?'

'Just one at the moment,' Benjamin said as he put the guard's pistol into his belt. He reloaded his own gun and stopped around the corner, just before the floor leading to the surface.

'Might want to cover your ears,' Benjamin said as he pointed his gun around the corner and towards the outside door.

'Ah, shit,' Borell said as he ducked his head a second before Benjamin pulled the trigger. The door exploded outwards in a fireball of splinters and metal shards. Not wasting any time, they took advantage of the disorientation of the guards and picked off any that had not been killed or knocked out by the concussive blast. Overall, seven guards lay scattered around and Benjamin had no doubts that more would be on their way.

'What else can that thing do?' Borell said as they ran across a courtyard to take cover under a monorail support structure. 'That's not standard issue.'

'One of Jackson's specials. It's got a few other tricks — maybe later.'

Benjamin took a moment to get his bearings and worked out the direction they needed to go to find the *Ascension*. It had been to the north when they flew in; being the only huge airship, it must be the one, so they headed off in that direction.

'This is going to take too long,' Borell said, really starting to feel the pain of his ribs with all the running. 'Come on.'

He had spotted a truck sitting idling outside one of the numbered buildings, its driver hurriedly loading crates onto the flat bed. Whilst the driver had his back turned to pick up another crate, Borell charged over, knocked him out with a quick blow from the butt of his revolver and rolled him onto the back of the truck, covering him with tarpaulin.

'I'll drive,' Borell said. 'You duck down out of sight; I'm still dressed the part.'

They jumped into the truck, Borell flooring the engine as they sped off along the road towards the *Ascension*.

'Any ideas on how we're getting aboard that behemoth?' Borell asked as they saw the might of the airship looming in front of them.

'They're loading cargo in a hurry — our best bet is to get onto one of the platforms lifting those crates into the hold.'

Benjamin pointed to where a hydraulic platform was descending from the belly of the *Ascension,* ready to be loaded with more crates waiting on the ground. He took off his jacket and put on a scruffy workman's coat that was stuffed into the footwell of the truck. He rubbed some grease from the floor onto his face and shirt to look less conspicuous. He was already beginning to look grubby from the time spent in the mines.

'Very pretty,' said Borell.

***

They were getting close to the *Ascension*, and the road was getting steadily busier as supplies and trucks carrying soldiers headed towards the docking bays. They were being loaded onto not just the *Ascension* but the other ships docked there as well. They continued past the smaller airships and headed towards the rear of the *Ascension*, keeping as far away from the stream of soldiers as possible. So far, no one had really noticed them amongst the bustle.

'Over there,' Benjamin said, pointing Borell to a stack of crates to park beside. They got out and casually walked to the back of the truck. Borell grabbed the cap from the man lying under the tarpaulin, knocking him out again as he started to come around, and threw it to Benjamin, who put it on.

'Better,' said Benjamin. 'Grab the other side of this crate.'

They each took a side and dragged the heavy crate from the truck. Steadily they struggled towards the handful of men organising the loading of the crates onto the platform, hoping to bluff their way on board.

'Hey!' shouted Benjamin towards the men. 'Give us a hand, will ya?'

Two of the men who were not loading anything at that moment ran over and grabbed a side each to help.

'Thanks. This thing weighs a tonne,' Borell said to the men jovially.

'What'cha got in 'ere,' one of the men asked him.

'Beats me. Been told to get this aboard for *Him* right away. Utmost importance or something.'

'Has to be taken to the State room as soon as it's aboard, is what we've been ordered,' added Benjamin.

'Yeah, lots of this kind of thing going up today,' said the other man.

The four of them shuffled along with the heavy crate until they made it onto the platform.

'Hold it, fellas,' said a man with a clipboard, checking off items being loaded. 'Where's the papers for that box?'

'Don't have any,' Borell said.

'Then it doesn't get aboard this boat.'

'Look, I ain't got time to argue this with ya,' Borell said, stepping up to the man. 'Under strict orders to get this aboard and not to fanny about on the way.'

Borell's attitude took the man aback. He looked at the clipboard then back at Borell. 'Yeah, but if it's not on my list and you don't have paperwork for it, it can't go up.'

Borell put his hand on the man's shoulder; Benjamin stiffened, praying he wouldn't do anything stupid.

'Listen to me, my friend. You hear all those alarms going off? There is some bad shit coming our way. Do you want to stand here whilst *he* waits for this special cargo to be delivered?'

'Erm,' the man, looking flustered.

'If you want to sit on it and wait for paperwork, whilst I go up and tell *him* personally that his crate is sat with some bureaucratic paper pusher on the ground, that's fine with us. Back on the truck she goes,' Borell said as he turned to Benjamin.

'W-wait,' the man with the clipboard shouted. 'It's just one crate and if it's on direct orders, then I'm sure it's fine.' The man looked anything but confident, but wasn't about to challenge Shranlon, not whilst a general alarm was sounding.

'We'll be riding up with it,' Benjamin said. 'Not to leave it alone, we're told.'

'Yes, yes, fine,' said the man, returning to the supervision of the other crews, glancing back at them as they waited for the ride up.

'You look nervous, old friend,' Borell said casually as

they waited for the remaining crates and supplies to be loaded.

'I was wondering how you were going to approach that negotiation. At least you didn't kill anyone.'

Borell smiled. 'Listen, there's something that I think your friend Jackson isn't telling you. Whilst I was waiting for your friends up in that madman's lair, he said something that sounded very personal to Jackson. He said something about family and "did he ever tell him". They were talking about your father. No idea what they meant by it, but Jackson took it very badly. The guy's name was Shranlon or something. Mean anything to you?'

Benjamin looked at Borell for a moment. 'Are you sure his name was Shranlon?'

'That's what Jackson called him. Everyone else seems to call him He or Him. Seemed to work on these guys,' he said, nodding towards clipboard man.

'I know that name from a long time ago. I'm sure it was the name of the guy at the Siege of Sorent.'

Borell looked at him blankly and shrugged his shoulders.

'Did you do anything but kill people in your training?' Benjamin asked in a hushed voice.

'Didn't go much in for the history stuff — more of a practical man, me.'

'Figures. He was supposed to have been killed at the siege. He was bad news back then... If it's the same guy we definitively need to find him and stop him.'

'Okay, let's add him to our list,' Borell said.

Their conversation was interrupted as the platform beneath them silently erupted into life.

'Best hold on ta summin',' the man with the clipboard shouted as the platform rose through the air and began closing on the hold of the *Ascension*. The scissor mechanisms beneath them extended smoothly and quietly, pushing them higher and higher.

'This thing is so much more massive when you're

right up to it,' Borell said as he craned his neck to look up at the belly of the ship. 'Where are we gonna start looking for this device?'

'I don't know, but we'd better split up. I'll go fore, you go aft.'

'Okay, sounds fair.'

Borell looked over the side of the platform at the ground moving away from them. He could see soldiers unloading a truck with what appeared to be prisoners, towards the front section of the main gondola.

'We've got another problem,' Borell said, pointing towards the two prisoners on the ground.

'Shit, that didn't take long,' Benjamin said, looking over at Lilly and Andris being escorted to the passenger lifts.

'You go find the kids. I'll find the device,' Borell said.

'Okay, I'll meet you back at the airship. And see if you can find out what they've done with Jackson. I'm hoping he's with his device.'

'I'll see what I can find out, but you might want to ask Shranlon if you find him first,' Borell said, handing Benjamin a miniature device from his pocket. 'And you might want this.'

Benjamin looked at it and realised what it was. 'Where did you put them?'

'Somewhere that'll make a hell of a mess. Just make sure you're nowhere near a steam pipe when you use it,' he smiled. 'I didn't want to use it until we knew were Jackson and the kids were.'

'We may not have a choice if we can't stop them any other way.'

'Okay, just try and give me a heads up if you decide to crack this nut open.'

Benjamin looked over the side of the platform, which was now a hundred feet or so above the ground and could see more soldiers arriving and falling into formation below the other airships. 'Do what you can to disable the ship and destroy the device — it can't leave this compound! I'll blow it as a last resort.'

The platform was now closing on the opening in the bottom of the cargo hold and men inside who had been standing clear of the edge moved in with speed and efficiency to begin moving the crates into the hold. Benjamin and Borell grabbed the crate they were escorting, lugged it to a space away from the throng of workers and went their separate ways.

***

The loud sirens had been replaced with spinning red lights along the corridors and steel gantries of the *Ascension*. Benjamin made his way towards the forward section of the hold on one of the gantries that was as high up as you could get. Looking down, he could see hundreds of stacked crates and dozens of vehicles stowed and tied down to the deck in the cavernous hold.

'Where the hell you goin'?' demanded a burly man wearing dirty overalls, walking towards him.

'For a piss.'

'Then you're goin' the wrong bloody way,' he said. Benjamin walked towards him, kicked him in the groin and brought his gun down hard on the back of his head. Fortunately, there was enough noise from the crews unloading that he wasn't noticed. He dragged the man's heavy body towards the door ahead of him, hoping no one would see.

Once inside the corridor at the end of the gantry, he closed the door and quietness fell. He found a small closet that was just big enough to stuff the man inside and cover with brooms, buckets and sheets. It seemed that this deck housed the quarters assigned to engineers and general aircrew. Bare metal and canvas walls, unadorned with anything remotely aesthetic led away towards a set of stairs leading up and down.

Benjamin guessed that if he was to find Lilly and Andris he would have to head up to the passenger decks and staterooms and look there. He realised he was going to look out of place again where he was going, wearing scruffy, dirty clothes. He dipped inside one of the open crew rooms and rummaged around in the lockers. It didn't take long to find some decent clothes that were his size. He made a quick change, washed his face and headed back out into the corridor.

A sign at the end of the corridor to the left of the stairs said he was on 'D' deck, so he headed up past 'C' deck and 'B' deck until the decor improved to the point that he no longer looked out of place. Stepping out on to 'A' deck, there were staff busying themselves preparing the large open dining rooms for departure. They were too busy to care that Benjamin was walking past and he took advantage of this.

He headed to the front of the dining room, which had windows along both sides, offering a fantastic view of wherever you were flying over whilst dining. Shranlon had not skimped on luxury for his vessel. Several stewards pushed past him with exasperated faces at being called to service before they were clearly ready.

Two corridors led away from the front of the dining room along the windowed sides of the deck. The corridors were wide and had a table and two or three lounge chairs around each for a view outside. Through the windows to the staterooms on the inside of the deck, he could see that some were fitted out for use, but many were empty. He looked in each as he continued his way forward.

As he came closer to the front of the deck, the corridor began to curve around the front aspect of the gondola. He decided to loop around, check the rooms on the opposite side and then make his way down to the next level. Ahead of him, he saw two guards standing to attention in an alcove. He picked up a box of supplies sitting on a table and held it on his shoulder as he approached them, hiding his face. They saw him but maintained their post until he was right alongside. Being the first guards Benjamin had encountered inside, he took a chance that they were guarding Lilly and Andris, maybe even Jackson.

He threw the box at one of the guards and ploughed his weight into the other, knocking him backwards into the wall. One guard finished fumbling with the box and moved in to grab hold of Benjamin. Benjamin kicked out, catching the guard a lucky strike on the chin and sending him tumbling into an unconscious heap at the foot of the stairs. Benjamin reeled from a kidney punch and returned as many quick jabs as he could against the other guard. The two wrestled for a little longer before Benjamin managed to free the guard's grip and get him in a chokehold, rendering him unconscious a few seconds later.

Catching his breath for a moment, Benjamin rubbed his bruised ribs and took out his gun before loading several rounds and cocking the hammer. In front of him was a short set of stairs leading up to a lift. He hoped this was the way to Shranlon's private deck, where Lilly, Andris and Jackson might be. He realised he might have to deal with Shranlon first. There was only one button inside the lift; as he pressed it, the lift shot upwards.

Prepared for more guards, Benjamin waited, pistol poised and his back to the lift side wall to provide a tiny amount of cover. Not the best situation to be in, but he had little choice.

The lift came to a stop, and the doors opened onto a large room with a glass ceiling. No guards were waiting for him, which Benjamin didn't like — it smelt like a trap.

'Come in, Benjamin,' came a voice from the shadows. 'I've been expecting you.'

He looked around the edge of the lift door for an ambush, but saw there was none.

'There is no need for your weapon; I intend you no harm,' the shadowy voice said.

Benjamin trained his pistol on the silhouetted figure sat in the middle of the room. He looked around for anyone else lurking in the shadows, but Shranlon appeared to be sitting alone. The morning sun was rising above them, but the windows above had been designed to leave an area for Shranlon to sit in the cool darkness.

'If it's all the same, my gun will stay where it is, Shranlon — if that's who you are.'

Shranlon continued to sit in the dark, only a vague outline in the surrounding light. Benjamin slowly stepped a few feet to his left to change his point of view, keeping his weapon pointed at his target.

'I have been following your career with interest, Benjamin; you are certainly an asset to be proud of in your organisation...and someone who would be a great asset in mine.'

'Since when are we on first name terms?'

'I do apologise. Would *Agent Sorrow* be more in keeping with our dynamic?' Shranlon said with a mocking tone.

'It might,' Benjamin said, stepping a little closer.

'I promise you, you will not need your weapon, *Agent Sorrow*.'

'And of course, I should trust you.'

'I see no reason why you should trust me. I am simply stating a fact. I am unarmed and alone and at present, no direct threat to you.'

Benjamin realised that holding his arm out to support his pistol was only going to tire it, so slowly lowered it to his side, but kept it out of its holster just in case.

'Don't think I won't hesitate to shoot you if you so much as move,' he said.

'Tsk tsk, Agent Sorrow. I've come to expect better than threats from you.'

'A promise, not a threat.'

'Perhaps,' Shranlon said. 'What do you think of the *Ascension*? A magnificent machine, is she not?' he said changing the subject.

'Impressive, I will give you that. Impressive too, that you have managed to keep your microcosm of a city hidden from us until now.'

'You are here because I wanted you here, Agent Sorrow. I foresaw this moment and the many leading to it.'

'Your *ability* to predict the future. I've heard about your parlour trick.'

'Not predict — foresee. I foresee many versions of the future and by no means a definitive version of events to come. What I do see gives me a perspective that others do not have. When you take a course of action, you want a certain outcome. I see the various outcomes first and can plan accordingly. And I can assure you, it is far from a "parlour trick".'

'From what I've read about your *ability*, it was all disproved as nothing more than clever tricks and staged events, designed to give the illusion of power.'

'Whether you believe in the mind's ability to do such things or not, does not stop them from existing. Your friend Jackson Burns didn't believe in my abilities, but even he has his doubts now.'

'Sorry to shit on your master plan, by the way. The whole unlimited power thing must have been a huge part of your plans.'

'Perhaps.' Shranlon gave a chuckle. 'You caused a small delay in my schedule; it was one of the foreseen eventualities. But as you saw, we are already beginning our first phase, which does not require more than a single device. As I said, I can see many versions of events and I plan accordingly.'

'There must be times when outcomes don't fit one of your *visions*. There must be an infinite number of possibilities to even everyday events, you cannot see them all.'

'You are correct. I see — likely outcomes. Just like the one that showed me you detonating the explosives your friend placed around our facility, with the trigger in your pocket.'

Benjamin looked around nervously, reached into his coat pocket with his free hand and pulled out the remote trigger Borell had given him.

'You see? A likely eventuality,' Shranlon said.

'So you're saying that, even though you knew I had this and that it would destroy everything you worked for, you still let me walk in here?' Benjamin was weighing up the odds of Shranlon guessing he had some kind of backup plan.

'Correct. Although the fact that it is no longer a threat negates any leverage you think you have over me.'

Benjamin tried to hide his look of concern. If Shranlon did foresee this moment and the remote trigger, it also makes sense that he would have taken steps to stop him using it.

'Go ahead,' said Shranlon. 'Use it if you must, if only to prove to yourself that the abilities of which I speak are genuine.'

Benjamin held the trigger tightly, his mind pondering the possibility that there really was some kind of force at work for Shranlon. 'What's to stop me detonating this and then shooting you?'

'Apart from the fact I do not believe you would shoot someone in cold blood, nothing. My death today is not a likely outcome.'

Benjamin didn't hesitate and flipped the switch on the remote trigger.

Something happened, but not what Benjamin expected. He felt the ship around him begin to move. He tried the switch a few more times and realised his efforts were futile.

'Phase one of my plan is underway and you will not be able to stop it now. And in case you were wondering, this room has been shielded from transmissions. Your detonator is useless.'

Benjamin quickly walked over to the large glass windows that merged with the glass roof and looked outside. The city below them was quickly moving away as they climbed above it.

Shranlon slowly laughed as Benjamin put the detonator back in his pocket and pointed his pistol at him again. 'My dear boy,' he sighed. 'Are you not satisfied now that my abilities exist?'

'I agree you are a very clever man. You may have planned for many outcomes, but you can't foresee the future, predict it or whatever.'

'You are very much like your father. Your physical resemblance and attitude is like reliving conversations from many years ago.'

Benjamin looked at Shranlon's shadowed outline and hesitated.

'Oh yes, I knew your father well. It was such a shame when we had to go our separate ways; he just didn't agree with me on my world view. He was very much like you in many ways — misguided to the end.'

Benjamin was about to say something when the floor beneath him shook him to his knees. An almighty explosion detonated in the city far below, followed by several other large explosions.

Benjamin smiled as he stood and walked towards Shranlon. 'It looks like your abilities have failed you.'

'Ah yes, your *friend*. He has proven most unpredictable,' Shranlon was sounding calm, far too calm.

Benjamin pointed his pistol at Shranlon again and pulled the trigger.

Chapter Thirty-Three

Shranlon writhed around in his chair, his scream sounding more animal than human, as the electrical energy discharged from the three-pronged round protruding from his chest.

'I said I wouldn't hesitate to shoot you. Didn't say I was going to kill you,' Benjamin said as the glow from the electrical discharge lit the dark face hidden underneath Shranlon's hood and faded away. His body sat slumped in the shadows. Benjamin cautiously checked him; he was still alive. Another one of Jackson's creations proving its worth.

Below them, explosions were sounding off rapidly. Borell must have had another trigger and felt the need to use it. He really hoped that meant Borell had found Andris, Lilly and Jackson on board. Through the windows he could see plumes of fire rising all around them as the ship began a rapid turn; Benjamin struggled to remain on his feet.

Shranlon fell forwards from his chair as the ship climbed and Benjamin caught him, putting the limp body over his shoulder. He didn't weigh very much and Benjamin could feel Shranlon's bony ribs and legs as he adjusted the weight across his shoulders.

Grabbing Shranlon's arm and hooking his own through one of his legs, he headed towards the rear of the room. As the direction of the ship changed, the rear of the room was illuminated by the sun and the entrance to a corridor appeared in the far wall. All about him, the walls shook. He placed a hand onto an exposed section of superstructure.

'That's inside the ship. What the hell did you do, Borell?'

The ship listed suddenly, forcing Benjamin against the corridor wall. He regained his balance and shifted the weight on his shoulders, heading towards the stairs at the end of the corridor. Sirens began sounding again as the ship shook vigorously. He put all his effort into climbing the stairs, which were now at a challenging angle.

Another shift in the balance of the ship levelled them off slightly as the crew tried to maintain integrity of the balloon by dumping portside ballast. Climbing the stairs became much easier and Benjamin put a hurried effort into getting to the top as quickly as possible.

His legs were tiring as he rounded the last corner of the staircase and kicked open the door. It looked as though Shranlon had his own personal airship moored in a section of the envelope that formed a hanger. The *Ascension* was nothing less than impressive, even if it was beginning to turn into an impressive disaster.

Unsecured crates slid along the deck as the ship began dipping its nose. Crewmembers were nowhere to be seen; they were most likely trying to save the ship or themselves. The air was warm and thick with ash and smoke as the destruction of the city below them bellowed up into the atmosphere.

Why didn't Shranlon have more guards? Was he that sure of himself?

Benjamin forced himself to focus, his mind beginning to ask questions he didn't have time to deduce an answer to right now. The small airship was still tethered to the deck, but it was moving around as it floated a few feet above it, taught against its lines. He had to hope that Borell was already making good his escape; a ship this size would probably be a flaming ball of gas before he could find them, if he even had that much time.

The lines groaned as they fought against the buoyancy of the ship. Benjamin prayed that they didn't snap before he was on board. He practically threw Shranlon's limp body through the door and into the cockpit before lunging inside. He closed the door and sat in the pilot's chair, the sounds from outside becoming muffled and dull. This airship was as automated as the one he had borrowed and would have no doubt been Shranlon's personal escape vehicle. *Proving,* he thought to himself, *that he can't know the future if he needed an escape option.*

He started the engines and released the tethers, sending the small ship on a jostling ride through the opening above them as he gave the engines as much power as he could. He couldn't see from his position how close he was to the opening in the *Ascension*'s envelope and, within seconds, he felt the balloon of his own ship bounce firmly from it.

With its gondola swinging like a pendulum, the automated systems on the ship tried desperately to correct. Within a few seconds, the stomach-churning ride was beginning to calm down and the propellers returned to the pilot's control. As his ship rose clear of the *Ascension*, Benjamin could see that it was heading straight for the volcano. Quickly, he turned the small ship around and flew almost directly along the spine of the *Ascension* towards its tail.

Ahead of him, he could see small planes taking off from the landing strip on the top of the envelope. He was close enough to see men and women panicking and many of them falling to their deaths as the *Ascension* lurched here and there. He could only imagine what state the rest of the crew were in as they tried to abandon ship. In the sky around him, he could see other airships heading for the mountain pass in an attempt to escape the all-encompassing destruction.

Benjamin's ship surged forwards as a massive shockwave buffeted them from behind. The nose section of the *Ascension* had exploded and it was now beginning a slow nosedive towards the ground. Benjamin gave the engines as much throttle as he could and the ship reluctantly pulled away from the burning wreck.

The panic below caught his attention as he began turning away.

'Shit!'

He caught sight of Borell, Andris and Lilly shooting their way across the flight deck. Benjamin was relieved to see them alive. It looked like they were heading for an aeroplane, but who was going to fly it? Without a second thought, Benjamin turned back towards the deck of the *Ascension*, spinning around almost on the spot. He tried his best to line up with the failing *Ascension* and reduced his altitude until he was sitting a few feet above the flight deck.

He set the controls as best he could to maintain the current heading and descent, but knew he didn't have long before they would run out of altitude. Opening the door to the cockpit, he threw out the emergency rope ladder and hung out of the door, holding onto the frame.

'Get a move on!' he shouted at Borell whilst firing a couple of rounds at men running towards them. At this point most of the guards and crew were too busy saving their own skins and were more interested in the ship Benjamin was flying than Borell and his group.

Lilly was the first to make it to the rope ladder, closely followed by Andris and Borell. She made light work of it, even as the declination of the ships made the ladder hang at an awkward angle. Benjamin grabbed her wrist and helped her with the last step into the cockpit. Andris was trying to get a start on the ladder, but it was taking him longer to get a sure footing.

'Hate to state the obvious, kid, but we're running out of sky,' Borell shouted over the noise of the engines and air rushing past outside.

'Yeah I know!' he shouted back, climbing as quickly as he could now he had made a start on the ladder.

Another explosion shook the deck as a rear section of the *Ascension* tore itself apart in a fireball. Suddenly the nose was no longer heavy and the rear began sinking quicker. Benjamin's ship ploughed into the deck as it continued on its nose-down attitude, throwing Borell to the floor.

'Where the hell is Jackson?' Benjamin shouted at Borell as he regained his footing.

'Not on board,' he shouted back, out of breath. 'Already gone!'

'Get your ass in here now!' Benjamin shouted over the din of explosions as he returned to the pilot's chair and started adjusting the buoyancy to compensate for the new angle and rate of descent. The envelope was deflating quicker than it should and they wouldn't be able to take off until it reached positive buoyancy again.

Borell clambered into the cockpit without needing the cumbersome ladder and detached it from the doorframe. He closed the door as several men charged at them in a last-ditch attempt to hitch a ride. He put his gun through a small window in the door and fired several rounds in their general direction. They soon got the message.

Their ship was now drifting away from the *Ascension* as they increased lift, with engines at maximum power. They could see the deck getting farther away as more explosions ripped through the envelope of the stricken airship below them. The cockpit was crowded and Benjamin had dropped all the available ballast to get them airborne again as quickly as possible.

To their port side, a balloon exploded underneath the deck, ripping it apart and making the *Ascension* list dramatically as its centre of balance shifted again. Benjamin turned the engines as far as he could and pushed them to the red line. They began vibrating horribly, shaking the cockpit and its passengers.

'Almost clear,' Benjamin said through gritted teeth as everyone huddled on the floor for stability.

'Is that —?' Lilly started as she noticed the shrouded body lying on the floor, having been too panicked to notice before.

'Shranlon,' Benjamin said, struggling to keep a grip on the control stick.

When Lilly heard this, she backed away as far as the limited floor space allowed.

'Don't worry, he'll be out cold for a while.'

Benjamin reduced the engine throttle as they were now far enough away from the *Ascension* to be out of immediate danger. He levelled the ship out and looked out of the port window.

'How much explosive did you use down there?' he said looking at Borell.

'It's not how much, it's where I put it.'

'Okay, *where* did you put it?'

'Where it counts,' Borell said, grinning. An updraft shook their ship as a warm orange glow illuminated the cockpit. 'Oh and maybe a little bit on one of the volcanic heat exchangers,' he added with his nose pressed against the glass, having a good look at his handiwork. The walls of the volcano had ruptured and they could see molten lava flowing from a steadily growing fissure in the base of the mountain. It was destroying everything in its path — buildings, airships, tanks and men.

'The mine...' said Andris. 'All those people!'

'Yep, most likely swimming at the bottom of a lava pool by now. Just as well there wasn't anyone down there we liked.'

'You really are a cold-hearted bastard, aren't you?' Andris said.

Borell shrugged his shoulders.

'You're sure Jackson wasn't down there?' Benjamin asked.

'I made some *inquiries*, and it looks like he was taken elsewhere, along with his device.'

'Shit,' Benjamin said.

'They split us up as soon as they caught us, Uncle Ben,' Lilly explained. 'If he was still down there, I swear I'll kill you myself,' she added, looking at Borell without fear or hesitation. Borell ignored her.

They all watched in astonishment as the basin in which a city once thrived became a hot orange pool of molten rock; the frame of the *Ascension* slowly melting and disappearing into the lava.

'Tie him up, just in case he comes around,' Benjamin said, looking at Borell.

Borell turned away from the window and grabbed some rope hanging on the wall to tie Shranlon up, trying to think of the best way to restrain him. He decided to lash Shranlon's hand to his waist, wrapping the rope around him a couple of times, ending in a secure knot. He tied his feet with the remaining rope, just to be sure.

'Benjie —'

'What is it?' Benjamin had gone back to the pilot's seat to get them away from the rising heat of the lava pool.

'Shranlon is bleeding — a lot.' Borell wiped the blood from his hands onto Shranlon's robes and uncovered the stump of his arm where it had been lost near the shoulder. A surgical wound had been torn open in the escape and blood had been gushing from it. His robes were soaked with a warm, sticky mess. Borell knelt next to the man and rolled him on to his back. 'Shranlon lost his arm in his escape thirty years ago, right?' he said towards Benjamin.

'So?'

'This is a fresh wound, it can't be more than a few days old. The stitches have torn apart. And that's not the worst of it.'

'What is the worst of it?'

'He's dead. Stopped bleeding — no pulse.'

Borell checked the man again, but he wasn't breathing and definitely had no pulse. He uncovered the shrouded face, revealing an old man — in his late seventies by the look of his weathered features. His eyes had rolled back into their sockets.

'Was the man you saw really Shranlon?' Benjamin asked.

'How would I know? I've never met him before. But Jackson seemed pretty convinced it was him.'

'So this guy pretends to be Shranlon, what — so he can cover his escape?' Lilly said.

'Maybe that was his plan all along,' Borell said. 'He seemed pretty convinced of his predictions. Another diversion? Another fake death? A bit last minute by the looks of this poor sod.'

'So if that's not him, he must have died down there — right?' Andris said hopefully.

'Not likely,' Benjamin said. 'He wouldn't go to all the effort of having a double, even with one arm removed, to fall foul of the hell Borell unleashed down there. He stopped me using the detonator, but must have somehow known this was all coming.' Benjamin paused. 'Or he let it happen.'

'It doesn't make sense,' Lilly said.

'If I remember *my* history correctly, one of the things Shranlon claimed to be able to do was project his mind onto another person. He could never prove it, of course, but this was thirty years ago.'

'So what you're saying is this guy was a puppet. Shranlon and Jackson could be anywhere by now,' Borell said, sitting back against the bulkhead and stretching his neck. Benjamin didn't reply, he just concentrated on their path out of the volcano. 'Hold tight to something, we're coming up on the mountain pass.'

Everyone looked out of whatever windows were available, expecting to see shots being fired at them from any of the guards still at their posts. What they saw were numerous ruinous buildings and plumes of steam erupting from what used to be gun emplacements. The steam pipes that Borell had sabotaged had cascaded to the outposts along the pass used for heating. Ruptured pipes and fires tore the buildings apart; men were running along mountain paths with sheer drops to the valley below, trying to escape the carnage.

Not a single shot was fired.

Chapter Thirty-Four

After a few hours of travel in their cramped airship, they arrived at Till, a little town about an hour outside the capital of Nartill. They had all agreed that they needed to stop for supplies and to clean up, although they were keen to get home. They had not eaten properly in a while and they were beginning to hate the dirt and smell they carried around with them from their incarceration. They also desperately needed to do something about the body of the imposter laying on the floor.

'I know someone who can help us with supplies,' Benjamin said as he brought the airship to land at the aerodrome in Till. 'Lilly, you and I will go fetch what we need for the trip home. Borell, see if you can get *him* wrapped up and outside for the trip back. He's really starting to smell.'

'I get all the fun jobs, don't I?' Borell said.

'Andris can stay and help you clean up the blood.' Andris didn't say anything, but just looked at the body, then at Borell, exhausted and expressionless.

'As soon as we're back, you two can go and get cleaned up,' Benjamin said. 'Lilly and I need to talk.'

Clunk.

The docking clamp grabbed hold of the nose securely and men scurried around on the ground, tying off guy ropes. Lilly and Benjamin climbed down and took a walk towards the town centre.

'I will get him back, Lilly,' he said in answer to her unspoken question.

'I know you will. It's just —'

'What?'

'There's a nagging question in the back of my mind. Something Shranlon, or whoever he was, said to Grandpa.'

'About me?'

'Yes, how did you know?'

'Borell told me what he heard before he rescued you both. I have questions for Jackson too. There's a history between him and Shranlon that involves my family. I want to know what that is.'

They walked in silence for several minutes, looking at the townsfolk going about their business.

'It's very pretty here,' Lilly said, breaking the silence with conversation.

'It is. I've been here a few times before. There's a shop I'm looking for — there it is,' he said, pointing to the open frontage of a blacksmith's a hundred yards ahead of them, bellowing smoke into the open air.

'Benjamin, my old friend. 'Tis good to see you again,' said the dirty hulk of a man as they approached. He stopped swinging his hammer onto the red-hot iron on his anvil and quenched it in a bucket of water.

'Vinny,' Benjamin said, shaking his hand. 'This is Lilly.'

'Pleasure to meet you, miss,' Vinny said, nodding his head.

'This isn't a social call I'm afraid, old friend. I need a favour.'

Vinny nodded, put his hammer down and escorted them to the back of his workshop, through a door and into a large storeroom. Benjamin explained their situation, the need for supplies and the fact that they had no money to spend. Vinny was more than happy to help, having been a friend for as many years as he could remember.

'We need enough to buy food and supplies for a trip back to Menillis, somewhere to clean up and some new clothes. I will send you the money as soon as we are home.'

'That I have no trouble with my friend. Wait here,

I'll be back in a few minutes.' Vinney walked out of the storeroom, leaving Benjamin and Lilly alone.

'How do you know him?' she asked.

'He used to work in Menillis, before his smithing business was destroyed, ironically, by a fire. He moved here about ten years ago to start over. We've known each other since we were kids.'

'You trust him?'

'With my life.' Benjamin could see a look of concern in Lilly's face. 'What is it?'

'Oh nothing, probably. Didn't he seem a bit nervous to you?'

'Not that I noticed.'

'Like I said, probably nothing then.'

Several minutes passed, and Lilly used the time to look around the storeroom. There was only one little dirty window in the wall, and the light streaming in was poor. She could see lots of raw materials and finished goods on the shelves. A coalbunker stood in another corner, with bags of charcoal and other unmarked sacks next to it.

'This is taking too long,' Benjamin said, starting to have concerns of his own. 'Come on.'

Just as Benjamin got to the door to the shop, it opened and Vinny stood there with a plain leather pouch in his hand.

'Here you go, fella,' Vinny said, offering the pouch to Benjamin. 'Come on, there's a place around the corner where you two can clean up.' Vinny turned and walked to the front of his shop. Lilly and Benjamin followed.

The barrels of the guns, forced to the sides of Lilly and Benjamin's heads by the unseen men standing either side of the door, made them freeze on the spot. Two other men stepped in front of them and quickly removed Benjamin's weapons.

'I should have listened to you, Lilly,' Benjamin said bitterly.

'Sorry, old friend,' he said taking the pouch from Benjamin's hand. 'I had no choice.'

'Selling out your own friends?' Lilly said.

'Just get them out of here,' Vinny said to the four men, turning to look away from Benjamin. One of them bound Benjamin and Lilly's wrists and then roughly pushed them in the back to get them moving. Stepping out into the street, Benjamin thought hard about a way out of this situation, but a gunshot broke his train of thought.

One of the men standing behind Benjamin dropped to the floor, like a puppet with his strings cut, and the man next to him followed suit moments later, neither man getting a shot off in return. Benjamin pushed into Lilly and dropped to the floor with her, out of the line of fire. One of the remaining men drew his weapons and tried to take cover inside the shop but he wasn't quick enough. A bullet caught him in the shoulder, sending him tumbling over an anvil.

The last man standing decided to make a run for it, but Vinny was having none of it. He threw his heavy smithing hammer with pinpoint accuracy and caught the man in the back of the head as he fled.

'They have my daughter, Ben!' shouted Vinny as he grabbed the wounded man sprawled by his anvil and lifted him into the air by his throat, his muscles bulging with the strain.

'Where is she, you bastard?' he said. The man didn't answer and started to lose consciousness. 'Oh no you don't!' Vinny said as he pressed his finger into the gunshot wound, making the man scream in pain.

'Three streets over — black wagon!' he cried.

'How many men?' Vinny shouted.

'Two, just two,' said the man before Vinny threw him back to the floor, knocking him unconscious.

'I'm sorry, Ben, I had no choice.'

Borell and Andris quickly appeared around the corner of the shop front with weapons drawn. Benjamin thanked Vinny as he cut the bindings on their wrists.

'Thought you'd get into trouble somehow,' Borell said.

'Questions later. Andris, get back to the airship with Lilly, Borell and I will be right back. Come on, we've got one more thing to do.'

'Yeah I heard. This day just won't end, will it?' Borell said with a sly grin.

The three of them ran across town looking for the black wagon, which they found right where the wounded man said it would be. They hid around a corner, watching. Benjamin was about to outline a plan of attack, but Vinny had other ideas.

'Shit,' said Borell as they chased Vinny across the street, firing at the men as they span around in horror to see Vinny bearing down on them. Benjamin caught a lucky shot on one of the men, spinning him around like a top. The other man took a shot at Vinny, but it merely tore the muscle on one of his huge arms, not even slowing him down. The man didn't get a chance to pull the trigger again, Vinny made sure of that.

'Dad!' shouted Milly as he opened the wagon door. She jumped down and put her arms around his thick neck.

'You need to leave Nartill now,' Vinny said to Benjamin. 'These guys turned up an hour ago, they knew you were coming. It's not safe for you here.'

'It's not safe for us anywhere,' said Borell, checking the men lying on the floor.

'What about you?' Benjamin asked.

'I can get us some place safe. I have contacts who can help. Just get your friends out of town. Here,' Vinny said, taking the pouch of money from his pocket and handing it to Benjamin. 'I'll collect another day.'

'Thanks, Vinny. Look after him, Milly.'

Milly smiled, too shaken up by her ordeal to reply. Benjamin and Borell put their weapons away and ran back towards the main street. They took as little time as possible, buying enough food for their trip home. A change of clothes and a bath would have to wait.

In short order, they made it back to the waiting airship,

glad to see that Lilly and Andris were inside waiting for them. Borell had wrapped the body of the imposter in a canvas sack and tied it to the storage rack underneath the cabin. The blood pool on the cabin floor had been hastily cleaned, leaving a dirty red stain behind.

Benjamin started the engines and released the docking clamps, sending them on their way home.

***

The journey home inside the cramped airship was uncomfortable, but they were relieved when they landed at a private aerodrome in Menillis. Benjamin had sent a message ahead to Kodey to make sure they had agents waiting for them when they arrived.

'Ben! Glad to have you home,' Kodey said as Benjamin climbed down onto the landing area. 'Sorry to hear about Jackson — we've been making inquiries as to his whereabouts, but I'm afraid we have nothing yet.'

'Thanks, Kodey. This is Borell,' he said, pointing to his old friend as he climbed down from the cabin.

'Hey, nice to finally meet ya,' he said, shaking Kodey's hand.

'Prefect Hoyt is keen to debrief you in person. There's a carriage waiting for you over there.'

'An audience with the boss... No rest for the wicked,' Borell said as he turned to Benjamin. 'I'll see you again. Maybe not as Borell...'

'Thank you.' Benjamin smiled.

'If you're going after Shranlon, and I have no doubts that you are, leave the kids at home.' Borell smiled as he walked over to his waiting carriage.

'We've made arrangements for you to stay at a safe house,' Kodey started to say. 'It's a little way out of the city but —'

'Actually, we're going to the country house. I know the area and the house; we'll be just as safe there.'

'I had a feeling you'd say that. Mary is already there, getting the place ready for your arrival,' Kodey said.

'I'm glad you're on our team, Kodey,' Benjamin said, shaking his hand.

Chapter Thirty-Five

Benjamin sipped his tea as he looked through the stack of reports delivered to him the day before. Mary was fussing around bringing toast and cereal and refilling teacups. She had been told to take it easy by her doctors, but looking after her family had been her life and she felt no need to change things because of a few bruises and a concussion. Her family had swelled by two since their return and she was happy they were all together again — all apart from Jackson, that is.

There was no way they could have stayed at the main house. It had been a total loss once the fire had run its course. Fortunately, one of the advantages of being a Sorrow was having property elsewhere in Menillis. In this case, the Sorrow country house situated an hour outside of Trellern, by the coast.

Andris came down the stairs looking very smart in a new suit, adjusting his tie as he sat at the table.

'You know you don't have to go back to Dolare yet, Andris. You are welcome to stay here for as long as you need,' Benjamin said.

'Thank you, Benjamin, but I need to get back to my studies. I've had quite enough excitement for a while. A change of pace will do me good.'

'I have arranged for someone to accompany you, covertly of course. It would be safer for you to stay here, but I won't force this upon you.'

'I appreciate the help. It does settle my nerves a little knowing there's someone watching out for us.'

'Us?' Benjamin said, putting his papers down.

'Erm — yes.'

'She's going back, isn't she?' Benjamin said without surprise.

'Maybe I should let her —' Andris started.

'It's okay, Andris,' Lilly said, walking into the room and putting down a small travel bag. 'I can't hide from the world forever, Uncle Ben. Mia is doing well and I really want to be there as she recovers.'

'I understand.'

'Besides, it sounds like we've got a nanny too?'

'There will be agents keeping an eye on you two. Don't worry, they'll stay out of your way. They'll be investigating the men who attacked you too, so you won't even know they are there.'

The men who attacked Lilly and Mia had been found, but one was killed whilst trying to escape; the other was being held in an interrogation cell at a Society office just outside Dolare. They were assuming that the attempted kidnapping was part of Shranlon's plan, so were not taking any chances with his underling.

Lilly gave Benjamin a big hug and kissed him on the cheek. 'Thanks, Uncle Ben. You will come and see us soon?'

'I promise. I've got lots of work to do here for now. Your grandfather and Shranlon are still out there, they are my only priority right now. It looks like I'm out of retirement.'

'Good. It didn't suit you,' said Mary as she walked back into the room. 'I've made you lunch to take with you, dears, and your carriage has just arrived,' she said, handing two brown paper bags to Andris.

Lilly ran over and hugged Mary.

'Gently, dear,' said Mary as Lilly squeezed her tired and aching body.

'I'll miss you,' Lilly said.

'I'll miss you too, dear. Come back and visit any time.'

Benjamin stood and shook Andris by the hand. 'Look

after her.'

'Yes, sir.'

'You two had better be off then. Arthur will sort out a ticket for you at the station, Lilly,' Benjamin said.

Lilly grabbed Andris by the hand and dragged him out into the hallway, her bag over his shoulder, and into the chilly sea breeze outside. Arthur Bourne had already loaded what little of Andris' luggage he had acquired onto the roof of the carriage, and was standing beside the open door waiting for them.

Benjamin and Mary stood on the porch to wave them off.

'They will be alright, won't they?' Mary asked.

'They are in good hands,' he said. 'Whatever we do, we can't keep them cooped up in here forever.'

Lilly and Andris climbed into the back of the carriage and closed the door. Arthur Bourne put his hand on the brow of his hat and tipped it towards Benjamin.

Benjamin knew they would be just fine.

Chapter Thirty-Six

It had been a week since their escape from Shranlon's mountain city, but Benjamin's world had changed dramatically.

It was revealed that part of Shranlon's great plan was a cull of key men and women within the Society and the government. In total, eight high-ranking agents and three prefects had been killed. The entire Society was working on tracking their killers with some moderate success already. Attempts had been made on two Royal family members, but their security had been airtight and the attempts failed. Needless to say the Royal family were more paranoid about security than ever now.

Word had passed from many of the other kingdoms about similar events; targeted assassinations, street robberies gone wrong...they all coincided with the destruction of the mountain city in Nartill.

In light of Benjamin's recent actions and the now vacant prefect positions, he was offered a position within the upper ranks of the Society alongside Kodey, but he had declined. If Shranlon had escaped, which they firmly believed he had, then it made sense he was prepared for the destruction of his city, maybe even allowed it, to cover up his real plans. It also stood to reason that the energy device hadn't been destroyed in the loss of his facility.

Jackson was Benjamin's main concern, if not a little selfishly. He had concluded that if Shranlon had gone to all this trouble to obtain Jackson, he would be safe enough for now. Shranlon no doubt had plans for Jackson that didn't include killing him. Benjamin had to believe that; he wouldn't accept another version of the possibilities.

Benjamin also had burning questions that he needed answering; what was the link between his father and Shranlon all those years ago? How did they know each other and why? He had obtained some of the reports surrounding the Siege of Sorrent and Shranlon from the Society vaults, and awaited further documents that had been classified beyond his reach. He had yet to visit the family vault at the city bank in Trellern, where his father would have kept anything he didn't want the Society to see; that would be his next stop.

Looking out across the veranda at the sun setting over the sea, he missed the familiar view of the clock tower and the city.

He had a lot of work ahead of him.

A lot of questions needed answering.

Author Profile

Born in 1975, Paul Challis is a Software Engineer by day, and a writer by night. Living near Huntington, Paul has a full house with one wife, two kids, one dog, three chickens and one rather under-loved vegetable garden. Working his way through his wife's library of books, Paul only developed a passion for reading a few years ago, and is now pursuing and encouraging the love of writing he had when he won a poetry competition at the age of 13.

Paul loves everything technological; a self-professed 'gadget man' and Twitter addict, you will find it hard to keep up with all the activity on his social media sites.

Most of his spare time is now spent with his family, doing the necessary home owner's DIY work (using carpentry skills he learnt from his father), and also disappearing into his workshop to build something strange and unusable.

Paul is hoping his first novel, Benjamin Sorrow: One for Sorrow, will encourage his passion for writing, as he has found this to be an interesting experience so far.

Follow and interact with Paul Challis:
    Book website: http://www.benjamin-sorrow.com
    Blog: http://blog.beakz.net
    Twitter: @beakz
    Facebook: https://www.facebook.com/BenjaminSorrowSeries

Publisher Information

Rowanvale Books provides publishing services to independent authors, writers and poets all over the globe. We deliver a personal, honest and efficient service that allows authors to see their work published, while remaining in control of the process and retaining their creativity. By making publishing services available to authors in a cost-effective and ethical way, we at Rowanvale Books hope to ensure that the local, national and international community benefits from a steady stream of good quality literature.

For more information about us, our authors or our publications, please get in touch.

www.rowanvalebooks.com
info@rowanvalebooks.com